A Tracy Brubaker Mystery

Book 2

Crossed Stitch

John Carter Stell

Midnight Marquee Press
Baltimore, MD, USA · London, United Kingdon

Tracy Brubacker Mysteries

#1 The Big Nap
#2 Crossed Stitch

ISBN 978-1-936168-67-5
Library of Congress Catalog Card Number 2016916580
First Printing June, 2017

Dedication

To my earliest guinea pigs,
Mom, Sue, Margie, and Tony.
Thanks for the encouragement.

If you can't dazzle them with brilliance,
baffle them with bullshit. —W.C. Fields

Chapter 1

Martin Nestle couldn't keep up with her. He was trying to return some of his client's charging documents to his black leather briefcase while following Tracy Brubaker through the halls of the Baltimore Central Booking & Intake Center. She obviously knew her way around here; him, not so much. Like her, he had very little experience with criminal law; his specialty was business matters. Finally she stopped and turned, saw his predicament, and waited long enough for him to do what he'd been trying to do for the last couple of minutes. "Sorry," he said to her, slightly embarrassed.

"That's okay, Marty," she responded, smiling. "Whenever you're ready." He finally got his case latched, papers inside, and they then continued to make their way to where Massimo Paganini was being held. When Tracy and Nestle arrived at their destination, they showed the attending guard their visitor passes and he then escorted them to the small room where Paganini was seated, anxiously awaiting his lawyer's visit. When he heard the door open, he looked up and gave Tracy a big smile.

"Tracy!"

"Hello, Mr. P. How are you doing?" She gave Paganini a quick hug and everyone sat down at the small table.

"Doing? I don't know what I'm doing *here*, I can tell you that," he answered, sounding somewhere between amused and irritated. "Marty tells me the police think I killed Randy Pepper."

"Of course they're absolutely *wrong* about that," Tracy told him.

"*Idioti!*"

"Max, calm down," Nestle said, as if scolding a naughty child. "Now that Ms. Brubaker is here we'll get this thing all worked out."

"What 'Ms. Brubaker'? This is little Tracy, but all grown up now, huh?" Massimo was smiling, looking at the woman he was remembering as a four year old coming into his shop with her father, waiting patiently for the lollipop Mr. P had waiting for her.

"In body if not mind, Mr. P," she answered him, returning his smile.

"You call me Max, okay? This young fellow with you isn't much older than you and *he* calls me Max. Why shouldn't you?"

"Max it is then."

"So Tracy, how many kids you got?" Max asked her. Tracy thought this had to be some kind of set up. She knew Max—or at least his wife—must have contact with her mother Violetta on a somewhat regular basis; that's how Max had learned that Tracy was a lawyer and that she had recently solved a murder case — and thus prevented a great injustice, no doubt. But Tracy also knew her mother would lament, to any one who would listen, her unwed daughter and the absence of grandchildren. Tracy was her only child after all.

"I'm not married Max."

"What? A pretty girl like you not married yet?" he asked appearing stunned. "What is it with the generation of today? Don't you appreciate the importance of family? I've been married to my Gloria for 41 years and I tell you *that* is what gives life its meaning." Max was moving his right arm up and down, his hand making motions like small karate chops.

Nestle cleared his throat. "I think we should talk about the charges against you now, Max. Tracy had to push back some previously scheduled appointments to see you."

"Ah, Tracy; you're such a dear," Max said, clearly touched.

She patted his hand. "Marty was showing me the list of charges they have against you. It seems the police have evidence you called and set up a meeting with Pepper the Wednesday he was killed."

"I never called that bastard that day."

"They have your cell phone records, Max," Nestle told him. "You called Pepper at 10:25 a.m."

"The records are wrong. The police are wrong. I never called him."

Nestle added, "They have people at Pepper's place of business who have said in their sworn statements that Pepper told them *you* called him and wanted to meet."

"Are you not listening to me, Marty? I told you I didn't call that *asino!*" Tracy couldn't help but laugh. The years had not dulled Max's bravado.

"But —" Nestle started to stay.

"But nothing," Max interrupted. He turned to Tracy. "Tracy, who are you gonna believe: me or the phone company?"

Tracy paused a moment. "Why, you of course Max."

Max smiled at Nestle while pointing at Tracy. "You see that Marty. That's the faith right there."

Tracy looked at Nestle, giving him a quick elbow to his ribs. Then she turned back to Max and said, "But Marty's right to be concerned. You said your phone wasn't out of your sight one minute the day of the murder. But the phone company has the call being placed from your mobile phone. And, like Marty said, people will substantiate that. You have a long history of fighting with Pepper. And you were the only one in your shop when Pepper arrived and got himself shot."

Max turned so he was not looking at either of them, and then waved his right hand dismissively. "If I was gonna kill that *asino* I'd have done it years ago."

"On the other hand," Tracy continued, "there are no witnesses to the actual crime. And other people who were in your office that day could have made the call."

"Nobody who works for me would have done it either."

"That's the only other explanation Max," Tracy said sympathetically.

"No! You don't think I know my own people? No, the explanation is that the police are lying or the phone company is lying, or they're *all* lying."

"Why would either or both of them do that?" Nestle asked.

"Aren't I paying you two to find that out?" Max asked looking at each of them.

"Are you sure you don't want someone with more criminal experience than me, Max?" Tracy asked him. "I don't typically get involved in murder cases."

"But you got that Shane kid cleared."

"That was an unusual situation. I knew him."

"And you know me; and you're Pete Brubaker's daughter. He was one of the best cops that ever set foot in my shop. You always used to tell me that you were going to be just like Daddy someday."

Tracy quietly said, "Things didn't quite turn out that way, Max." After her father's murder while on the job, Tracy knew following her father's path would probably put her worry-wart mother in an early grave. She therefore had chosen a different profession.

"Well, *I* believe you can help me," Max told her. "But if you don't want to…"

She smiled at him. "Of course I'll help you, Max."

"*Meraviglioso!* It's settled then." Max looked at Nestle. "Marty, I appreciate all your help up until now but Tracy can handle things from here. You stick to the business side of things."

"Right Max," Nestle said.

"But you give her whatever help she needs. She may have questions about the business that only you can answer. And you can tell her all about that *dolore nel culo* Pepper. He must have lots of people who didn't want him around."

"Sure Max."

Tracy then said, "You're going to have a bail review hearing tomorrow and we'll see if we can get you released. I'm optimistic that we can. The judge we see may even end up being one of your customers."

Max again smiled. "See, you're helping me already. Now go to your other meetings and I'll see you tomorrow."

"What about Gloria and your boys?" she asked him.

"I've been keeping them apprised," Nestle volunteered. "I'll make sure Gloria knows about tomorrow. She can make sure one of her sons is available if Max makes bail."

"That sounds fine then," Tracy nodded. She rose and, before leaving, gave Max another hug; Nestle settled for a handshake. As the attorneys were moving toward the exit Tracy asked, "Do you have time now to tell me all about Max's feud with Randolph Pepper? It's about 11:30 and there's a coffee shop not too far from here that has a nice lunch menu."

Nestle checked his watch. "Hey, that sounds like a great idea. Should we drive together?"

"Sure," Tracy said. "I'll play chauffeur since I know the way, then I'll drop you off at your car afterward."

Nestle smiled and nodded. This day was turning out not to be so bad after all.

"So how long have you been representing Max?" Tracy asked Nestle. She took her first bite of her roast beef and Swiss bagelwich as he answered.

"About three years now; his former attorney retired—at 81 no less—and I took over."

"How'd you manage that?"

"I worked for Mark Mustabaugh, his attorney. I started working there part-time during law school. Eventually Max was one of my regulars, so when Mark finally called it quits and I started my own firm, Max came with me."

"How big is your practice? What kind of work do you do?"

"Oh my goodness it's just me and Callie, my administrative assistant, secretary, and basically everything else. I handle mostly general business matters—contracts, estates, wills, some work with charities—enough to keep me pretty busy anyway."

"It sounds like we do the same kind of work for the most part."

"You have your own firm too, don't you?"

"Yep; there's me, my right hand man Neal, and Rebecca who fills out the rest of the body, so to speak."

Nestle smiled. "Yeah; law school doesn't really teach you about all the administrative garbage you have to sort through."

"Amen to that. I don't like dealing with all the paperwork and such so I basically have Neal and Rebecca to handle all of that, although Neal is fully licensed to practice law." Tracy drank from her bottle of lemonade and then asked, "So, what is the story between Max and Randy Pepper?"

Nestle took another bite of his ham and cheese croissant and then said, "The history starts before I knew Max. But I think I got the gist of it. About 10 or so years ago Pepper got a franchise from one of the big clothiers—Mason & Bond for Men—and opened it up a few blocks from where Max has his store. Pepper came in to introduce himself and then, in no time, offered to buy Max's place. Of course the intent was to close it down and eliminate the competition. Max turned him down, probably not in the most diplomatic way." Tracy smiled and nodded. She could imagine Max huffing and puffing at the wolf who entered his territory. "That was the start of it. But Max survived, thanks to a loyal customer base and his outstanding reputation for quality."

Tracy added, "And the help he gave to the community. I don't know if you know this or not Marty, but Max gave discounts to police and fire personnel. I'd be in there when I was little and no matter who came in he always knew their name, their spouse's name, even their kids and grandkids names, without fail. And if he didn't know you, he'd come over to you and introduce himself with a warm handshake and a smile. I love Max."

"Max *is* great. And he still pretty much operates the same way, except one of his sons is more likely to be greeting you these days. Max is mostly in the back office trying to do what he can to make ends meet, this economy and all."

"Oh: is he really struggling?"

Nestle nodded slowly. "Unfortunately, yes. Fact is, Max should really let some people go. He doesn't really need two salespeople or two tailors on staff full time. But he can't bring himself to do it." Nestle paused a moment and then continued. "Come to think of it, Pepper came in the other week, made some very unkind comments about the empty store, and how he probably didn't need to buy Max out because Max would be closing shop on his own any day now."

Tracy gave Nestle a questioning look. "After all these years, Pepper was *still* trying to shut Max down?"

"Oh yeah, Tracy. It was an ego thing pure and simple—two pit bull alpha males who weren't going to stop until only one remained standing."

Tracy shook her head. "Poor Max."

"His customer base has slowly been eroding for years. Some died, some moved to the suburbs, some retired and moved to Florida and places like that. And with more and more companies allowing the business casual look, or letting people work from home, there's been less and less a demand for the exquisitely tailored—albeit expensive—suits Max offers."

"Ain't progress grand?" Tracy mused.

"But I think Max is more worried about his sons having the wherewithal to support their own families. Max and Gloria's oldest, Antonio, is the only one working full time at the store. Roberto and Germano work part time there, helping out when they can. They have other jobs."

"So Max is what now, 63, 64?"

"64. Tony is 39, Rob is 36, and Jerry is 32."

"All married with kids?"

"Jerry isn't, but he always seems to be going on a date whenever I'm dropping by Max's office late in the day. Tony has two daughters; Rob, a son."

"Well good for them. How are they all dealing with everything?"

Nestle frowned and shook his head. "Not well at all, as you can probably imagine." He sighed and then said, "They're good people Tracy. I've gotten to know them pretty well through the years and I feel so awful for them. I wish Max had told me about you right away instead of waiting until after they locked him up. But since he didn't do it I guess he figured nothing would happen. I totally blew it at the initial appearance yesterday."

"You couldn't have done anything for him really," Tracy said sympathetically. "A District Court commissioner cannot set bail in a first degree murder case in Maryland. That's up to a judge."

"Thanks for saying that, Tracy. I did manage to get the preliminary hearing scheduled for next Wednesday."

Tracy's eyes widened. "How'd you manage to do *that*? That's nothing short of a miracle."

"Luck…and playing up Max's age and health issues. They had a sudden opening in the docket due to the State bungling something or other.

A Tracy Brubaker Mystery

And Max has friends where it matters. Still: I'm glad you're here now to help him."

"I'll certainly do my best." Tracy paused a moment to finish her food and drink and then said, "I'm going to need a list of the employees who were at the store the day of the murder. Is that something you might be able to pull together for me since you're familiar with his business?"

"Sure, I can do that. I mean, if Max didn't make the call, someone else there had to have made it. So that would be nearly all of his employees, except for Paul Iris."

"Why's that?"

"He's not there Wednesdays. So he couldn't have been the one to use Max's phone."

Tracy nodded. "I see. Where does Max keep his cell phone?"

"It's usually sitting by or in its charger on a small table next to his office door. Nobody really calls him on it except his wife maybe, or me sometimes. Max has been letting Tony deal with most of the day-to-day stuff so Max's phone doesn't ring that much anymore."

"Did he tell you if he left the office for any extended period of time?"

"I'm not sure. But he doesn't normally go out once he gets there. He usually orders lunch in and eats at his desk. Sometimes an old customer will come in and want to catch up and Max will go to talk. I think he may have some arthritis in his legs. I notice sometimes he seems to be in pain when he walks. And his eyes aren't so good either."

"More bad news; that stinks. But I'll talk to Max more about the details tomorrow; hopefully, after he's had some of Gloria's home cooking."

"Have you ever tasted her herb chicken over pasta with that light sauce she makes?" Nestle asked.

"It's supreme, isn't it? Whenever my mom got sick Gloria would be over with some heaven-sent meal. Not to knock my mom's cooking or anything, but Gloria could have opened her own place in Little Italy if she wanted to."

Nestle laughed. "You know, I never thought about that but you're absolutely right."

Tracy checked her watch; almost 12:30. "Shall we head out? I have a 1:30."

"Oh sure. I'll email you that list if you want to give me your contact info."

"Of course." The two exchanged business cards, and then they moved toward Tracy's blue Audi parked on the street. Tracy shortly thereafter pulled into the BPD parking lot and drove Nestle to his car. "You can't beat Tracy's limo service, can you Marty?" she asked him grinning.

"No way," he responded chuckling. "It was great meeting you Tracy. I'll be in touch." He offered her his hand and the two shook their goodbyes.

"Great meeting you too, Marty. And thanks in advance for that list."

"You bet," he said while exiting her vehicle. The list would no doubt give Tracy a narrow field of alternate suspects from which to choose. And she'd be able to thin it out further once she learned who was in the store at 10:25 a.m., the time the alleged call summoning Randy Pepper to his doom was made. But now it was time to get back to the home base, advise Neal and Rebecca on their new client, and make her first afternoon appointment. Tracy couldn't help herself from wondering though, during her drive to the office, what Gloria Paganini was serving for dinner tonight.

Rebecca Dietz was on the phone when Tracy arrived shortly after 1:00 in the afternoon. She gave Tracy a wave as the attorney made her way to her office. Tracy's associate Neal Bennett was not in, so she sat down to check her emails and phone messages, neatly written on pink Return Call slips and stacked on her desk. Her next appointment was a Charles Betts, who would be at her office shortly, so there was no point returning any potentially lengthy calls. Betts had told her he wanted to open a seafood stall at Lexington Market, a Baltimore landmark founded in 1782, which today was the largest marketplace of its kind in the world. He needed legal advice in completing his lease application and securing the proper business permits and licenses. It was pretty basic stuff and Betts could probably have found most of his answers online. But Tracy got the impression when speaking to him that he had no interest in spending an afternoon doing his own research.

Charles Betts arrived promptly and Rebecca showed him to Tracy's office. Betts looked to be in his mid-40s, had short dark hair with matching mustache, and was a slim 5'10". After the customary exchange of pleasantries ("Call me Charlie!") Tracy handed Betts a folder Neal had pulled together.

"Lexington Market has a pretty detailed and clear process for opening a business there or purchasing an existing one, Charlie," Tracy began. "In the folder you'll find a copy of the application with the relevant contact info. You'll also need to obtain your Baltimore business license and food permit, so you'll need to schedule an appointment with the Baltimore City

Health Department. But that is also covered in the application. Have you set up your business yet or at least looked into what legal form you want—Partnership, Limited Liability Company, etc?"

"No," Betts answered shaking his head. "I'm not even sure I want to do this. I came into some money recently and I want to do something constructive with it."

"What made you think of buying a place at the Market?"

"Several things—I've always liked visiting there when I was in the city for whatever reason. It's been around for well over 200 years which tells me it ain't going anywhere. Plus you have the built-in customer base that visits regularly; that would of course be a big advantage to someone starting out." Betts paused and then looked around the office. "But I also know it's risky, the odds are against a new eatery being successful, especially now."

"Yes, you're absolutely right about the risk when it comes to first time restaurant owners, although I understand the 90% failure rate is exaggerated."

Betts paused a moment, and leaned forward in his chair. "Is that your father?" he asked pointing to the picture on Tracy's desk. He smiled at her.

"Yes, it is."

"Is that you with him or is that a granddaughter?"

"That's me. I was six."

Charlie leaned back. "My, what a pretty little thing you were." Tracy felt herself blushing. "I see you wear a cross," he said now pointing to her necklace. "It's quite beautiful."

Tracy was starting to feel a bit uncomfortable. "Thank you," was all she said in response.

"Let me guess, a gift from your father."

Tracy smiled. "As a matter of fact, it was."

Charlie nodded. "Strange. Your dad was a cop, and you're a person of faith. Yet you try to free criminals for a living."

Now Tracy was visibility irritated. "That's not exactly true, Charlie."

"Oh, don't misunderstand me, Tracy. I'm not judging. I didn't mean to offend you. In fact, I think faith is important. Sometimes that's all you have when life does terrible things to you. I mean, I know it's especially hard for you Catholics these days, what with all the scandals and exposed hypocrisy."

Tracy squirmed again. She didn't like this. She didn't like this at all.

"Oh dear," Charlie finally said. "I seem to have upset you again. I apologize. Sometimes I don't know when to keep what I'm thinking to myself."

Tracy forced a smile. "That's okay, Charlie."

Then Betts looked around her office again and said, "I guess I still have some more thinking to do about this restaurant business. Maybe this meeting was a tad premature."

Tracy looked at him curiously. "If you're not comfortable with the idea of the eatery I wouldn't recommend using your newfound cash for such a thing," she offered.

"I'll look over what your firm put together and let you know if I'm going to move forward. In the meantime feel free to send me a bill for all the work you've already done." He handed her a business card. "My address is on this; just send the bill there."

"Okay Charlie; I'll do that," she said as she accepted the card. She gave him another curious look. "Is there anything else I can do for you?"

He smiled again. His eyes met hers. "No; there's nothing else for the moment." And with that Betts arose from his seat and quickly made his way to the exit. Tracy usually saw clients—especially new ones—to the door but Betts' haste had caught her off guard. He was already entering the down staircase by the time Tracy reached the reception area.

A voice behind her asked, "Was that Charles Betts?"

Tracy turned to see her associate Neal Bennett standing behind her. "Oh, you're back," she said to him. "Yes, that was Charlie."

Neal studied her. "What's wrong?"

She turned to look at the now-deserted hallway, and then turned back to Neal. "I don't know exactly. He barely looked at the information we put together for him and then basically said he changed his mind about the whole thing. And he asked some personal questions. It was just…odd."

Neal pursed his lips. "You think he was here for another reason?"

She nodded. "Well, ever since the Shane case we've had to turn away potential clients who thought I would help them beat their murder charge."

"Yeah. But in all those cases you felt they were guilty."

"I *knew* they were guilty," Tracy cut in. "Maybe this is a case of someone taking a different approach, although I can't figure it."

Neal sighed. "This was always a risk of taking Brian's case. You got some good publicity and this is the result." Neal cleared his throat. "And now I hear this morning you met with some businessman who supposedly killed a competitor; another exception?"

Neal was very much aware of Tracy's reluctance to get involved with clients accused of murder. Her father had been a decorated detective with

A Tracy Brubaker Mystery

the Baltimore Police Department before being killed in the line of duty. And while, for her mother's sake, she had chosen the legal profession in lieu of a career in police work, she didn't typically take on murder cases for fear her skills would free a murderer, something she felt would be a betrayal to her father. But she had recently made an exception when the man she once loved, and probably still did, was accused of killing his own father. She was successful in not only getting the charges against Brian Shane dropped, but also in uncovering the real culprit in the process. Her resulting 15 minutes of fame had the unwanted consequence of several potential clients seeking her aid. But she had turned them all down for the simple reason that her experience and instinct told her the police had arrested the right person.

Tracy looked at Neal. "Yes," she answered him, with a hint of defiance in her tone. "He's a friend of the family, a man I've known nearly all of my life. He's something of a character but he is also a person *of* character. I can't believe he'd kill someone."

"Uh huh," was all Neal said in response.

"Now don't you two start again," Rebecca jumped in. They looked at her.

"You're right Beck," Tracy finally said. Then she gave Neal a big smile. "Neutral corners for now, Neal. Besides, I think you'll like Max Paganini."

Neal smiled back. "Sorry Tracy. I didn't mean to start anything; really."

Rebecca made an obviously insincere sniffling sound upon observing Tracy and Neal's truce. They looked at her and the three of them shared a brief but hearty laugh. "Alright you jokesters, back to work," Tracy said pleasantly as she prepared to return to her office. Neal and Rebecca had been with her nearly five years now, since she started her own practice. Her relationship with them had grown to the point where she thought of Neal and Rebecca more as family rather than employees. As she was younger than both, she sometimes felt they thought of her as their uppity kid sister.

Sitting down at her desk, she again considered the mysterious Charlie Betts. What was his game? She had enough initial meetings with future clients to know there was something strange about the one she just had. Thinking back to the phone call she received from him a little over a week ago, she remembered he made no mention of why he chose her as his potential attorney. That in and of itself didn't mean anything. But now she was beginning to wonder if Betts had been after something else this afternoon. Still, there was little point to dwelling on it. Maybe she was just getting paranoid. There were more important things to worry about now, namely how could she help Mr. Paganini? She took a quick look at her office email and was pleased to see Martin Nestle had emailed her the list of employees she asked for. A quick look at the list told her eight employees were there the previous Wednesday when the phone call had been placed. Among them were Max's three sons, two salespeople, two onsite tailors, and Max's office manager/bookkeeper. Most of them had been with Max for many years; the idea that one of them would turn on him seemed unlikely. But that *had* to be the case. Tracy wasn't looking forward to what would most likely be butting heads with Max over his employees. She forwarded Nestle's list to Neal and asked him to start doing the standard background checks. After all, the State's Attorney would be calling several if not all of them to verify Max's whereabouts that Wednesday as well as to confirm his open animosity toward the victim. Tracy had just sent the email when Rebecca buzzed.

"Tracy, there are two gentlemen here to see you."

"I didn't forget about an appointment did I?" Tracy asked, sounding embarrassed and panicked. "I don't have anything else listed on my calendar for today. I thought I pushed all this morning's originally scheduled appointments to later in the week."

"No, Tracy. These are unscheduled visitors; the kind with shiny jewelry in their wallets."

"Oh," Tracy remarked, sitting herself up straight. "Okay, bring 'em on back then."

Rebecca shortly thereafter brought two men into Tracy's quarters, and the first thought that popped into the attorney's head was that her visitors could be from secret agent central casting. They were tall; were well-dressed in dark business suits; and boasted crew cut hair. Alas they were not wearing sunglasses; other than that though they appeared to be either FBI or CIA. But what surprised Tracy most was that she had been absolutely right.

"I'm Agent Roper; this is Agent Lennon," the one with the lighter hair said. They both showed Tracy their badges, Federal Bureau of Investigation. She looked at them briefly and then offered them the two seats that were in front of her desk. "We'll stand," Roper said.

"Egads," Tracy thought. She told them, "Well I'm going to sit if you don't mind." After doing just that she asked, "What can I do for you?"

    A Tracy Brubaker Mystery

Lennon spoke this time. "You had a meeting with Carlton Brandice earlier this afternoon." They both looked at her awaiting a response.

"I had no meeting today with anyone with that name," she said flatly.

Roper then said, "We observed him entering your office around 1:30 this afternoon."

Tracy tried to maintain her poker face. "No one with that name came to see me today. In fact, I've never seen anyone with that name."

The two agents looked at each other. "Perhaps he used a different name," Roper offered.

"You go to the head of the class," Tracy thought. But she said, "I can't tell you the names of any of my clients just because you ask. You boys should know that."

They again exchanged looks. "May we sit down Ms. Brubaker?" Lennon asked as the two agents helped themselves to the previously offered seats. Tracy just frowned. "Do you know who Carlton Brandice *is*?" Lennon inquired.

"No; I can't say that I do."

Roper said, "He works for Reginald Walters. Have you heard of *him*?"

Yes, she had heard of him. In September 2013 he made headlines when he was arrested, tried, but ultimately acquitted in a case involving a real estate deal that netted one of Walters' companies millions, and resulted in at least one corpse. Walters had somehow found out a national developer was interested in constructing a shopping mall and casino in a burgeoning Maryland suburb near Baltimore City and started buying all the land—both vacant and occupied—he could. The charges stemmed from accusations that Walters used threats, intimidation, and actual violence against those who wouldn't sell. There were even some fatalities connected to the case, although Walters was formally charged with only one of them. But witnesses against him developed memory problems and the State wound up with egg on its face. But Walters had been known long before this as someone to whom you didn't say "no".

"Yes, I've heard of him. Brandice works for him?"

"He's not someone we recommend you take on as a client, Ms. Brubaker," Roper responded. "Quite honestly, we were a bit surprised given your reputation among your peers and local law enforcement that you'd even meet with Brandice. But if you didn't know who he was then that may explain it."

Tracy was confused. If the FBI was tracking Brandice why would they let someone they thought was his attorney know this? Or if they were just confirming their suspicion that she knew nothing why even continue the interview after they'd established Brandice used a false name? Surely Carlton Brandice and Charlie Betts was the same person. And just what did Betts, and perhaps by extension did Reginald Walters, want with *her*? The implication was that Brandice helped Walters physically persuade people to see the latter's point of view. In a nutshell, she didn't know what the hell was going on.

"Look agents, I'll tell you straight out, neither Carlton Brandice nor Reginald Walters are clients of mine. And they never will be. If you have in fact done your homework you know that's the truth." She paused and looked at each of them. "And that's all I feel comfortable saying at this point unless you want to tell me what all of this is about."

The two agents rose in unison. "Thank you for your time, Ms. Brubaker," Roper said. "We'll let you know if we need anything else from you. No need to show us out." And with that the dapper duo left her alone.

Neal was in her office in seconds asking, "What was *that* all about?"

"You got me there. I haven't the slightest idea. Charlie Betts is apparently really Carlton Brandice, who supposedly works for Reginald Walters, who allegedly is a thug in fine clothing."

"The same Walters who dodged a lengthy prison term last year?"

"Yup."

"But we've never dealt with Walters in any way, have we?"

"Not that I recall. But we've stalled some foreclosures in recent years. Maybe we ticked off Walters somehow. Or maybe he's just looking for new counsel."

Some of the color drained from Neal's face. "Good Lord. What do we do now?"

Tracy shrugged her shoulders. "I have no idea about that either, Neal. But I'm probably not going to be able to sleep tonight wondering just what the heck Carlton aka Charlie was really doing in my office earlier today."

As Neal shook his head, Tracy glimpsed at the desk photo of her and her father—one that had been taken while on vacation in Ocean City, Maryland. And that's when it hit her, her father was wearing a tank top and swimsuit in the photo. He was not in uniform. But Charlie or whatever the hell his name was had known he had been a cop. Tracy hadn't told him this, but he knew it. This visitor hadn't just shown up today; he had done his homework. Why? Why did he care about the life history of Tracy Brubaker? And she tensed at the realization that she would probably be learning the reason soon enough.

Chapter 2

Tracy wished she could blank out her mind. But she couldn't, and sleep would not come. She tossed and turned; she stared at the ceiling; she was even desperate enough to try warm milk. Nothing helped. It wasn't just that she couldn't figure out the puzzle that was Carlton Brandice. She felt uneasy, nervous, and uncomfortable; something was going on that she had no control over and that she didn't understand. It was a position she rarely found herself in and she wasn't dealing with it very well.

When her alarm sounded at 6:30 a.m. she immediately opened her eyes. How much sleep had she gotten? She wasn't sure; two or three hours maybe. She slapped the 'off' button like it just insulted her and she sat up, rubbing her eyes. An extended hot shower and extra cup of coffee did little to rouse her. This day was going to be a struggle. And she wanted to be operating at 100% for Max's bail review hearing. She dressed in a gray business suit with fabulous new purple heels she had just bought. On her way out she grabbed a bagel and two oranges before the start of this important day. She didn't feel like eating, but would force herself at some point if need be.

Tracy was the first to arrive at her office, and the most pressing order of business was to get the coffee brewing. Reviewing her email she found mostly junk, and there were no new voicemails since the last time she checked. She planned on being at The Central Booking and Intake Facility by 10:00 a.m., the time when Massimo Paganini would most likely be placed in a holding cell pending his bail review hearing. She'd spend the next couple of hours reviewing the notes she had made regarding his long history in the community. At least, that's what she had planned to do until she heard a voice call her name. "Tracy, you here?"

She recognized the voice as belonging to Detective Elias Tanner, her father's former partner. He didn't have an appointment that she recalled but that didn't matter. He was family. "Back here, El!" she answered him as she arose from behind her desk. She went to the coffee pot right outside her office to pour a cup for her always-welcome visitor. She had it in hand by the time he made his way to the back. "Here you go, handsome," she said smiling while handing him the mug.

Tanner chuckled. "Glad you're in a good mood," he said taking her offering. "Can we talk a few minutes?"

"Surely; just follow me to my boudoir." She flopped into her chair while Tanner parked himself in front of her desk. He took a few sips of his java and began.

"Did you have any well-dressed visitors recently?"

She looked at him a bit. There was obvious concern in his voice. This wasn't going to be the light conversation she originally thought. "Yes I did; yesterday." She looked at him a bit more. "What's going on, El?"

"I can't tell you much, Tracy," he began. "In fact I've already bent the rules a bit."

"What do you mean?"

"Well, that person that came to see you yesterday, Brandice, let's just say he's a really bad guy."

"I gathered that."

"What I'm about to tell you needs to be kept between us, just as if I were a client."

"Okay."

"State and Federal people have been watching Reginald Walters and Carlton Brandice pretty much since Walters' acquittal. When it was learned Brandice made an appointment to see you, well, they wanted to know what was going on."

"I didn't know who he was, El. He didn't use his real name."

"Oh, I understand that Tracy. And I told everyone who you were and who your father was — and that there was no way you'd get involved with people like that."

She glanced down and said, "Thanks El."

"And then I told them that you should be warned about Brandice. That didn't go over too well. So I told them that if they didn't warn you then I would. And that if they didn't like it I'd be willing to put in my papers."

Tracy looked back up at him, clearly moved. "You did that for me, El? You're not going to get into any trouble are you?"

"No. Everything's fine. But I find the melodramatic tends to get the point across."

She smiled at him. "I don't know how to thank you El. I was freaking out not knowing what was going on, although, come to think of it, I guess I *still* don't really know what's going on."

He nodded. "Can you tell me anything about Brandice's visit?"

"He came in under the pretense of wanting some basic legal advice. But he didn't seem to care about what I was saying. Technically, he's not even a client. No contracts have been signed. I don't know if I'll ever see him again."

Tanner thought a bit. "What does your gut tell you about the real reason he was here yesterday?"

Tracy thought a bit. "Like maybe he was sizing me up. He kinda looked around the office, the degrees on the wall. He was pleasant enough. He started making some personal comments at one point. Maybe that's when I realized something was off. And he knew Dad was a detective, even though I never told him." Tanner nodded and then Tracy asked, "Do you know if Walters and Brandice know that they're being watched?"

"Hard to say." Tanner leaned forward. "Hopefully you'll never see him again."

"That's not going to satisfy me," Tracy said firmly.

"What does that mean?"

"I'd really like to know why he came to see me."

"You're not working on anything real estate related, are you?"

"Just your basic foreclosure stuff. But that concerns individual homes in mostly impoverished areas, not the kind of costly stuff Walters is into."

Tanner shook his head. "Believe me Tracy, if I knew why Brandice picked you I'd tell you."

She studied him a moment, noting the frustration in his voice. "El, if he does call back to make another appointment, what should I do?"

"Why not tell him you have too many clients and can't take him right now?"

"But if he doesn't know you're watching, won't denying him tip him off? I mean, I was able to accept the initial meeting with no problem."

Tanner sighed. "Mm; you make a good point. I'll tell you what, if he *does* call back, go ahead and make your next appointment. Then call *me,* and let me know the details. We'll think of something."

Tracy nodded. She studied her hands a bit. Then she looked back at Tanner. "Should I be worried, El?"

Tanner shook his head. "No Tracy. There's nothing for you to worry about. The feds are involved since Walters and his compatriots deal in multiple states and they have people on Brandice 24/7—at least, that's my understanding. There is no reason at this point to think he means you any harm."

She continued looking at him. "But here you are, El."

"A precaution, Tracy; that's all. A heads up, if you prefer it put that way. I just didn't like the idea of you not knowing who came into your office yesterday."

She smiled at him. "Okay El. Thanks for looking out for me."

Tanner stood up, as did Tracy, and she moved in for their customary good-bye embrace. "Give my love to that beautiful wife of yours and that dashing fellow known as Elias, Jr."

Tanner laughed, and then squeezed her a bit tighter. "Take care of yourself Tracy. And you call me if Brandice wants to see you again."

She nodded as Tanner exited her office, giving her a quick last smile before he left. She sat down, leaned back in her chair, and started rocking slightly. "Let's see," she thought. "If the appointment was made Tuesday last week, today's Thursday, that's nine days ago…what clients, if any, had anything dramatic happen that Tuesday or in the days before?" Tracy started swiveling back and forth in her chair. Nothing was springing to mind.

"Morning, Tracy!" Rebecca called out.

"Same to you Beck," Tracy called back. Then she got up and headed toward the reception area. "Is Max all set up in the system yet?"

"Yes. I took care of that yesterday afternoon."

"Great; thanks Beck."

"Righto. You have his bail hearing today?"

"Yeah. I'll leave here around 9:30 and then probably will be gone for most of the day. I'll have my phone off too. So just leave me a message if anything urgent pops up and I'll get back to you."

"Gotcha." Rebecca sipped from her mug. "Hey Tracy, nice work on the coffee beans." That got a chuckle and a 'thank you' from Tracy as she returned to her desk. She sat down and sighed. Then she started planning her presentation to make sure Max got bail.

Max was seated in his cell at The Central Booking and Intake Facility. Tracy was allowed entry at about 10:20. He rose and smiled at her. "Tracy, what a sight for these eyes you are."

"Oh Max you're so sweet." She seated herself, doing her best to be cheerful. "How did you like the video they just showed you? Do you have any questions I can answer?"

"Nah, I'm fine."

"You understand how this is all going to work then?"

"I think so."

"Well, just to be sure why don't I run through it quickly?"

"Sure, that's fine."

"Okay. Sometime after 11:00 you'll be called to the courtroom and I will go with you. The Judge will read off your name and the charges. Someone known as a Pre-Trial agent will speak about what information was gathered during interviews with you, any criminal history, and whatever else he or she deems relevant. Someone from the State Attorney's office may or may not offer a bail recommendation. After all of that, I will speak on your behalf. I will be talking about you personally, not the charges against you. In a nutshell, I'll tell them what a great guy you are, that you've never been in trouble with the authorities a day in your life, and that you're not a dangerous person. And I'll point out all the help you've given to the community over the years, your donations of clothing to the poor, your work with various charities, stuff like that. And after telling the Judge how wonderful you are, I'm going to ask that you be released ROR."

"Huh? What is that?"

"It means released on your own recognizance."

"What does *that* mean?"

"I'm asking for no bail; that you can be trusted to return for your court date."

Max twiddled his thumbs. "You think I have a chance with that?"

"Yes, I really think you do."

He looked at her and she was smiling at him. "You're a real sweet girl, Tracy. If Gloria and I had been blessed with a daughter, I would have wanted her to be just like you." He looked back down at his hands.

"Oh Max," she said as she arose and then kneeled down beside him. "I'd be proud to call you my father." She rubbed his back briefly and then let the quiet encircle them as they waited.

The review process commenced for Massimo Paganini just after 11:30, and went as Tracy described it. She presented Max as nothing less than a saint. But she also decided a little sympathy play couldn't hurt. "And I also want to mention, Your Honor, that Mr. Paganini is an elderly man in declining health. He is certainly no flight risk. Given the exemplary life he's lead, the grand citizen he's been in this state for his entire life, we are asking that you release Mr. Paganini on his own recognizance." Tracy wasn't totally surprised when the Assistant State Attorney present put up little fight. And then the Judge sent Max home.

While Max awaited his formal release, Tracy phoned Rebecca and told her the news. She also said she had volunteered to take Max home so that she could stay with him and gather some more specifics about the case. She wouldn't be back today. Neal would be able to handle things. Tracy then called Gloria Paganini at the number Max had given her, and told her that she would be bringing her husband home for a late lunch.

"Where are the boys?" Max asked his wife as he entered their home.

"They'll be here for dinner. I told them all you were coming home today but that you might be tired."

"Oh."

Gloria turned her attention to Tracy. "Tracy, come in here and sit down and let me get you something."

Tracy took a seat in the kitchen. "Thank you Mrs. P. Anything you put in front of me will be gladly devoured." Gloria laughed and gently patted Tracy's head. Max joined Tracy, and the three of them shared a quiet meal, during which the elderly pair held hands the entire time. After lunch, Tracy asked Max if they could go somewhere to talk.

"Are you tired Max; would you like to take a nap?" Tracy asked, noting his haggard expression.

"Nap? What am I, a baby?"

Tracy smiled at him. "No Max; of course not. But you've been through an awful few days and maybe getting some rest is the best thing for you. I know I need a nap most days myself."

He shook his head. "Nah—I'll go to bed early tonight and get a good night's sleep, and I'll be fine."

"Okay Max. Can we talk about last Wednesday?"

"I guess so."

"Was it your typical Wednesday?"

"Yeah."

"Come on Max; I need more than one-word answers. How about you just tell me about your day? When did you get to the office? What did you do? Who was there?"

"Yeah, I get it. Maybe you want something to drink?"

"I'm fine Max."

Max snorted. "Well, Antonio picked me up from here at 7:30 in the morning. We got to the store a little before 8:00. Damn construction slows everything down. So we got there and cleaned the store up a bit. The other two boys got there by 8:30, and then we started organizing the front racks for the items that were going on sale that day. Our sales run Wednesday to Tuesday. Do you remember that Tracy?"

"Sorry Max. I mostly remember the lollipops and piggyback rides."

Max slapped his knee and laughed. "Yeah—you were scared the first couple of times. You would slap me on my head. You got so mad." And Max continued to laugh.

Tracy, frowning, waited for him to calm down. "Okay, okay. When did everyone else get there?"

"I don't know exactly. Jeff and Craig—the tailors—were there by 9, and so was Lester, my bookkeeper. Now Sonny and Abe—the sales associates—they got there by 9:30, when we open."

Tracy stopped her note taking. "Max, don't you have any women on your staff?"

"Nah."

"Why not? Wouldn't a beautiful young gal telling a guy how handsome he looked in one of your fine suits be a great sales technique?"

"What are you talking about? Men like men fitting them."

"Max, I don't think that's necessarily true."

"Listen, you want to know something? Every time I hire a girl to sell for me, you know what happens?"

"No, Max."

"They marry my sons and leave me looking for someone else. And Germano, well he tries to date all the ones my other boys didn't want and when he dumps them, or they dump him, they quit." Now Tracy started laughing. "You find that funny, huh? Well no more girls for Max until Germano finally grows up and settles down. Then maybe I reconsider."

Tracy got serious. "So who's worked at your store the least amount of time?"

"Let me think. Abe's been here about a year and a half. But I knew him before he came to work for me. Sonny's been here almost three years."

Tracy nodded as she made her notes. "And how about everyone else?"

"Lester's been with me for more than 15 years; Jeff and Craig for almost 20. Believe me when I tell you Tracy that none of them could be involved in this anymore than I am."

She nodded again but it wasn't because she agreed with him. She just didn't feel like arguing. "Okay Max. So what did you do after setting up the sales racks?"

"Well, Marty came to see me about 9. He had some bank papers I had to sign for our loan extension."

"Okay, then what?"

"Well, after he left, I met with Lester to get him to cut a manual check for the extension fee that had to go with the bank forms. Then we went through the bills that had to be paid this week. We have to do this on Wednesdays so they can be printed and signed and mailed by Friday."

"Hmm. Why doesn't Tony do that yet?"

He looked at her. "I can still take care of my shop," he said a little defensively.

Tracy stopped writing. "I didn't mean anything by the question, Max. It's just I understood Tony was taking over a lot of the day-to-day stuff and wondered why he didn't deal with Lester."

"I still like keeping my eyes on the money while I still have them to do it."

"Okay, Max. I completely understand. So you approved the bills Lester could pay and then…?"

"Well, he left my office around 10 I guess. Then I was looking at some material orders we were going to make when Marty called me and said I should probably sign the papers today so he could get them to the bank that afternoon."

Tracy paused her scribbling again. "Why the sudden urgency?"

Max looked away from her. "Well, when Marty called the bank to tell them the extension payment was on its way, whoever he talked to said one of the board members was making noise about granting loan extensions to…" Max stopped speaking.

"What Max?"

"I think the term he used was high-risk people."

Tracy felt her face go pale. "Max, was Randall Pepper on the bank's board?" All he did was nod. "Oh, Max."

"There's nothing I could do about that."

"So you think Pepper was trying to block your loan extension?"

"I didn't think anything. I mean, what could the bastard have done when the bank already said they'd extend me?"

"How long was the extension for?"

"Six months."

"And so you'd have to go through this process again in six months?"

"Yeah, sure. I guess."

So this was Max's perceived motive. A life-long adversary had weaseled his way onto the board of directors at Max's bank, in spite of his unpleasant notoriety, and was trying to get the bank to force payment. And then Max would, file for bankruptcy? Close the shop down? Fire some employees? So, Max called Pepper to have it out. "So Marty told you he wanted to pick up the paperwork and check that day." Max nodded. "What did you do after Marty's call?"

"I called Lester and told him to cut the check. And then I called Antonio and said I wanted him to grab the check from Lester and bring it to me at lunch time. Antonio helps review some of the legal stuff sometimes. He's a smart boy, Tracy."

"And you just used your office phone to call them?"

"Yeah. You just push a button and there they are."

"And those calls didn't take very long?"

"No; a couple of minutes, maybe."

Tracy sighed. "So now it's, about, say, 10:20. What did you do then?"

"I went back to looking over the supply order."

"You didn't leave the office to talk to someone, to visit the showroom, to use the bathroom?"

"Nah."

"And no one came in to see you around that time?"

"No."

"Okay, Max. So you spent the rest of the morning in your office?" He nodded. "What about lunch?"

"You hungry, Tracy? I can get you something."

Tracy chuckled. "No, Max. I mean, what did you do for lunch that day?"

"Oh. I had Antonio grab me something from the deli down the street. He brought it to me when he met me to go over the bank stuff."

"And he brought Lester's check to you then?"

"Right, Tracy. We had everything together for Marty. He picked it up in the early afternoon."

Tracy stretched her arms, tilted her neck from side to side, and then leaned forward. "Max, was everyone at your store aware of what was going on? I mean, did they know about you and Pepper, and the whole loan extension business?"

"Probably. My boys knew, and Lester knew. And Lester doesn't always know when to keep his mouth shut. So I don't know."

A Tracy Brubaker Mystery

She gave him a sympathetic look. "Okay Max. Now we'll do the hard part. Tell me about that night at the store after everyone went home. You close at 6:00 in the evening?"

He placed his folded hands on the table and shuffled in his seat. "Yeah; everyone's usually gone by 7. But I stay late on Wednesdays."

"Why's that?"

"Its Gloria's bible study night at the house. All those ladies yacking in my living room, going in and out of my kitchen; I just stay here."

Tracy found herself chuckling again. "I think that sounds rather nice for Gloria."

"Nice for her, sure," he said while flipping his hand in the air.

"Okay, so you're at your store and everyone's gone…"

"I guess it's about 8:30. I hear a noise in the back—in the storeroom. I get up to see if something fell over. Then I see something on the floor. I pick it up and it's a gun. Then I see something else on the floor. I look closer and it's Pepper. But I don't pick *him* up." He stopped talking and started rubbing his thumbs together. Tracy reached over and rubbed his hands. He looked at her. "So I wait for Antonio to show up to pick me up. Then he calls the police. A few days later the cops are saying I killed him."

"What time did Tony get there?"

"He picks me up at 9:30 usually, so it must have been around then."

"Why didn't you call the police yourself?"

He shook his head. "I don't know. There's no phone in the storeroom. I was upset and felt a little dizzy, so I just sat down."

"I understand. Was the store all locked up when you were alone there?"

"It should have been. But I didn't check every door."

"Was the alarm on?"

"No. It has motion detectors so it gets turned on only when there's nobody there."

"Okay. Who has keys to the store?"

"Me and the boys – that's it."

"I suppose someone could have made a copy of the key to the back storeroom at some point."

"Huh? What do you mean?"

"Max, we know that Pepper told his employees that you called him and wanted to meet with him, probably at 8:30. Now, I'm guessing whoever called him told him to come to the back entrance near the storeroom because that was the furthest location from your office. This person would have to have had a key to open the storeroom and wait for Pepper. Pepper shows up; the killer lets him in and shoots him; and then he leaves the gun behind. He takes off while you're making your way to the back room."

Max looked at her impressed. "So you think that's what happened, Tracy?"

"It's my best guess for now."

"Well; can't you tell the cops that?"

Tracy gave him a smile. "I wish it were that simple." Now she gave him a serious look. "They have your prints on the gun, the phone call, a motive…You were the only one in the store. It's what they call a circumstantial case."

Max shook his head. "I told you I found the gun. I told you I didn't call him."

"*I believe you Max. You don't have to convince me.*"

"You're so sure huh? You haven't seen me for years. Maybe I got real cranky."

Tracy laughed gently. "Max, if you did kill Pepper then you wouldn't be so insistent that your phone was in your office the entire day. You could easily lie and say you left the office to do something during the time of the call."

"Hey young lady, I may not be crazy about those bible studies but I don't lie."

"I know Max. That's why I believe you and am here to help you."

He looked at her, a little embarrassed by his misunderstanding. "Oh. I'm sorry Tracy. You're the last person I should be cranky with right now."

She smiled reassuringly. "It's okay Max. I realize this can't be easy for you."

He looked in the direction of the kitchen and whispered, "…Or for my Gloria."

Tracy pursed her lips. "Marty told me you have someone else who works for you, Paul Iris."

"Yeah."

"He wasn't there Wednesday?"

"No. He's there Tuesdays and Thursdays. He's just part-time."

"What does he do?"

"Everything else."

Tracy sighed. "What does *that* mean?"

     A Tracy Brubaker Mystery

"He cleans the whole store; he makes deliveries and does pick-up sometimes. He runs errands. I do my best to keep him busy."

"He needs the job?"

"Yeah. He has at least one other part-time job. It's just him and his eight-year-old girl."

"I see. How long has he worked for you?"

"Couple of years. He used to be a customer. Then he got laid off and I could tell he needed help. So I offered him what I could. But it's not much."

Tracy gulped. "Okay. Is there anyone else we haven't talked about?"

"No; that's everyone. All good people."

She nodded. "It would seem so."

"So you agree with me then? Nobody at my store could be involved in this."

Tracy managed a grin. "I guess so, Max."

He smiled and nodded. "Okay then, what's next?"

"We have a preliminary hearing at district court next week. At that time the State's Attorney will present all the evidence they have against you. This will probably include some witnesses. After that, the court will decide if there's enough evidence to charge you. If they do, then you will enter a plea, and then they'll schedule a date to start the trial."

Max nodded. "Do you think I'll get charged?"

Tracy looked at him. Then, she bowed her head slightly. "Yes, Max. I think they have enough to formally charge you." She lifted her head. "But we will be entering a Not Guilty plea. And I promise I'll do everything I can to make sure you don't spend another day in jail."

Max turned away from her and nodded a few times. "Tracy…"

"What is it Max?"

"I'm a sick man. Things just seem to have stopped working well for me. I want to spend what time I have left with Gloria and my grandkids."

"I want that for you too, Max."

"It looks bad for me though, doesn't it?"

"Don't think like that, Max. The police have done what they do. I haven't had a chance to do what I do yet."

Max laughed. A mental image of an angry four-year-old girl on his back appeared. "You gonna slap them all on the head, Tracy?"

She laughed as a similar memory came to her. "If I have to, I will. But I'm older now Max. And these hands are gonna hurt."

Chapter 3

Tracy arrived at Paganini & Sons Fine Clothiers and Tailoring at 9:00 in the morning on Friday. While Neal would be spending the early part of the day running the background checks, she would be talking to whomever she could. Max and Tony Paganini had already arrived; the latter let her in.

"Hi Tracy," Max's eldest son began. "I don't know if you remember me. I'm Tony." He offered her his hand and there was a brief shake. "Pop's back here." Tony relocked the front door and then led her back to Max's office.

"Tracy's here, Pop," Tony said after briefly knocking on and then opening the door.

Max rose from his seat. "Tracy, *buongiorno!*"

"Hi Max," she greeted. "Did you get any rest last night?"

"I did okay."

She nodded, smiling.

"Do you want any coffee, Tracy? It's fresh."

"Sure, Max. That'd be great."

"Antonio! Get Tracy some coffee, huh."

After receiving a steaming mug, Tracy took a seat in front of Max's desk. "Okay Max," she began. "I'd like to talk to some of your staff this morning. I'd like to start with Lester, if that'd be alright."

"Sure, Tracy. He should be here any minute now. He'll have the week's checks for me to sign, and after that you can talk to him as long as you need."

"Supreme," Tracy chirped. She turned to look toward the office door, and then she noted the small table to its left. She arose and moved toward the stand. On it were Max's cell phone — which sat next to its charger — some mail, a stack of sticky notes, and a picture of what must have been his grandchildren. She smiled. So that's why Max was so sure about the phone being there the morning of the murder, he probably snuck frequent looks at that photograph. She turned back to Max. "Max, they're beautiful," she told him.

"Yeah, I think so."

"What are their names?"

Max leaned back in his chair. "The girls are Antonio's, Rosa and Angelina. The boy is Roberto, Jr. The girls are six and four. Little Roberto is three." And then Max put his head down and started rubbing his eyes. Tracy moved toward him.

"What's wrong Max?" she asked him. He shook his head and then cleared his throat.

"I can hardly see them. I look over there all the time thinking I'll be able to see them plain as day like I used to. But..."

Tracy looked at him sympathetically. "I'm sorry, Max." He shook his head some more, but said nothing. "I see your phone there," Tracy said, changing the subject. "Is that where you always keep it?"

"Yes," Max nodded. "I don't have much use for it. But I got one any-way."

"Do you get many calls on it?"

"Nah. Gloria may call me after the shop closes or if there's no one up front answering the phone. She doesn't have the patience to wait for the directory options to come on so she just calls that thing. I guess she's afraid something will burn while she waits." He started chuckling. "Marty calls me on it. I made the mistake of giving him the number the first time we met and he programmed it into that phone of his. So when he wants to call me he just pushes a button. Dag gone pain in the...well, you know."

Tracy was chuckling. "That's it? Marty and Gloria?"

"The boys call me on it sometimes if I'm not at my desk. No matter how many times I tell them I don't carry that thing around with me all the time they still call me on it. They don't listen." Tracy laughed some more. "And then I get these calls that I don't know what they are, I won a vacation, I won a car, I won this, I won that...What the hell *is* that?"

"Telemarketers have moved into the 21st century, Max. That's why I look at the phone number or name on the screen when I get a call. If I don't recognize it, I don't answer. That's what voice mail is for."

"Voice mail?"

"Like an answering machine inside your phone."

"Oh, the message thing. I always forget to check that." Max scratched his chin. "Tracy, why all the questions about the phone?"

"Because one of the main reasons you're in trouble is because of the call you said you never made. So someone else made it. Once I find out who that was, I'll be able to make all this go away."

Max shook his head. "I've been through all this with you, Marty, the cops; I keep telling you, the phone was in my office all morning. Nobody borrowed the phone."

"I know, Max. I know." Before Tracy could continue there was a knock at the door.

"Come in Lester," Max shouted. "Come in and meet Tracy. She wants to talk to you and I want you to answer all her questions. *Capice*?"

"Right, Max," Lester Grossman said as he made his way toward his employer's desk. He placed the stack of paper in front of Max and then went to where Tracy was now standing.

"Lester Grossman at your service," he started. "And you are Miss…?"

"Tracy Brubaker. But please call me Tracy."

"Very well then; you can call me Lester." Grossman moved back to Max, who was starting to sign the checks. "Any questions, Max?"

"Lester, do I ever have any questions when I'm signing these damn things? Why can't you get me a stamp or something?"

"Max, I told you. If you don't want to sign, I can get Tony to do it."

"Tony says we could pay most of this stuff through wire or the computer or some such thing."

"I am old fashioned, Max," Grossman said firmly. "I do not like the idea of money going out of here through cyberspace or any of its relatives. It creates the risk someone could help themselves."

"Help themselves to what, Lester? There ain't nothing there."

"Just sign the checks Max. If we are going to make any changes to our accounting procedures we can discuss that at a later time; privately."

"It's always 'later' around here. You all are just waiting for me to die so you can do what you want."

Grossman took a step back from Max, who was still hunched over his desk signing. "I will not even respond to that," Lester snapped, clearly offended. Tracy turned from the two men and let out a light chuckle. "Good ole' Max, cantankerous as ever," Tracy thought.

After Max handed the signed checks back to Grossman, the bookkeeper started making his way back to his office. Tracy followed him to what was a room not much larger than a supply closet. Or rather, that's the way it appeared, because there were volumes of binders stacked up against the walls, as the bookcases were already at their respective limits. She wondered if all this represented 15 years of recordkeeping. There was a computer on Grossman's desk, but it was not on. He took his seat and motioned to the single chair in front of his desk. "Please have a seat. We can talk while I double check everything against my list here and stuff the envelopes."

Tracy nodded. "That'd be supreme, Lester." Tracy pulled out her notebook and pen, at which point Grossman gave her a huge smile.

A Tracy Brubaker Mystery

"I see you don't like technology much either," he told her.

"I'm sorry…"

"You're going to take notes the old-fashioned way, I see. I thought you'd be pounding away on one of those little keyboards or something." Grossman started wiggling fingers mid-air, as if he were typing on an imaginary keyboard.

"Oh," she said nodding. "I've been doing this since I was in school and it always seems to work for me; if ain't broke and all that."

He nodded approvingly. "You know, I was at the doctor's just last month. He barely looked at me. He had some electronic clipboard which he kept tapping away at with his pen. He'd ask questions; I'd answer, but his eyes hardly ever left that board. Just…aggravating."

Tracy nodded and said, "I hear you, Lester." She did see his point, although she wondered if Lester Grossman was just a man reluctant to make any kind of change. "Can I ask you some questions about last Wednesday morning?"

Grossman nodded. "Certainly. What is it you want to know?"

"I'm focusing on the call that Max was supposed to have made at 10:25 a.m. When did you last see Max in his office?"

"It would have been well before that. I meet him on Wednesday's shortly after 9 to go over the bills that can be paid for the week. Then I print them out, double check them, and have Max sign them Thursday afternoon or Friday morning. Of course, Tony actually approved the bills this week because of…the situation."

Tracy was nodding as Grossman spoke. "And that's how it went this particular Wednesday morning?"

"Yes, I think — oh, wait a moment. He was meeting with his lawyer around the time we usually met. So I met with him a little later and I probably didn't leave Max until closer to 10. And I remember that I had to fill out a manual check for the loan extension fee. Originally I thought I had until the end of the day but the lawyer called back and said he would pick up everything that afternoon, which he did."

"Yes, this all sounds in line with what Max told me." She stopped to look up at Grossman, who was putting checks in envelopes he had already prepared. "So you left Max's office around 10, and you didn't see him again until when?"

"Hmm; I remember Tony came and got the check from me around lunchtime. So they went over everything they needed for the lawyer around then. I probably saw Max in the afternoon at some point. Does that answer your question?"

"Yes, Lester. Did you notice anyone maybe go in Max's office as you were leaving?"

Grossman shook his head. "No, I don't remember seeing anyone. By that time the store would be open and most people would be up front, not in the back offices."

Tracy sighed. "So how is it really looking financially for Max, Lester? Is it as bad as I understand it to be?"

Grossman ceased stuffing and looked at her. Part of him wanted to refuse to answer such a personal business question. But Max had been pretty clear that she should be cooperated with fully. "Let me put it this way," he began. "After each loan extension fee, we start trying to figure out how we're going to pay the next one, forget about paying the principal down. I've told him he should let one of the tailors and one of the salespeople go—and especially that Iris person; all that would certainly help. But he won't do it because there's nothing wrong with the work they do."

"Must be frustrating when you know how to help him but he doesn't take your advice," Tracy said, taking his side more for building trust than really thinking Max was wrong.

He smiled at her again. "Yes it is. I see you understand."

"I own my own firm; I understand *exactly* what you're saying here." Tracy leaned in. "Off the record, Lester, have you considered looking elsewhere for work? Maybe find a place that appreciates what you bring to the table more than Max does?"

He studied her a moment. "I guess I've thought of it. But I haven't really done anything about it. I like Max very much. I wish he didn't see me as just a number cruncher. I'm not just a cruncher. I have tried to meet with him to discuss a solid business plan many times. And when I approach Tony about my plans he says that while his father is running things we'll have to respect his wishes. I understand the position, of course. But I just hope there's something left for Tony to take over when Max finally does decide he's ready to retire."

"I love Max very much myself," Tracy offered. "But I know he's hard-headed about some things. Take for example this phone call I alluded to earlier…"

"Oh, the one made at 10:25 a.m.?"

A Tracy Brubaker Mystery

"Yes. Anyone could really have made it. Max's phone is right on the desk there. But Max swears up and down that nobody did, as if admitting he didn't know where his phone was 24/7 was some kind of fault or something." Tracy paused to study Grossman's reaction.

Finally he said, "So that's what you think happened, someone used Max's phone and called that Pepper fellow?"

"Yes, that is what I think. Do you know if anyone else here knew and/or disliked Randall Pepper?"

"Well, we all knew *who* he was. He'd come in here once in a while. I didn't see him at every visit but the people up front would of course. I did see him once or twice, but I never introduced myself or anything. I really can't say what the others felt. I never actually witnessed anything."

Tracy made some final scribbles and then closed her pad. "I think that's enough for now, Lester. I really appreciate your time and honesty." She rose to her feet.

"Not at all; not at all young lady," he said while standing also. "If you have any more questions please just let me know. Can I take you somewhere?"

"I'm good Lester, thanks. I'll just make my way back to Max and see how he's doing."

"Fine then. It was very nice talking to you." And then Grossman sat and resumed his stuffing.

"You too," Tracy smiled. And then she returned to Max's office.

Interviewing the people on the floor would be difficult during the sales day. In spite of the supposedly slow business each tailor had work that needed to be done and Tracy didn't want to bother them. Tony Paganini came into his father's office around 11:30 a.m. "Pop, I'd like to take Tracy to lunch. I'm sure she's got questions for me and it will make things a little nicer." Tracy smiled at that suggestion.

"Sure; that'd be fine. Just bring me back something," Max said.

"Okay Pop." Tony turned to the hungry visitor. "Ready Tracy? The deli's just down the block a bit. It's not too cold outside for the walk."

"Let's do it," Tracy said while grabbing her coat. "We'll see you in a bite—I mean, a bit—Max."

"Take your time," Max said. "Enjoy your meal." Tracy followed Tony out the door to their impromptu lunch meeting.

"Everything's good here," Tony told her as they entered Dominique's Deli. "Their roast beef is especially good. If you don't eat meat they have some nice vegetarian choices too."

"Oh, I haven't made the move to a vegetable-only diet yet, Tony. I think I may take you up on the roast beef."

"Great! And this is my treat. It's the least I can do for someone who's helping Pop." Tracy gave Tony an appreciative smile and the two placed their orders. After their food was ready, they found seats by the window overlooking the street. "You know Pop was really tickled when he saw your name in the paper a few months ago," Tony continued.

"Really?" Tracy said mildly surprised.

"Yeah. He was telling everyone how he knew your father; what a great man he was. I guess I never got to tell you how sorry I was to hear what happened."

"Thanks Tony."

"Pop cried about that, you know. He was really upset about it. Anyway: now he talks about how you're going to be doing great things like your dad."

"Oh, I don't know about that."

"Well, Brian Shane – that was his name right?" Tracy nodded. "Well, he said in those interviews that you saved his life. That's pretty great."

Tracy was feeling a little embarrassed. She hadn't planned for the adulation. "I did what an attorney's supposed to do, zealously represent her client."

Tony looked at her and grinned. "I think you did more than that. But I think I may be embarrassing you. So I'll stop. But you can see why Pop wanted you when he got arrested. I know having you on his side is helping him deal with it better."

"Tony," Tracy said after a brief moment of quiet, "how is your father really doing? Is he as sick as he's intimated?"

Tony put his food down and took a drink of water. "His body seems to be shutting down. First, there was the arthritis in his legs that made walking difficult. But he seemed to learn to deal with it because he doesn't seem to complain about it much anymore. Then his wrists started hurting. But he just learned to deal with that too. The latest thing is his eyes. He says he can't see that well. I've been driving him to and from work for the last couple of months. But of course, he keeps putting off seeing a doctor."

          A Tracy Brubaker Mystery

"Oh Tony, you and your brothers *have* to drag him to one. There could be things that can be done for him."

Tony nodded. "I hear you, Tracy. But the truth is that Pop is scared of what they might find. It's like he'd rather go on not knowing than getting some official diagnosis."

Tracy sighed. "I guess I can understand that. But speaking as someone who's lost a father long before she should have, I'd want as much time as I could with him."

Tony stared at her a moment. "Would you tell him that, Tracy? Would you tell him how hurtful it is not to have your father around?" Tony paused. "Oh forget I asked that of you. That's not fair of me. I really didn't mean to sound so heartless."

"Oh, no, Tony; I understand what you meant. I'm at the point where I can talk about my dad without totally losing it. You didn't offend me."

Tony sighed with relief. "Oh good; I just think you telling him your feelings may make him understand things better, from a daughter's perspective."

She smiled and added, "You were right about the roast beef, very good."

Tony laughed. "So is there anything I can help you with? I want to, you know."

"What I really need is an alternate suspect, someone who was there when the call was made and had something against Randy Pepper. But so far I've only talked with Lester Grossman and he didn't have any ideas for me. Any thoughts?"

Tony sighed. "Boy, that's tough. I mean, if you just wanted a list of people I knew personally that didn't like him I could provide some names. But as far as people who were in the store, I can't think of anyone."

"Well, let me ask you this, is it possible some of the people you're thinking of know someone who works at the store?"

Tony thought a bit. "That's interesting. I don't know if I could answer that."

"This might be the break I was hoping for," she thought. She said to Tony, "Well, could you make a list of those names then? I have someone who could look into things. Maybe he could find something."

"Oh, sure." Tony pulled out a piece of paper and a pen from his inside coat pocket and started writing down names; he then handed the list to Tracy.

"Wow, thanks Tony! I'll get on this right away."

"You know I want to help you on this, Tracy. I want you to call me any-time for anything, okay?"

"You bet, Tony. Contrary to what the papers may have led you to be-lieve, I don't do this work alone. I'll take all the help I can get. I will call you just like you asked."

Tony looked at his lunch companion. "I know you're going to get Pop out of this. I just know it."

Tracy and Tony returned to the store shortly after 1:00. Tony dropped his father's customary chicken salad sandwich off to him before returning to the sales floor. Tracy asked for and received permission from Max to talk to Abe Denberg, the person who'd been on the company payroll for the least amount of time. As Tony was not using his office he offered it for Tracy to use for any interviews. She and Abe sat down beside each other after the introductions.

"Max tells me he knew you before you started working here," Tracy began. "How long have you been friends?"

"Oh, it must be five years at least," Denberg answered. "My family and I moved to his neighborhood about that time. My wife and his wife talked, and when Gloria found out I worked for a clothiers, Max made a point of introducing himself. When the place I was working for closed down last year, Max said I could work for him if I wanted to. It was just one of those things that affirm one's belief someone is looking out for you, you know?"

Tracy smiled and nodded. "Did the place you used to work change locations?"

"No. We went out of business. We couldn't compete with that Mason & Bond for Men. Their quality is nowhere near as good as ours was but the prices were just so much cheaper. What can you do? The owner was just losing too much money."

So Denberg's former boss was effectively run out of business by Randy Pepper's store. But what would Denberg accomplish by killing Pepper and framing his new employer? The revenge angle she could understand but not the frame. "How long had you worked at your old store?"

"About 11 years, I think; maybe longer. It was a nice place to work. And Mr. Grimes was a fine man. I think he moved to Florida."

"That's a real shame about the store. I guess you knew Randy Pepper then?"

     A Tracy Brubaker Mystery

Denberg made a sour face. "Yes, I knew him. After he opened his store he came to see Mr. Grimes and offered to buy his place. But from what I remember the offer was ridiculously low, so Mr. Grimes turned him down. I think that Pepper fellow flipped houses during the '90s. So I suspect that's what he had in mind when trying to buy the store."

"Interesting," Tracy thought. Neal was currently doing the research on Pepper so she didn't have all the facts about him yet. "Mr. Grimes owned his store and the property, just like Max?"

Denberg nodded. "Yes. Some of the standalone places around here are actually owned instead of leased. I dare not hazard a guess as to how Pepper dealt with local shops that leased."

"Do you remember the last time Pepper came into Max's store?"

He shook his head. "No, I can't say that I do."

"How's business been lately, Abe?" Tracy asked switching gears.

"Not too bad, actually. I think the holidays approaching and the economy getting better have helped. We actually have seen things pick up since…"

"Since Max got arrested?"

"Yes. Not that everyone who's come in has bought something. But there have definitely been more people through here in the last few days."

Tracy scratched her chin with her pen. "Do you remember much about last Wednesday, Abe?"

Denberg shook his head again. "No, not really. It was just an ordinary day."

"Do you recall if something happened which required Max to come out of his office? For example, did a friend or customer come in and ask to see him?"

"Oh, I don't recall. That doesn't happen too much anymore; the visits I mean. Besides, Tony is the face of the store now, and he definitely inherited his father's charisma. I think Tony is going to be a fine boss someday."

Denberg was smiling so Tracy smiled back. "I should let you get back to the floor. If I think of anything else maybe we can talk again."

"That would be fine," Denberg said while he stood up to leave. "I sure hope you find what you need to get Max out of this. Nobody here believes he killed that Pepper fellow."

"I'm really glad to hear that, Abe. Thanks again." Denberg gave a quick nod and another smile, and then left the office. Tracy remained in the chair. So Randy Pepper flipped houses in a former life. Flipping in and of itself wasn't illegal in Maryland. But certain practices involved in such an activity could make it so. Tracy felt a return to the office to learn Pepper's background might be the better option than continuing the interviews. Those could wait until Monday. Tracy pulled out her cell phone, dialed Neal, and told him she was headed back to the office and wanted the complete Randall Pepper story.

"I'll be waiting with bated breath," Neal told her.

"There are breath mints in my top drawer if you need one, smarty pants," she returned.

"My hands are going nowhere near your drawers," he challenged.

Tracy blushed. "You're dangerously close to crossing the line, Bennett."

"Gulp. I'll see you soon then."

"Yup," she laughed. After ending the call she said her goodbyes to Max and Tony and told them she'd call if anything came up. She wanted to come back at some point to talk to the rest of the staff. That should be no problem. And then Tracy was off.

Tracy lobbed a "hello" at Rebecca as she passed the reception desk and the secretary served her one back. Neal saw Tracy zip by his door, so he picked up his notes and entered her office as she was hanging her coat on the rack.

"I'm all set to go when you are," he greeted.

She grinned at him remembering their call. "Uh-huh. Sit boy."

"Is this your way of saying I'm in the doghouse?"

She just smiled and sat down. "Okay. Randy Pepper. What's there to tell?"

"Subject: born June 1963 in Arlington Virginia; only child to Mark and Lois Pepper. The family moved to Baltimore in 1974. Graduated Listner College in 1985, and went to work for an accounting firm in the fall of that same year. After a couple years there he then went to work for one of the firm's clients, a construction contractor, where he did the accounting. He stayed there for a few years and then went to work for a mortgage brokerage company. During the 1990s the company did a lot of flipping in Baltimore City, but from what I could find it was all on the up and up. I guess he put all his money away because when the brokerage firm he worked closed its doors in 2003 he started investing and/or purchasing various businesses, including getting the men's store franchise. But he also has other investments and holdings as well, his own construction company, an appraisal firm and a nightclub."

"A nightclub?"

"Yep. Cascade Thunder off of Fleet Street."

"Cascade Thunder?"

"I didn't make that up."

"So Randy Pepper has his hands in quite a bit. And a lot of it involves real estate." Tracy leaned forward in her chair. "And Charlie Betts works for Reginald Walters."

Neal raised his eyebrows. "But didn't Betts make his appointment to see you *before* Pepper got himself killed?"

"Curious, isn't it? A rather large coincidence, I think."

"And now I suppose you want me to see if I can find any link between Pepper and Walters?"

"Correct, gold star for you today. You're out of the doghouse."

"Oh joy. And what if I *do* find something?"

Tracy paused a moment. "Then *I'm* going to be in the doghouse with El. I told him I wouldn't tell anybody what he shared with me in confidence. But if Walters is involved in my case, I'm going to have to do just that; but first things first, Neal."

"Okay."

"Look, it's almost 5. Unless there's anything earth shattering involving the other names I gave you, why don't we wait until Monday. The preliminary hearing isn't until Wednesday and I have no doubt Max will be formally charged no matter what we find out between now and then."

"No, there's nothing that's going to turn any heads."

"Okay then." Tracy pulled a piece of paper from her briefcase and handed it to Neal. "Also on Monday, see if you can find any connection between any of the four names on this list and Max's employees. Tony Paganini says these people didn't care for Pepper."

"Gotcha."

"And then there's the possibility that one of Pepper's own employees is involved since several of them told the police they knew about the appointment."

"Wow, we have quite a bit of work ahead of us on this, don't we?"

Tracy nodded. "Yes, we do. So go home and have a nice weekend. I sense overtime in both of our futures."

"And what do you have planned?"

"I'm spending most of tomorrow with Mom."

"Is that going to be what you'd call relaxing?"

"Oh, it's not so bad."

Neal gave Tracy a smile as he prepared to leave. Then he turned back to her before exiting her office. "So it looks like this is going to go to trial; your first murder trial."

Tracy gave Neal a brief stare. "You're right. I didn't even realize that until now."

"I'll see you Monday then. Goodnight."

"Goodnight, Neal. Have a supreme weekend." Tracy leaned back in her chair feeling slightly rattled. Even though a potential trial was months away and anything could happen during those months, she nevertheless felt a mix of dread and anticipation at the thought of defending Max in open court. What if she lost and Max went to jail? "Stop thinking that way," she told herself. She closed her eyes and started thinking of her mother; the visit tomorrow would be welcome. But when her mother learned of her helping Max, would she understand or would Tracy be in the doghouse?

A Tracy Brubaker Mystery

Chapter 4

Tracy's mother had lived in Aberdeen, Maryland for over five years, in an apartment she shared with Maria Raccio. It was nearly an hour's drive for Tracy so she usually visited her mother on the weekend. That way she could arrive early Saturday and spend most of the day with her. Tracy rang the doorbell and the door was opened almost immediately. "Hi Mom!" she said as the two shared the customary welcoming embrace.

"Tracy, come in and get out of the cold," Violetta Brubaker ordered.

"It's not too bad really." Tracy followed her mother into the small living room and the two sat down on the beige couch that could accommodate three. "How are you doing Mom? Everything okay?"

"Oh, I'm fine. I'm a little sore on this elbow." She was pointing at her right arm, and Tracy noticed a bruise.

"What happened?"

"I bumped it on the counter when I was trying to open a can of olives."

"Ouch!"

"It's not so bad."

Tracy looked around. "Where's Mrs. Raccio today?"

"She went with her daughter and grandchildren to the church bazaar. Then they'll go to lunch."

"Would you like me to take you to the bazaar, Mom? I don't mind driving you over."

"Why would I go? Who do I have to buy for? You never liked that kind of stuff, and I don't have any grandchildren."

"Not that you know about anyway."

Violetta looked at her daughter who was wearing an impish grin. "Oh, you think you are funny."

"No, Mom. I'm not funny at all. That's why men don't like me and I don't have kids. Face it Mom. I may have to adopt and raise humorless children. Of course I'd have to hire a humorless nanny so they wouldn't prefer her over me. Maybe I should just get a dog instead; a droopy one, like a Basset Hound or something. A dog won't care about how unfunny I am. They can't laugh anyway."

Violetta blew air through her lips. "Oh stop with your nonsense." Tracy started chuckling. "Why do you like to tease me so much?"

"Why do you always try to make me feel guilty because I don't have children? If it's meant to be then it will happen."

Crossed Stitch

"I just hope I'm still around."

"Oh don't start with that." Tracy forced a smile on her face. "So, what shall we do today? Is there anywhere you'd like to go? Do you feel like going to a movie, or do some shopping — anything?"

"No. I think I want to hear about you and Massimo Paganini."

Tracy looked to the floor. "How'd you learn about that?"

"There was something about him in the paper about getting out, and you were mentioned. And then Gloria called to tell me thank you, as if I have any say in your life."

"You're not mad are you? Max is an old and dear family friend."

Violetta shook her head. "No; why should I be mad? You just be sure to take care of yourself."

Tracy smiled. "I'll be fine Mom."

"Did you eat breakfast? There's cereal and pastries."

"I'm good; ate before I got in the car."

"How is your business doing?"

"We're doing well, Mom. We've been pretty busy. In fact I may go into the office tomorrow."

"On Sunday?"

"I figure we can go to mass at 5:00 p.m. and then go to dinner. I'll even take you to bingo if you want. Doesn't that sound like a nice evening?"

"I guess so."

Tracy frowned. "Mom, what's wrong?"

"Nothing's wrong. I just get bored being out here. I wish you'd come by more."

Tracy took her mother's hands. "It's the holidays coming up, isn't it? You're thinking about Dad a lot, aren't you?"

Violetta looked at their entangled fingers. "We used to go shopping for the turkey about this time. Your father didn't like waiting until the last minute. It would take up all that room in the fridge for two weeks and I had no room for anything else; he could be so difficult sometimes."

Tracy leaned in so that the two women's foreheads were pressed against each other. "I miss him too, Mom. You know Mom, you could come live with me if you wanted to. I could clear out the second bedroom and I could sleep in there. You could have the master bedroom and it could be like a little apartment for you."

"You don't want me there."

"That's not true. I wouldn't ask if I didn't want you there."

    A Tracy Brubaker Mystery

Violetta looked up at Tracy. "You're a good daughter, Tracy. But I'm fine here. Besides, Mrs. Raccio needs me. I'll be okay."

"Well, I want you to think about what I asked. Think of the fun we'd have, we could go to the Harbor restaurants, heat up the dance floor and we can be each other's wing woman."

Violetta smiled, turned her head, and then waved her hand. "Oh, Tracy." After a brief moment she continued, "Why don't we go to the bazaar? There might be some nice young men there from the church."

Tracy rolled her eyes but laughed. "Sure Mom. But I don't want you introducing me as your 'very single daughter' this time."

"I never…"

"Oh yes you did, at the church July 4th picnic we went to this year."

"You heard me wrong."

Tracy laughed as she pulled the door closed.

She switched on her lights a few minutes before 11:00 p.m. It had turned out to be a very nice Saturday with her mother. They had basically window shopped at the church fair. But they had met up with Mrs. Raccio and her family and enjoyed the company of her three grandchildren. Tracy loved bearing witness to their visits to Santa, who had made a guest appearance at the cozy neighborhood church bizarre, bearing candy canes and hearty ho-ho-hos. When they returned to the apartment they played cards until it was time to leave for the evening service, dinner and about 90 minutes of bingo. Tracy said goodbye to her mother and told her she'd pick her up Thanksgiving morning for their annual holiday meal with the Tanners. Warm embraces and I-love-yous ended the evening. "Yes," Tracy thought, "it had been a very good day."

Now she found herself in the spare bedroom which presently housed her DVD collection of mystery movies and TV shows that mostly once belonged to her father. Each title on the various shelves held some memory for her. She had spent Saturdays and Sundays, and more time when school was out, on her father's lap watching Nick Charles or The Falcon, or whatever happened to be on. She grew to share her father's love of detective stories and whodunits, but the real reason her collection meant so much to her was because it kept her father with her all the time. But she would have no problem boxing them up to make room for her mother. Her only reservation was that, with her at work so much, someone might not be at the unit if her mom needed help. Living with Mrs. Raccio seemed to be the better alternative since they could watch over each other and had much in common, two widows whose husbands were once Baltimore City detectives. Tracy liked Mrs. Raccio very much and thought her a perfect companion. But all her mother had to do was say the word and Tracy would make a place for her here.

Lying in bed on her back, however, Tracy's thoughts returned to Max Paganini and his situation. The revelation about Randy Pepper's resume had Tracy convinced that Reginald Walters was likely involved in this. If that were true then someone working for Max could really be in cahoots with Walters, in spite of Max's insistence that his employees were above reproach. First thing Monday she'd find out all the details Neal had assembled and then make a return visit to Max's shop. And, what *about* Walters? She'd been warned by Tanner as well as the federal fellows that he was dangerous. But she didn't have any real justification for trying to see him at this point anyway. She had heard nothing further from Carlton aka Charlie. But it had been only a few days. Still, her working theory was that Walters wanted Pepper dead and set up Max for it. Enough of this for now, though. Tracy rubbed her forehead, turned on her side, and closed her eyes. She was asleep in seconds.

"How was your weekend?" Rebecca asked as Tracy was pouring her first cup of Monday coffee.

"Very nice. I spent the day with Mom Saturday, and then came in here for a few hours yesterday to clean up my office and sign some of those forms you've been leaving all over my desk." Rebecca chuckled. "How was yours?"

"We all went shopping for Thanksgiving dinner necessities, and then we did some early Christmas shopping too. I'm almost done."

"I hate you," Tracy chided.

"How is it that you always manage to wait until the last minute when it's just *you*?"

Tracy thought a moment. "I guess I think better under pressure."

"Uh-huh. You work too much."

"No I don't."

"If you say so."

Tracy gave Rebecca a steely-eyed glare. "I left those signed forms on your chair."

"Yeah, I noticed that when a paperclip pinched my butt."

A Tracy Brubaker Mystery

Tracy laughed out loud. "Okay Ms. Smarty Skirt, back to work. Next time I may use thumbtacks." Then she went to wait for Neal's arrival.

When Neal poked his head in his employer's office, she was reviewing Maryland hearsay law. "Morning, boss. Shall we interface?"

Tracy looked up at him. "Um, what did you say?"

"Should we meet now?"

"Oh, sure."

Neal already had his papers with him. "What do you have there?"

"I'm seeing if there's any way to stop Pepper's employees from testifying about the phone call. They can testify as to the identity of the caller as Max only because Pepper *told* them it was Max. But someone could have *pretended* to be Max."

"But they have the phone records."

"That just proves someone made a call using Max's phone. It doesn't prove Max made the call. They need both to make a convincing case, you see?"

"I do see."

"Art will no doubt try to get the statements in via one of the exceptions, and he has several possibilities. But for now let's pick up where we left off on Friday. Tell me about Lester Grossman."

Neal flipped through his notepad. "Okay...Lester...Lester... Lester. Here we go. Lester Grossman, 56 years of age, lives in a city apartment, no wife or kids, been with Max since 1998. BM—"

"Excuse me?"

"Before Max, he worked at several public accounting firms starting in 1980, but ended up working for one of those places—Logan's Temporaries and More—that provides temporary help, secretaries, accounting personnel, etc. He worked there from 1994 until he landed with Max. He never got his certified public accountant license so I guess that's why he went private."

"Alright. I guess it would be next to impossible to get a list of the temp jobs he worked in his four or so years there."

"We'd have to subpoena the records, yes, if they even would still have them. But we'd have to have some justification to do that. You could ask Lester about it."

"And then he'd know I was digging around in his background. And if he had something to hide he'd keep on hiding it."

"Like you said, impossible."

"Nuts. Hey, didn't you tell me Pepper worked at an accounting firm at one point?"

Neal started flipping through his notes, checking the name of Pepper's old firm and then seeing if Grossman may have worked there too. "No, Tracy, no firm in common. But that doesn't mean they didn't meet at some point. Maybe they shared the same client or were involved on opposite sides of a divorce trial or something like that."

"I wonder if there's any way to find something like that out. But that would have been so long ago. Why would Lester have suddenly decided Pepper needed to die?"

Neal was making notes regarding Tracy's questions. "I'll do a little more work in this area. But don't get your hopes up."

"Oh come on Neal. Hope should be like a soaring balloon. Don't be a pin…head."

"Huh?"

"Tell me about the tailors."

"I don't know any Taylors, except Andy and Opie."

"Hardy-har-har."

"Okay, so it wasn't that funny."

"Right. Hardly-har-har then."

Neal started chuckling. "You win. Jeff Pollenfax and Craig Marwood have been…" Neal stopped talking when he noticed Tracy was quietly laughing. "What is it now?"

"He's ceased to be. He's expired and gone to meet his maker. He's bereft of life."

"Who? Pepper?"

"No, the parrot." And then she started laughing out loud.

"Dear Lord, Tracy, what *are* you talking about?"

She wiped the tears from her eyes. "I'm sorry Neal. I don't know what's with me all of a sudden. I'm sorry."

"Is there a parrot involved in this somehow?" Neal asked incredulously.

She shook her head while starting to laugh again. "No. It's just that Craig's last name is Marwood and I've heard of only one other person with that name before."

"Oh—who's that?"

"John Cleese, Marwood is his middle name. You know, Monty Python, the Parrot Sketch."

"Before my time," he said, looking at her quizzically. "Are you okay now?"

"I'll behave. I don't know why I have such a case of the sillies. Maybe it's the stress showing itself in a bizarre manner. Anyway, you were telling me about Jeff and Craig…"

"Yes…Max hired them both in 1994 around the same time. Both men are in their 50s. Jeff is married with three grown children. Craig is divorced with two adult kids. Now Pepper didn't enter the picture until years after Max hired them so I don't see how either of them could be involved. But I thought I might take it a step further and see about their kids."

"Hey, that's a real good thought there, family man. Maybe they would turn on Max if one of their kids is mixed up with Pepper or Walters and needed Dad's help."

"My thoughts exactly. It's a stretch…"

"It's a good thought, Neal."

"Thanks. Now we have Sonny Palin and Abe Idle…"

"Oh, you're cute. You want me to start singing *The Lumberjack Song* or do the Wink-Wink-Nudge-Nudge skit? I will you know."

"No, no, that's okay, again before my time."

"Then, say no *more!*"

Neal laughed. "Right. William "Sonny" Brookhouser has been with Max since 2011. He moved that year from Delaware where he had worked for one of the major clothiers."

"Any idea why he moved?"

"Not sure. His wife manages a chain restaurant downtown so maybe they moved so she could take that job. But I'm just guessing."

"Any kids?"

"A 14-year-old daughter."

"Okay…and Abe Denberg? He told me his former employer closed up shop."

"That checks. Went to work for Max last year."

"And Abe told me Pepper's store effectively closed down his former employer's."

"There was an article on the closing in the newspaper. The owner's name was Edward Grimes and he was interviewed. The store had been there for 20 years. I read it but didn't really find anything helpful to us in it. But he did mention something along the lines of the big guys trying to close the little guys down in *all* lines of business."

"One day your only choices will be the internet or *the* mega-store," Tracy said ruefully.

"You may be right about that."

"I know Abe is married. Any kids?"

"Nope."

"And no criminal records on any of these guys?"

"They're all clean in that regard. But like I mentioned, I haven't checked their kids yet."

"Mm; I guess that leaves Paul Iris. Max said he was a single father."

"True. He has a daughter named Pauline. The wife-mother died of some rare heart condition called Danon disease."

"Never heard of it."

"Neither had I. It had gone undiagnosed and when it was found, it was too late. She died of heart failure."

Tracy shook her head. "That's awful."

"The little girl was five when it happened. Her father's 36 now; works three jobs—the tailor shop, a gas station and a pizza place on the weekends."

"Who watches Pauline?"

"Iris has a sister with a family of her own. Pauline spends time with her aunt and cousins."

"Ah. What did Paul Iris used to do?"

"He managed a woman's shoe store not too far from where Max is located. The owners closed several of their stores a few years ago and Iris' was one of them."

"Women's shoes, huh? I don't think either Randy Pepper or Reginald Walters dabbled in footwear."

"Not that I could find."

"Paul's lucky though to have a sister who can help. At least he knows his daughter is in good hands."

"True. But it's also true that guy is struggling financially; not getting to spend time with the person he loves most in the world."

"I see where you're going with this, but the point is moot. Paul Iris wasn't even at Max's that Wednesday, so he couldn't have called Pepper."

"I suppose."

Tracy sighed. "Okay. I guess that's all fine with respect to the employees. But we still have the list Tony made that I gave you. I wonder what

 A Tracy Brubaker Mystery

luck I would have trying to speak with *Pepper's* employees, the ones who either overheard the call or were told about it."

"No idea."

"And I haven't even delved into alibis for the actual murder yet. The married ones most likely will have their spouses. Iris was probably with his daughter if he wasn't working. So that would leave Lester and Craig as the first two to check out."

"What about Max's sons? I know it's a horrible thing to suggest, but still."

Tracy turned to look out her window. "You're right to bring up the possibility of course. But let's work through the other options before we head in that direction. Max is stubborn enough with respect to his employees."

"Well, I'll just do some general checking then after I'm done with everything else. If I find something I'll let you know."

"That sounds like a plan."

"What about the preliminary hearing?"

"I'm not sure how much I want to say there. Art will probably put only a couple of the investigating officers on the stand and that should be enough to have Max arraigned. I just can't see how Max can avoid that."

"I'm sorry, Tracy. I know Max and your father were friends."

"Thanks, Neal. Right now it feels like defending Max will be like trying to chop down a tree with a herring."

Neal paused. "*Holy Grail*, right?"

Tracy nodded without smiling. The sillies had left her. "I think I'll try to meet with Max, Gloria, and Tony and tell them about how Wednesday is likely to go. Thanks again Neal. Thanks for being my MVP."

"Sure Tracy." Neal left her office, and then she picked up the phone to set up her next Paganini meeting.

"Will they put him in jail?" Gloria asked.

"No, I don't think so. I can't see the State's Attorney asking that."

"But it could happen," Tony offered.

"Let's not worry about that right now. I will have my arguments ready in case that unlikely scenario comes to pass. Right now I just want you all to understand how Wednesday is likely to go." Tracy, Max, Gloria and Tony were seated at the Paganini dining room table. Tracy had decided to eschew any more interviews with the shop's staff until after the preliminary hearing. She didn't think talking to Max's employees would be helpful at this point, and she was more interested in what Neal might find. Of course, Max had insisted Tracy join them for dinner, but she wanted to get the business done with first.

"Why don't you two let the poor girl talk?" Max said to his wife and eldest.

"It's okay, Max," Tracy said sympathetically. "They're worried about you."

"Fine. But I still say they should let you talk first."

"Sure Pop," Tony told him. "Okay, Tracy, no more interruptions until you're done."

"Fair enough," she responded. "Now the preliminary hearing is where the State will present its evidence against you, Max, fingerprints on the gun, the phone call, the opportunity to commit the crime since Pepper was killed at your store, and the antagonistic history. They'll try to show they have probable cause to charge you with the murder. I want to be truthful here, I believe the State has enough to have the case sent to trial." Tracy observed Gloria reach for her husband's hand and start crying. "I'm sorry Mrs. P. I wish things were different."

"What will happen then if you're right?" Tony asked.

"Max will then have what's called an arraignment scheduled where he'll enter his plea of Not Guilty. Sometime after that the State will probably offer a plea bargain. It would mean less jail time but Max would have to plead Guilty. But of course we won't be doing that. I'll try to get the trial date set up at the arraignment. I'm hoping for February or March. I will play up Max's age and health to force as early a court date as possible."

"Wait a minute," Max interrupted. "I don't want the whole world to know how I'm feeling."

Tony added, "Not too many people know about Pop's problems. I mean, they can see he has trouble walking but they don't know about his eyes or hands or anything else. Only people who work at the store know about that. We'd like to keep it that way for now, if at all possible."

"Okay. I'll be as vague as possible in that regard," Tracy offered.

Now Gloria chimed in, scolding her husband. "You let her do what she has to do. Don't tell her how to do her job. All she's trying to do is help you..." Gloria couldn't finish her thought.

There was quiet at the table now. Tracy broke the silence. "The hearing is at 10:00 a.m. I'll meet you, Max, at the courthouse."

A Tracy Brubaker Mystery

"Do you want me there, Pop? Would it be alright to leave the store?"

"You *and* your brothers; one of you can drive us all to the courthouse. The store will be fine."

Tracy rose from her chair to leave, suddenly feeling like the unwelcome messenger of doom. "Tracy, where are you going?" Max asked.

"Just home, Max."

"No; you stay here and eat with us. Roberto and Germano are coming; they should be here soon. We'll forget about all of this for a while. I have some homemade wine for you to try too. You're old enough for it now."

She didn't want to stay. The tension in the air was palpable and she felt like being there, regardless of what Max said, would make the meal feel like the Last Supper.

"Tracy, please stay," Gloria said.

"How can you turn down Ma's cooking, Tracy?" Tony asked smiling.

"Well, you got me there," Tracy admitted. "But you have to let me help set the table and help clean up afterward. Those are my conditions."

Max laughed. "Of course, of course." And then Max went to put his arm around his dinner guest.

Roberto and Jerry arrived together at their parents' home as Tracy was helping Tony set the table. "You two are just in time to eat, as always," Max called out while greeting them. "Go see if you can help your brother or mother. And say 'hello' to Tracy."

"Hey, its Jerry's fault Pop," Roberto said defensively. "He was late picking me up."

"I got stuck in traffic," Germano said testily.

"Oh stop you two," Max said as he headed back to the kitchen. "Always with the excuses."

Tracy and Tony had finished with the table when the two younger sons entered the dining room. There were warm greetings all around, but Roberto and Germano asked Tracy practically simultaneously about their father. Before she could answer Tony spoke. "Pop's going to be fine. Tracy's a great lawyer and she's doing everything she can. Now let's not talk about it for the rest of the night. Agreed?"

Tony's brothers nodded. Everyone made their way to the kitchen to see what help they could be to the Paganini matriarch. "Why didn't you bring the family, Roberto?" Gloria asked while kissing her second oldest.

"Roberto, Jr. has a cold Ma and is not feeling well. Besides, I thought maybe Pop would like it to be a little quieter around here."

"I'll send some soup back with you for Roberto, Jr."

"Sure Ma; that'd be great."

Germano, meanwhile, was staring at Tracy who was holding a bottle of Max's homemade wine. "Wow; you're all grown up now, huh?" he finally said.

"Yeah," she answered with a slight chuckle. "It happens."

Tracy started making her way back to the dining room table to deposit the wine bottle. Germano followed empty handed. "I haven't seen you since school days."

"You're right; it's been quite a while, hasn't it?"

"You look…real nice."

Tracy smiled again. Then she looked at him, hand on her hip. "You didn't used to think so."

Germano blushed. "Hey, what the heck did I know? I was just a dumb kid. I guess it's too late to apologize for picking on you like I used to."

Tracy laughed. "Hey, it's okay; I'm just getting a little good-natured revenge is all." Then she gave him a flirtatious smile and headed back to the kitchen saying, "You didn't turn out so bad yourself."

Upon her return to the kitchen Tracy asked Roberto, "What are you doing with yourself these days?"

"Oh, I'm an architect."

"Hey, that sounds fascinating. Any structures that have your fingerprints on them I may recognize?"

"A couple of new hotels in the area have some courtyards and the like around them for aesthetic purposes; the firm I work for was involved in those designs. And there were some city renovation projects we were involved with too."

"You were always very creative from what I remember."

Roberto smiled and laughed. "I really like it."

"And you still find time to help your dad out too."

"Mostly on weekends. And I do take some Wednesdays off by working late other days to get my time in. My employer is very good about that."

"I think that's a terrific thing you're doing, Roberto; both you and Jerry. Not all sons would do that for their dads."

"Well, I do what I can." Roberto changed the subject. "So do you work for a big law firm?"

"No; just me and a couple of other people. I interned at one and worked there a couple of years while I finished law school. But I like being my own

A Tracy Brubaker Mystery

boss and having control over the cases I take on. I don't know if you remember how stubborn I could be."

Roberto laughed. "I remember you being really smart; that's what I remember about you."

Tracy blushed. "I don't know about that." She cleared her throat. "What does Jerry do for a living?"

"Computers; works for a company that takes care of your computer if it has problems, whether individual or corporate."

"That's a job that has total future security; we'll be needing computer help for the rest of our lives."

Roberto nodded. "It's a good job, sure; some crazy hours though. Sometimes he'll have to work nights after a business closes down for the day. But like me, he's arranged it so he can help Pop out."

Tracy started laughing. "Your dad tells me you and Tony stole his sales help away, via marriage."

"Yeah," Roberto answered chuckling. "What can I say? Pop always had an eye for the ladies. I walked into the store one day and there was Rachael. And that was it."

"And it was like that for Tony too?"

"He asked Donna out the first or second day she worked there," Roberto answered, resuming his laughter.

"Well, Max has some good looking sons," Tracy offered, laughing herself.

"When Jerry started dating Laura, that was it; Pop was pissed."

Tracy suddenly ceased her merriment. "Max didn't fire Laura, did he?"

"Oh, no; she just quit."

Her smile returned. "Oh good. I could see him doing something like that in a moment of fury."

"No, Pop would never do something like that; he was mad at Jerry not Laura. Laura's gorgeous; like I said, Pop has the eye."

"But his heart belongs to your mother."

Roberto looked at Tracy with a serious expression. "Yes. They still hold hands all the time. Ma was a gorgeous woman too you know."

"She still is."

"Of course; Ma *is* a gorgeous woman. And what about you Tracy? Are you married? Any kids?"

She shook her head. "No."

"Well you're seeing somebody, right?"

Another headshake. "I'm working through something currently."

"Oh, okay." Roberto, sensing he was in touchy territory, cleared his throat. "Well, watch out for Jerry then. He may be with Laura but he still comes across like he's…well—"

"On the make?"

"Yeah, 'the make'," Roberto nodded, his smile now returning.

"Hey Roberto," Max interrupted, "dinner is ready; let Tracy sit down and eat."

"Let's go Tracy; his majesty grows hungry." Roberto took Tracy's arm and escorted her to the feast.

Tracy and the Paganini family partook of Gloria Paganini's homemade penne and meat sauce. Bread, salad, and wine were also enjoyed. While there was some laughter during the repast, the tone was nevertheless somber. Max put up a brave front, telling stories about his grandkids and anything that seemed to amuse him. His family smiled and tried to join in with Max's ebullience. But the murder charge was still in the room, hovering over the dinner table like some invisible party crasher. When the dinner had ended, Tracy helped Gloria with the dishes as agreed to, and then she thanked and said goodnight to the Paganini family. She wasn't in the best of moods.

Back at her condo Tracy sat on her couch staring into space. She had hoped preparing Max and his family for Wednesday was the right thing to do, to help them know what to expect. But she wasn't so sure she made the right decision. She couldn't let them down. "I can't take on these personal cases anymore," she thought. "After this I should just go back to doing what I know and what I'm good at. Who do I think I am? I got lucky with Brian's case because the killer made a stupid mistake. But this…" She shook her head, and then changed into her pajamas and tried to think of how much she enjoyed the holidays, which were just around the corner. If she were little once again she could make this all better by just writing a letter: "Dear Santa, Please let Max be okay."

Wednesday morning Arthur Pankow addressed the court. "The State is ready to proceed with the preliminary hearing, Your Honor." His premier witness was the first officer to arrive at the Paganini shop the night of the murder.

"Officer Ross, what time did you arrive at the tailor shop the evening of Wednesday November 5?"

A Tracy Brubaker Mystery

"At 9:54 p.m."

"Who had called you there?"

"911 dispatcher. She said a homicide had been reported at that location."

"Who called 911 to report the homicide?"

"Antonio Paganini."

"Who was at the tailor shop when you arrived?"

"Mr. Massimo Paganini and Antonio, his son."

"Had they been there together the whole evening?"

"No. Antonio said he arrived there around 9:30."

"So then Mr. Paganini had been alone in the store for how long?"

"From about 7:00 in the evening until his son arrived."

"I see. And the victim, Randall Pepper, was he already dead when the son arrived?"

"Yes. Both father and son confirmed that."

"Did Mr. Paganini tell you what happened?"

Ross withdrew a small notebook from his pocket. "He said he heard a noise at about 8:30, went to investigate, and found the victim in the storeroom."

Pankow paused a moment. "Are you saying Mr. Paganini found the body at 8:30, but that the police weren't called until the son arrived about an hour later?"

"Yes sir."

"Did Mr. Paganini offer some kind of explanation for this?"

"Not exactly. He said he was confused and he knew his son would be there soon and would know what to do."

Tracy looked over at Max who was looking at his folded hands, which were resting on his lap. She rubbed his shoulder as Pankow continued.

"I see. No more questions."

"Do you have any questions for this witness, Ms. Brubaker?" the presiding Judge Altman asked.

"Yes Your Honor." Tracy arose from her chair but remained in place. "Officer Ross, is it unusual for someone to be, to use the word you just used, confused after a crime, especially a violent one?"

"That depends."

"On what?"

"The circumstances."

"The circumstances in this case—an elderly gentleman all alone in his store at night, hears a noise and finds a body—would you, based on your experience, say such circumstances might lead one to be confused?"

"Objection!" Pankow shouted. "Counsel is asking for a conclusion from the witness."

"Only as it relates to his experience, Your Honor."

"Rephrase the question, Ms. Brubaker," the judge ordered.

"Officer Ross, based on your experience, when Mr. Paganini told you he was confused, did Mr. Paganini appear to be confused?"

"Objection!"

"No, I'll let him answer that," Altman told Pankow.

"He certainly seemed upset," Ross answered. "And yes, I would say he appeared to be a little confused as to what was going on."

"Thank you Officer. No more questions." Tracy returned to her seat.

"The State calls Detective Adam Garrison." Tracy was unfamiliar with Garrison but he cut an imposing figure, tall with broad shoulders, crew cut blonde hair. Military man, maybe? He walked quickly and took his seat in the witness box. Pankow began, "Detective Garrison, you are the lead detective assigned to this case?"

"Yes sir."

"Can you tell us what time the coroner put the time of death?"

"Between 8:00 and 9:00."

"So you would say that is consistent with the account given by Mr. Paganini."

"Yes sir."

"What was the weapon utilized in the death of Randall Pepper?"

"A 9mm Walther Centerfire Pistol."

"Did you retrieve the murder weapon?"

"Yes."

"Was it registered?"

"No sir."

"Did you find any fingerprints on the weapon?"

"Yes; we found Mr. Paganini's prints on the weapon."

"Detective, did you have chance to speak with some of the victim's employees in the days following the murder?"

"Yes, I did."

"Did they offer any explanation as to why Randall Pepper may have been at Mr. Paganini's shop the night of the murder?"

"Yes, they did."

"And what was the explanation, Detective?"

A Tracy Brubaker Mystery

"Several people we spoke with said Mr. Paganini called Mr. Pepper earlier that day and asked him to come to his shop that night at 8:30."

"Could they tell you why the meeting was called?"

"Paganini said he was ready to sell his store. And that Pepper better jump at the chance before he changed his mind; that was the gist of it anyway."

"Were Paganini and Pepper friends?"

Garrison smiled. "No sir. They were not. They had a long standing animosity based on what several people whom we talked to said. Mr. Paganini admitted to that himself."

"How can you be sure Mr. Paganini made the call setting the appointment for that night?"

"Mr. Paganini said he had had his phone all day, and the phone company records confirm a call was placed from Mr. Paganini's cell phone to Mr. Pepper's about the time Pepper's employees say he took the Paganini call."

"So is it your theory, then, Detective, that Mr. Paganini called Mr. Pepper to the meeting and then shot him due to their long standing animosity?"

"Yes sir. That is what the evidence suggests."

"Thank you, Detective. No more questions."

Tracy rose to ask *her* questions. "Detective, I'd like to go over a few points and get some clarification. You said the murder weapon had Mr. Paganini's fingerprints. Where exactly were those prints found?"

"On the handle and on the barrel."

"Not on the remaining cartridges inside the clip?"

"No."

"Hmm. Did you perform a paraffin test on Mr. Paganini?"

"Yes."

"What were the results?"

"The test was negative."

"I see. Detective, regarding the people you spoke to that knew about the meeting, would it be correct to say that the only reason they knew about the meeting details was that Randall Pepper *told* them about those details? In other words, nobody but Randall Pepper allegedly spoke to Mr. Paganini on the phone."

Garrison paused a moment. "That's correct, Mr. Pepper told the employees about the call."

"Detective, is it true that Mr. Paganini denied making the phone call that set up the meeting."

"Correct."

"And you claim the phone company's records show a call was made from Mr. Paganini's cell phone. But can you say for certain that Mr. Paganini made the call, since, as you just said, he denied making such a call?"

"We have what Mr. Pepper told some of his employees."

"But can you be certain that the call didn't come from someone *claiming* to be Massimo Paganini?"

Pankow arose. "How can the detective answer that question?"

Tracy turned to the judge. "That's exactly my point. I have no additional questions for Detective Garrison." She returned to her seat and let out a barely audible sigh. There wasn't much else she could do.

"The State believes it has shown it has probable cause in its case against Mr. Paganini and asks that he be arraigned in circuit court."

"I agree," Judge Altman said without hesitation. "Mr. Paganini, we can schedule the arraignment for Tuesday, December 2 at 9:30 a.m."

"Very well Your Honor," Tracy responded as she stood up. And that was, unfortunately, that.

Outside the district courthouse, Tracy met with Tony Paganini and his parents. "I guess we should be thankful they didn't try to put Pop in jail. You were right about everything Tracy."

"I'm sorry everyone. There was just too much circumstantial evidence to hope this wouldn't happen." There was silence, so she continued. "We'll next appear in circuit court on the second. As I told you before, we'll enter a Not Guilty plea. They will set the trial date at the arraignment also. In the meantime I'll move ahead with preparing our defense."

"Okay Tracy," Max said softly. "You call us if you need anything."

"I'm just getting started here so let's all try to stay positive. I'll be in touch." Tracy then went to give everyone a hug as the Paganinis started toward their car. She was watching them, a sympathetic and concerned expression on her face, when Arthur Pankow lightly tapped her on the shoulder. "Oh, hi Art," Tracy said as she turned.

"Tracy, we are open for a plea on this."

"He won't take a plea, Art. He says he didn't kill Pepper and I believe him. I'm not going to push a plea on him."

"Not even if we drop the charge to voluntary manslaughter? Maybe Paganini didn't intend to kill Pepper when he set up the appointment.

Maybe something occurred that ticked off Paganini and he shot him. We could talk about eight years for everything, the killing and all the handgun violations. That's certainly better than 30. "

"I'll tell him what you said Art but he won't do it. He won't say he did something he didn't do."

"Alright then. But please tell him the offer is open and that he has time to think about it. Just let me know for sure at the arraignment."

"Okay, Art. Thanks. And Happy Thanksgiving."

"Sure. And Happy Turkey Day to you too." Pankow smiled as he left Tracy standing on the steps. "Eight years was a good offer," she thought. "And with some prodding I might even get another year or two knocked off. Pepper doesn't have any family to scream injustice." But she shook her head. Max wouldn't hear of such a thing. She'd let him know about the offer nevertheless after the upcoming holiday.

Tracy was seated at her desk eating her lunch when Neal cautiously entered. She had said barely a word since returning from the hearing so he knew she was feeling down. "How are holding up, Tracy?" he asked her, not knowing any other way to start a conversation.

"I'm okay, I guess. I knew how it was going to go and all that; but I still feel like I let them down."

"I bet *they* don't feel that way."

She gave a faint smile. "You're probably right. And the SA is already making offers, eight years. I bet I could get him down to five."

"Would Max take that?"

"No."

"Tracy, please don't get angry with me, but I have to ask, are you positive Max didn't kill that guy?"

She put her chicken salad sandwich down and looked across at Neal. "Yes, I am."

"Can I ask why?"

"Because if he were guilty he could easily have told the police that he wasn't sure the phone was on his desk the whole morning."

Neal nodded. "Of course, he could be protecting someone."

"One of his sons, you mean?"

"They could have wanted to meet with Pepper. Maybe the intent wasn't to kill the guy. Things got out of hand. They tell their father and he protects one of his boys."

Tracy's face showed no reaction. "There's a big problem with that idea, Neal."

"Oh?"

"All of Max's sons have cell phones of their own. If the meeting was originally going to be just a harmless sit-down, why use Max's phone? Why not just use their own phone? And why tell Pepper it was *Max* who was calling? You get me?"

"Yeah; okay."

"And that would hold true for any of Max's employees too. Also, why would an otherwise honest person be carrying around an unregistered weapon?"

"Oh, I didn't realize that about the gun."

"It's true. I may have some wiggle room with the gun though, prints on the handle but not on the cartridges. No residue on Max's hands but his fingerprints on the handle. What'd he do, wear gloves while shooting Pepper, remove the gloves, and then grab the handle? Max's story about how his prints got on the gun is the most logical one. But damn it about that call; if I can find a way to explain *that* I would really have something."

Neal listened as she aired her frustrations. "I haven't found anything regarding Pepper, Walters, and the employee's grown children yet. But I'll keep looking."

Tracy gave her associate a smile. "Thanks Neal."

"*There* it is!" he said arising from his seat. "I knew you had at least one in you."

Now she was gently chuckling. "Okay, you got your smile, now resume the hunt."

"You bet. And remember, Tracy," Neal began as he exited humming, "*always look on the bright side of life.*"

Tracy smiled again although Neal wasn't there to see it. Yes, there was much good in her life she could try to focus on, the business was doing well; her employees were second to none; she had Thanksgiving with her mother and the Tanner family to look forward to; and much more than all of that. But Max Paganini? His business was struggling, and it was more than likely that one his employees framed him for murder. Is that what Max would be thinking about during *his* Thanksgiving dinner?

A Tracy Brubaker Mystery

"Welcome!" Rita Tanner called out as Tracy and her mother entered the Tanner homestead foyer. "Come here Violetta and give me a big hug." Violetta passed her homemade Italian wedding cookies to her daughter and the two women embraced. Next Rita demanded the same from Tracy. The cookies changed hands again, only this time Elias Tanner was on the receiving end. After the warm greetings and removal of coats, the Brubakers and Tanners made their way to the family room, where they all sat down. Vegetables and dip, cheese and crackers, as well as sliced sausage rested on the trays covering the coffee table. The first of many football games of the day was playing on the television. It was close to 3:00 so dinner was a couple hours away. Elias took drink orders, and then made his way to the kitchen with the baked goods.

"Hey!" Tracy called out looking around. "Where's El, Jr.?"

"He should be here in time for dinner," Rita responded. "He's with his girlfriend's family. They're having brunch over there and then the two of them will here for dinner."

"Oh, so he's got a lady now, huh? That's supreme!"

"Look at that," Violetta said gruffly. "*He* found someone."

Tracy looked at her mother long enough to scowl and then returned her attentions to Rita. "How long have they been dating?"

"I think six months. Right Elias?"

Tanner was bringing in the water glasses which he handed to the guests, and then sat next to Tracy. "Longer than that; closer to nine, I think. Didn't they start going out right after Valentine's Day?"

"Oh, that's right," Rita said in agreement.

"And this is the first I'm hearing about it? El, you get an F."

Tanner laughed. "I'm sorry, Tracy. I'll try to remember to keep you updated on Elias' love life." Tracy gave his knee a light slap, and then reached for a piece of cheese.

"Want something to eat Mom?"

"I'm fine."

"Here, try some cheese. It's cheddar — your favorite."

"Maybe later."

"How about now?" Tracy was forcing a cube of cheddar into her mother's hand.

"Oh, Tracy, you're impossible," Violetta said taking the chunk.

"How about another one?"

"Oh, you difficult child." Violetta got up from her seat and moved to the small couch where Rita was seated. "I'll be fine here, I think."

Tracy's face registered a mock-hurtful expression which started the Tanners guffawing. "Oh, Tracy you're adorable as ever," Rita managed to say amidst the laughs.

"Don't encourage her," Violetta said trying not to smile. But when she gave in her daughter pointed at her.

"Gotcha!" Tracy cried victoriously. And more laughter ensued.

When Elias, Jr. and his significant other Marleena arrived, they were greeted in much the same way as the Brubakers had been. Introductions were made, and then all returned to the family room.

Marleena sat next to Tracy, while Elias, Jr. sat next to his girlfriend. "Elias says you were like brother and sister growing up," she began. "I've heard a lot about you, Tracy."

"I wish I could say the same, Marleena. But brother and step-dad haven't been doing their duty."

Marleena laughed. "Oh, then you and I will have lots to talk about. And you can tell me all about Elias when he was little."

"Not everything I hope," the junior Tanner cut in, smiling.

"Oh, the stories I could tell; the tales I could spin. He was quite the rapscallion, you know."

"Tracy, don't cause trouble," Violetta scolded.

"Want some more *cheese* Mom?"

Violetta grunted and waved her hand dismissively while Rita started laughing again.

"The bird's ready," the senior Elias announced. "Everybody to your stations."

"Want to set the table with me Marleena?" Tracy asked enthusiastically.

"Sure!"

"I am a table setting master; I've got this down to a science. Follow me!" And Marleena and Tracy headed to the dining room. Father Elias handled the carving, while Rita and Violetta moved the sundry side dishes to serving bowls. Son Elias then brought said bowls to the table. The team quickly had the feast prepared and set out, and not quite as quickly plowed through it. This is just what Tracy needed, a house filled with love and laughter; her family together sharing warm memories. As was customary,

A Tracy Brubaker Mystery

Elias, Sr. raised a glass to the one person — Tracy's father — they all wished was there, "To Peter," he announced, his voice slightly cracking. That was all he had to say.

After the diners were stuffed and started leaving the table, Violetta insisted on helping Rita clean up, at which point Tanner put his arm around Tracy and led her to a small sitting room. "We haven't gotten a chance to talk much over the last few weeks. How are you doing? How is Max?"

"Oh El," she said while leaning into him. "I guess we're both doing alright. I wish you were on the case."

"Not possible since I'm friends with the suspect."

"I understand that. I was just sayin'…"

"Look, Tracy. If you need something, you let me know and I will see what I can do, unofficially of course."

She looked up at him. "Hey, thanks El. I just might do that."

He nodded. "Any more from Carlton Brandice?"

"Not a peep."

"I guess that's a good thing."

"Anything going on with the feds case against Walters that you can tell me about?"

"All is calm," he answered with a slight grin.

"I might need some help connecting Walters with someone who works for Max."

Rita Tanner entered the hideaway. "You two better not be talking shop in my house," she said, only semi-kidding.

"Just catching up regarding a mutual friend, love," her spouse responded. They exchanged smiles, and then both Tanner and Tracy made their way back to the gathering.

"I helped Mom with the cookies, El. You'll have to let Mom know how much better they taste this year."

"Are you trying to get me in trouble?" he chuckled.

"Always." And the troublemaker put her arm around his waist as they rejoined the festivities.

The party started to disband around 10:30 p.m. "It was great meeting you Tracy," Marleena said as Elias, Jr. helped her with her coat. "We should meet for lunch or something sometime soon."

"Hey, that's a great idea," Tracy agreed. "Let me give you one of my cards; it has all of my contact info on it."

"Thanks!"

"Bye bro," Tracy grinned as she hugged Elias, Jr. "Have a great Christmas and New Year if I don't see you before the first."

"You too Tracy; it was great seeing you. I'll be praying for you and Max." He turned, took Marleena's hand, and the two lovebirds glided down the stairs.

Tracy turned to Rita. "You and El raised a fine young man there. He and Marleena really seem happy."

Rita nodded. "I like her. Elias does too." But Rita stopped short of saying anything further.

"You could double date if you gave someone a chance," Violetta told her daughter.

"Good grief Mom."

"What did I say?"

Tracy shook her head in frustration, and then hugged her goodbyes to Rita and Elias senior. "Thanks as always Ms. Rita. Have fun in Florida this Christmas."

"You have a great Christmas, Tracy. It was so great being able to spend some time together."

While the elder women exchanged parting words, Tracy went to Tanner. "I know we'll be seeing each other soon."

"Safe travels, Tracy. See you soon."

Tracy was a bit apprehensive about the drive back to Aberdeen to return her mother to her home proper. She imagined she'd be listening to her mother go on about how lovely Elias, Jr. and Marleena looked together, how they were this and how they were that, and how Tracy wasn't this or wasn't that. But Violetta was asleep before Tracy even entered I-95. Tracy wasn't going to poke the matchmaking bear. Snoring beauty awoke just as Tracy turned off the engine. "Let me help you upstairs Mom."

"I can make it."

"I want to stretch my legs and steal a Coke if you have one. It's past my bedtime."

"Let me set up the sofa bed for you and you can sleep here."

"I'll be okay."

"You have such a long drive back to the city. Why don't you stay?"

"I'll probably go into the office tomorrow. Maybe next time, Mom."

"You never stay over. Is the sofa not comfortable?"

"Now how would I know *that* if I 'never stay over'?"

"Oh, you think you're so funny."

"I keep everyone in stitches except you Mom. You're a tough crowd."

Tracy was smiling as their typical back-and-forth came to an end. She entered her mother's apartment and then gave Violetta a long embrace. "I love you Mom. I'll call you soon."

Tears were forming in the elder woman's eyes. "I love you too dear child. I'm always sad when you leave. Grab what you need from the icebox."

"Thanks Mom. I'll talk to you soon." Tracy grabbed a can of cold caffeine as directed, gave her mother another quick hug, and then swiftly made her way to her car before she yielded to the temptation to stay.

Back at her own home, Tracy found herself thinking about Brian Shane, the man she spent almost three years with in college before ending their romance. She didn't want to end it. But his drinking had gotten so bad, and his personality so radically changed because of it, that she couldn't continue with the relationship. For the first two-and-a-half years she had been so happy that she let herself imagine a fairy-tale future. But those last six months had seen a change spurred by alcohol. The reasons for Brian's drinking were many, the constant putdowns by his father over his grades; a false accusation of sexual abuse which his own father thought him capable of; and the loss of his mother to cancer years earlier, the memory of which still haunted him. Ultimately the murder of Tracy's father and Brian not being there for her led to their breakup. Brian would call occasionally to apologize and suggest getting back together. But until he gave up his vice she wanted no such rendezvous. And the years were zipping by.

But when he phoned her earlier this year having been accused of his father's murder, she didn't hesitate to help him. There were many reasons for this—her belief he couldn't do such a thing; her personal desire to see him again; her need to know if it really was over between them; and the opportunity to play detective. She had wanted to follow in her father's footsteps and wear the badge that he did. But upon his death, she couldn't see joining the force and putting her mother through the ordeal of constant worry. But she had found the legal profession a way to help people, and to do something that really did matter and positively impact people's lives. And she was a very good attorney.

When Brian, thanks to her, had been cleared of the crime, he had joined Alcoholics Anonymous and made no secret that he still loved her. Gradually she had to admit to herself she still loved him too, and wanted back the feelings and joys she experienced during those first two-and-a-half years together. But she had told him he needed his own time to sober up and figure out what he wanted from his life. After that, then maybe they could start seeing each other again.

Now she found herself wondering how he was doing with the program. Was he still sober? Did he still want her? Should she call him or wait to hear from him? Seeing Elias, Jr. and Marleena together, so happy, had been difficult for her, although she was successful in showing no signs of such feelings. She actually *would* like to double date, with Brian as *her* companion. "If it's meant to be it will be," she finally told herself. "I'll just have to have faith that it will all turn out as it's meant to. Sometimes faith in something is all you can have."

Chapter 6

The arraignment of Massimo Paganini went as Tracy anticipated. The Not Guilty plea was entered, and a trial commencement date had been set for Monday, March 16, 2015. If she were lucky this could all be over before Easter; maybe earlier, *if* she got even luckier. Tracy had told Max of Pankow's offer of eight years, and how he might even agree to a shorter sentence. But as she had predicted, Max refused to even discuss a plea. He would not admit to something he did not do. "Besides," he told Tracy, "you're going to make things right. I have faith in you, Tracy." All she could do was smile and promise she would do everything she could. She hoped he didn't notice how scared for him she was.

Upon returning to her office this first Tuesday afternoon in December, Tracy called Neal in to discuss the overall strategy based on the facts known. Tracy had taken her dry erase board out of the office storeroom and brought it into hers. Neal sat at attention as she picked up a black marker.

"Okay, we have two areas of focus as I see it, the phone call at 10:25 a.m. made from Max's cell, and the five employees, not counting Max's sons, who were at the shop the time of the call." Tracy wrote the aforementioned time on the board and below it the employees' names—Sonny, Abe, Craig, Jeff, and Lester. "Now, we know Max had to have his cell at 10:15 a.m. to receive Marty Nestle's call about the loan extension."

"You confirmed the time then?"

"Yup; I asked Tony to get me a copy of the December bill from online that had the November charges on it."

"I see."

While writing 10:15 a.m. on the board above the other items Tracy continued. "Marty called Max from his office in Baltimore County according to the number listed—Marty's office land line—on the bill. So that means between 10:15 and 10:25 someone came into the office and borrowed Max's phone. The call to Pepper was less than two minutes so it wouldn't have been out of Max's sight for long."

"Why do you think Max is so adamant the phone never left the office?"

"I'm not sure. At first I thought maybe he was having memory issues and didn't want to admit that. But his recollection of all the events that took place the Wednesday of the murder seem pretty solid, and jibe with what the others I've talked to told me. So I haven't figured Max's stubbornness out yet."

"I have to ask again, could Max be protecting someone? He knows who borrowed his phone but won't say anything for some reason we don't know about."

"I've debated asking Max that question myself. But I can't find a way yet to do that without implying Max is a liar, or at least a hider, and offending him. Besides, Max just doesn't strike me as a man who would keep quiet about a murder."

"Not even if he were threatened?"

"Oh, you mean by someone like Reginald Walters or Carlton Brandice?"

"Right."

"Well, if you're saying someone killed Pepper and then Max was told to keep his mouth shut, I'd think Max would be more scared than angry about his situation. But I guess I should ask Max flat out the questions you raised, even if I think I know the answers already."

"Fair enough."

"Regardless though, we're faced with discovering which of the five people listed here may have a reason to kill Pepper."

"I agree," Neal nodded. "I'm going to start from scratch and look at each of the five again."

"Good idea. And let me throw out another possibility, one that we haven't considered yet."

"What's that?"

"That Max is the real target here and Pepper was a means to an end. What I mean is, what if someone wanted Max out of the way, but thought that killing Max could lead to the discovery of whatever the killer's motive is. So our mystery person, who knows about the feud with Pepper, kills Pepper and frames Max. Everybody is looking at who wanted Pepper dead when we should be asking, who would want to hurt Max?"

"That's an interesting angle. But we're still left with the same list."

"True."

"And that wouldn't explain Brandice's visit."

"Also true. But until we can find a definite connection between Pepper and Walters, I have to consider the other scenario. Maybe Walters is involved with some other thing we're working on or have been involved with, real estate wise."

"Okay. But I haven't found anything in our records yet. What about the other elements of the case?"

A Tracy Brubaker Mystery

"Not much I can do there. The body was found at the shop that was locked up for the night, and Max waited until his son got there before calling the police. The animosity can be attested to by people who knew Max and Pepper. I can point out the inconsistencies with the prints on the gun versus lack of GSR, but I'm not sure if that's much of a convincer. The phone records of course are what they are, and would meet the business exception rule for hearsay if challenged. Now I've reviewed the hearsay rules again and again and looked into case law. Bottom line is I don't think I'll be successful trying to get the Pepper employees' testimony about the phone call kicked out. I'm not sure the statements are even hearsay since they are not specific statements, just a more general plan, i.e. meeting with Max at 8:30. I don't think the judge would buy that naming Max and the exact time qualifies it as hearsay."

"Which exception do you think Pankow will use if challenged?"

"If it were me I'd use the statement to explain future intentions exception. Pepper tells people he plans to attend the meeting Max set up that evening. And Pepper's not around to expand on his state of mind. Or, if someone actually overheard the call, one might squeak by on the excited utterance exception, that Pepper's responses to Max's remarks during the calls were spontaneous responses, something like that."

"I have to say I think those statements are going to be allowed, Tracy. Pankow's just establishing why Pepper was there that night. It's not like he's trying to get people to say Max threatened Pepper over the phone."

Tracy nodded. "I agree. But I'll go for it anyway. And of course we'll have to go through the material the SA has when everything is sent over. But I can't see there being much more."

"What about someone from Pepper's office being involved in this?"

"I've thought about that again and again; I just don't see that, unless all of Pankow's witnesses are lying about the nature of the call; that Pepper actually spoke to someone else that morning and they know it. But I highly doubt that. Or, if one of the employees merely took advantage of the meeting and followed Pepper, we are still left with how the killer opened the door to let Pepper in. They would have to have had the opportunity to make a copy of the key. And that brings us right back to the shop's employees."

Neal nodded and then sighed. "I see what you mean. I have to admit Tracy, it's a good frame."

"Yes, Neal—one that must have been planned in advance, not a spur of the moment thing." Tracy paused and then added, "We need to spend the rest of the month cleaning up what cases we have outstanding so we can be focused come the New Year. I'll keep in touch with Max of course, but I think waiting a bit before I do any re-interviews may be the way to go; maybe someone will let their guard down, confident that Max is going to be convicted. Besides, with the holiday shopping season officially under-way, I don't want to bother Max's people and interfere with the business."

"It's going to be a tough holiday for Max and his family. They're not going to able to pretend there's nothing wrong."

"I know, Neal. But that's the thing about the Christmas season, it's a time for miracles."

Alas, the holidays came and went without any miracles, at least not for Tracy and her client Massimo Paganini. So on Monday, January 5, Tracy met Max at his shop to continue her interviews with the staff. She had talk-ed to Lester Grossman and Abe Denberg, so that left the tailors (Jeff Pol-lenfax and Craig Marwood) and Sonny Brookhouser, the other sales asso-ciate. Neal continued to strike out with finding direct connections between anyone at Max's shop and the ethereal, mysterious Reginald Walters. Nor could he find a link between any of the names Tony had given them to any of Max's employees. Thus it was back to the trenches, as Tracy would say, to dig deeper still. She had to be right about her theory; she was convinced of that. Tracy entered the shop before they formally opened for the day at 9:30. Tony Paganini greeted her at the door. "Come on in Tracy. How was your Christmas?"

"Nice and loud," she answered. "Mom and I were invited to the Rac-cio's—my mother's roommate's family—for dinner. So there were a lot of little ones running around, decking the halls with howls of laughter. I got a kick out of it, at least until Mom brought out her favorite Christmas carol, *Tracy, My Unwed Daughter.* Do you know that one, Tony?"

"No," he answered starting to grin.

Tracy began.

"Tracy, my unwed daughter
Doesn't have a fam-i-lee
And if you ask her about it
She'll give you a slap on the knee…"

    A Tracy Brubaker Mystery

Tony laughed loudly. "I'll never be able to listen to *Rudolph the Red-Nosed Reindeer* again without thinking of you, Tracy." Tony's continued laughter got the attention of everyone as he made his way to his father's office.

"What's all the noise about?" Max asked grumpily as his son opened the door.

"Oh, Tracy, meet the Grinch," Tony said as he left.

"What is all this about?" Max asked his giggling attorney.

"Happy New Year, Max! How's my favorite curmudgeon?"

"What?"

"How are you doing, Max?"

"I'm okay. How was your Christmas, Tracy?"

"I was just telling Tony all about it, complete with song."

Max shook his head. "Tracy, I don't mean to be rude but I'm very busy."

"I'm sorry Max. I don't mean to bother you."

"Oh, I didn't mean it like that. Please tell me what you need."

"I'd like to talk to Jeff, Craig, and Sonny today, if possible. It doesn't matter to me in which order. Unless of course things haven't calmed down yet from the holidays and they're too busy."

"No; that will be fine. Come, I'll take you to the tailoring area and we'll get you started."

"Great, Max; I'm right behind you."

As Tracy followed Max she started singing again—but more quietly this time.

"All of the other people
Have a bunch of lovely kids
But not my poor dear Tracy
She would rather play with squids..."

"Squids? I'm going to have to work on that," she murmured.

"Tracy, what are you mumbling?" Max asked.

"Nothing Max," she answered, amused with her improvisation. Max pulled aside a curtain and Tracy saw two gentlemen who could have been brothers.

"Jeff," Max said to the man on the left, "and Craig," he addressed the man on the right, "this is my attorney Tracy. She wants to ask you some questions. Tell her whatever she wants to know." They both nodded. "Good. Jeff, you can be first since we'll be here all day if I leave it up to you two to decide." Then Max turned and left.

Tracy offered her hand to both Pollenfax and Marwood; each accepted. "Where's a good place to talk, Jeff? I don't want to distract Craig. It shouldn't take very long."

"Oh, well, just follow me. We can talk just outside here." Pollenfax pushed through the curtains and went a few feet and then turned. "We can talk right here, if you don't mind standing."

"Is there a chair I could borrow?" Tracy asked. "It's easier to take notes sitting down."

"Oh, how thoughtless of me." And Pollenfax was gone and back quickly with two folding chairs. He set them both up and motioned with his hand for Tracy to take a seat.

"Thank you, Jeff."

"My pleasure. What can I tell you?"

"Well first, I just want you to be aware that the man prosecuting Max will most likely be calling you, and Craig too, as witnesses to testify as to Max's vocalized feelings about Randy Pepper."

"Yes, I know. We were told that back in November."

"Now it's important to be honest when you're asked questions on the stand. You won't be doing Max any favors if you try to dodge questions or feign ignorance when you know the answers. It may seem counterintuitive but doing those things would actually hurt Max because it would sound like you're trying to hide something."

Pollenfax nodded. "I see what you're saying."

"Good. Now, you were here the morning of the murder."

"Yes."

"Were you in that curtained area for most of the morning?"

"Either there or around the dressing rooms. If customers come in to pick up alterations, I, or Craig, would bring out their clothes and assist them with trying them on to make sure everything looks and feels right. And I believe there was some of that on that Wednesday."

"I see. So you didn't have any reason to see Max in his office that morning?"

"No. I very rarely have any reason to go in there."

Tracy nodded. "You didn't happen to notice anyone lurking about in the store in a place they might not usually be?"

Pollenfax raised his eyebrows slightly. "I'm not sure what you mean."

"Well, for example, you didn't see one of the salespeople back here, trying to sneak a smoke or something."

A Tracy Brubaker Mystery

"Oh, I understand now. Let me think a moment." And Pollenfax thought a moment. "No, I can't say I remember having that impression of anyone that day."

"How about any other day?"

"Uh, no; I don't think so."

"Rats," Tracy thought to herself. "Did you hear Max talking about Randy Pepper that day by any chance?" she asked aloud.

Pollenfax did some more pondering. "No, I can't recall anything specific from that day."

"How about in general, then? Did Max talk about Pepper a lot, a little, never?"

"Oh dear, Max would certainly go on anytime Pepper showed up in the store, or if Max found out Pepper had been there when Max was away for some reason."

"How exactly would he 'go on'?"

"Calling him a jackass in Italian; other names too, I think. But that's the one he used most often. At one point he tried to get some kind of order so that Pepper couldn't come into his store."

"Did Pepper ever threaten Max?" Tracy perked up.

"Oh no, nothing like that. He'd just come in smiling, saying how the store looked to be on its last legs and that we should all be sure we had jobs lined up for when the place finally closed. Then he'd laugh and say he was just kidding around. It was that kind of stuff. He just loved to get Max riled up."

"I see. And Max never threatened him, right?"

"Well, that's hard to say really. I mean, if Max started speaking in Italian I wouldn't be able to follow everything. You'd probably have to ask his sons about what he was saying."

"Hmmm. But you never heard him threaten Pepper with violence in English?"

"Oh no; never. You have to understand that Max was like that whenever he was upset. If the supplier sent us the wrong materials, or too much, or too little, Max would get riled up. If Lester was on Max to change something to save money Max would finally lose his temper and send Lester back to his office; you get the picture. But Max never hurt or said he'd hurt anybody. And I've been here over 20 years."

Tracy nodded, thinking this was all good news. She looked at Jeff. "The truth is, though, speaking of Lester, that the store is struggling a bit."

Pollenfax put his head down. "Yes, it is."

"Has Max tried to cut expenses back at all?"

"Well, last summer we did go briefly with a cheaper supplier of certain fabrics, the heavier ones tend to be more expensive. But we quickly learned why they were less expensive, more prone to staining, easier to tear. So we went back to our old supplier, and ended up throwing away the unused cheap stuff."

"Oh my. Lester probably wasn't happy about that, was he?"

"No. Max and Lester had some words." Then Pollenfax paused and started chuckling.

"What is it Jeff?" Tracy asked hoping to learn something worthwhile.

"I think Lester ended up taking the materials himself. Then he made Max really mad."

"How so?"

"He told Max he could probably sell the stuff to Randy Pepper and get some of their money back. I think it was the same supplier Pepper used."

"No kidding."

"Talking with you is bringing it back. I think Max said if Lester went to Pepper he could stay there; something like that."

Tracy shook her head. "Do you know what Lester ultimately did with the stuff?"

"I have no idea. The next day things went on as if nothing happened. That's how it goes with Max. He gets mad, he vents, and then he's fine until the next time."

"I hear you, Jeff." She quickly looked over the notes she'd taken thus far. "Jeff, the next question is sensitive and I don't mean to upset you or anything; but I have to ask it."

Pollenfax stiffened. "Well, okay."

"And this is between just you and me. Given what's been going on, financially speaking I mean, are you thinking of seeking employment elsewhere?"

Pollenfax turned red. "I…"

"I won't be telling Max anything Jeff. I promise."

"Well, I'm not sure what this has to with anything."

"Please, Jeff. What is it?"

"Well, the store's been in dire straits for so long."

"Yes, I know."

A Tracy Brubaker Mystery

"Well, some of us have been talking about starting our own store, outside of the city."

Tracy felt those pangs in her stomach she always got when she felt her case was about to take a major turn. "Who were the 'some of us' Jeff?"

Pollenfax regretted what he'd said. But it was too late now to backtrack. "Me and Craig, and Sonny too."

"Had you started making any definite plans or is it all just talk at this point?"

Pollenfax sighed. "We've just been looking into things, some available places to rent or buy in some of the counties, Howard, Carroll, and Baltimore. We asked some questions about financing; you know, what kind of credit score you need for loans, the kind of collateral or personal guarantees you'd have to put up or make; but nothing official."

Tracy leaned back in her chair. "Where did you make those financial inquiries?"

"I didn't make them."

"Who did?"

"Sonny."

"And do you know who Sonny talked to?"

"Someone at the bank, I think."

"The bank this shop uses?"

"Well, yes, I think so. But you should ask Sonny to be certain. And please don't let on I'm the one who told you."

"Don't worry Jeff. I will keep my promise to you. No one will know where I got my information."

Pollenfax sighed with relief. "Are we done then?"

Tracy stared off a bit, and then realized what Pollenfax had asked her. "Oh, yes, Jeff; we can be done for now. I'm sure you have plenty to do. Thank you very much. You've been very helpful."

"Maybe too helpful," he thought to himself as he left Tracy sitting there. "Sonny isn't going to like this," Pollenxfax complained as disappeared behind the curtain.

Tracy couldn't stop the ideas that were raising their little hands in her mind, all shouting, "Pick me! Pick me!" Was this what it was really all about, a possible mutiny that Randy Pepper discovered as a member of the bank board? Did he threaten or blackmail someone involved? Would this really be a reason to kill Pepper though? Sonny, Jeff, or Craig could just claim Pepper was full of it. But of course Max could find out from some-one at the bank, an old friend who worked there might know about what Sonny was asking. But then what? Max fires all three of them? One or more of them conspire to kill Pepper for fear of losing their jobs? It didn't sound likely, unless there was something deeper going on here. And Tracy had just learned about this. Suddenly her spirits were lifted; there were more possibilities to explore, more work to be done. Poor Max though, oblivious to what was going on around him. And then she thought of the court date, March 16, one day after the Ides of March. But who, in this case, was Max's Brutus?

A Tracy Brubaker Mystery

Tracy was moving quickly down the street outside Max's business, headed ostensibly to grab a quick bite. But the real reason was to call Neal and fill him in with respect to Jeff Pollenfax's admission, without having to worry about eavesdroppers. "Did you get all that Neal?" she asked after her major share.

"I think so. I'll see what I can find on any new business filings involving shops like Max's. But as far as confirming anything with the bank or potential landlords, I'm not sure what I can do there."

"Gotcha; I'm going to talk to Sonny first thing after I eat. And then I'll talk to Craig. Hopefully I'll get a contact name for the bank and we might be able to go from there."

"Okay. Just give me a ring with anything else you find."

"You betcha. I'm outta here." She put her phone in her coat pocket and entered the deli. She scanned the menu and suddenly realized, after several minutes of looking, that she had no idea what she had just read, her mind apparently on its own lunch break. So she just ordered the same roast beef sandwich she did when Tony brought her here before, quickly filled her stomach, and then was back at Max's to talk to Sonny Brookhouser. It may have been a personal lunch record in terms of speed.

"Sonny, can I have a few moments of your time?" Tracy asked the salesman after he finished with a customer.

He turned and flashed a smile. "Little lady you can have as many moments of my time as you need." Tracy kept her smile as she introduced herself. "Oh right, you're the lady lawyer I've been hearing about. Let me see if we can talk in Tony's office."

"Sure, Sonny; I'll just follow you."

"Please do," he said, flashing his smile. Now, Sonny Brookhouser was a handsome fellow, a full head of black hair topping off a svelte, sharply dressed, tanned figure who obviously fancied himself quite the ladies man. Of course he couldn't remove his wedding ring because of the tell tale tan line. But if this interview was going to consist of innuendos, come-ons, stale flirtations, and the like, Tracy was going to have a hard time keeping that roast beef down. When the duo arrived at the empty office of Tony Paganini, Brookhouser just went right in. "Tony will kick us out if he needs to. Why don't we sit right down here next to each other and you can ask me anything you want to." Brookhouser took a seat and then patted the cushion of the empty chair next to him. "Sit down. I don't bite."

"Yeah but I might if you lay one finger on me," Tracy thought as she smiled at Brookhouser and took a seat.

"What's that you're wearing?" Sonny asked her.

"I beg your pardon."

"The suit."

"Oh. It's an Armani."

"It's very nice." He leaned in and, without asking permission, started rubbing her lapel with his right thumb and index finger. Then he leaned back. "Yes, very nice." Then he looked at her legs. "You don't see too many below the knee skirts these days."

"Dear Merciful Lord," she thought. But she said, "Thanks Sonny."

"You have nice legs from what I can tell. You should show them off."

"Officer, I didn't want to stab him in both eyes with my pen but he asked for it. Can't you understand that? He deserved to scream in pain." But she just smiled. "Well, I walk a lot. It helps keep me fit."

"You sure are fit alright; yes siree."

"And I had to kick him in the groin because he wouldn't stop talking." Another smile; "Thanks Sonny; you're too kind. I know you're busy so I promise I won't keep you."

"Well, don't worry about it. Ask away!"

"Do your wife and daughter know what a sleaze you are?" she wondered. But she said, "I understand you've been with Max since 2011."

"Right."

"And you worked in sales in Delaware before you moved here."

"You've been checking me out, have you?" he asked not sounding offended.

"Just standard background stuff."

"Hey, I've got nothing to hide."

"Yeah you do you lizard," she thought. "Do you mind if I ask why you moved?"

She finally asked something that gave him pause. "Well, my wife had a business opportunity to run a restaurant that was opening in the city. It was a real big deal for her; so, what the hell, we packed up and moved here-" Tracy heard the ringtone emanating from Sonny's suit pocket, ZZ Top's *Legs.*

    A Tracy Brubaker Mystery

"And at this point officer I realized death was the only solution; permanent, irreversible death."

"Sorry there beautiful, I have to take this," he said, interrupting her fantasy.

"No problem." Tracy looked around to see if there was a large, thick blanket or rug she could wrap around herself lest his laser beam eyes manage to melt her clothes.

"Sorry about that," he finally said returning to his seat.

"Oh that's okay, Sonny. You were telling me that your wife got a job managing a restaurant. How did you end up working for Max?"

"The old-fashioned way, looked in the want ads. And here I am."

"Yes, you certainly are, aren't you?" She was getting tired of smiling at him. She needed a shower and she needed it now. "I'd like to ask you about the morning of the murder."

"Awful business."

"Yes. Did you have reason to see Max in his office that morning?"

"No, I'm too busy on the sales floor."

"Busy doing what?"

"Um, selling."

"I asked that because I've heard business had been kind of slow."

"People come in all the time; doesn't necessarily mean they buy something though."

"Yeah; I can now see why."

"What did you say?"

"Oh crap, I said that out loud," she thought. "I mean, the economy and all; people tend to browse instead of buy these days."

"Oh, yeah."

"Nice recovery," she secretly congratulated herself. "Did you notice if Max was out of his office that morning to see a customer or something?"

Sonny shook his head. "Max doesn't leave his office anymore. I can't remember the last time I saw him on the sales floor after we opened."

"And what was your take on Randy Pepper?"

The smile left Brookhouser's face. "I didn't like him. He was a jerk."

"Why do you say that?"

"The way he strutted about, with his coat hanging on his shoulders; you know the type."

"Oh this is just too good coming from you," she thought. "Did you know Pepper personally?"

"Why would you ask that?"

"Do you really want to know you Cro-Magnon?" But she actually said, "Well you seem like a guy with everything together, and you had experience with at least one major retailer while living in Delaware. So I cannot help but wonder, given your total awesomeness, if you didn't first try to get a job at Mason & Bond for Men?"

The look on Brookhouser's face changed. And Tracy realized she just screwed up—that line about awesomeness tipped him off, no doubt, to what she *really* thought of him. She had laid it on too thick. But Brookhouser was probably used to such reactions. And she suspected she hit the nail on the head about Pepper too, two similar slime balls with the one not wanting to compete with the other. So Brookhouser ended up here, occasionally being visited by a man who knew Brookhouser's first choice. Maybe not a motive for murder in and of itself, but if you add that to the bank loan inquiry…

"Anything else you want to know?" he finally asked, not answering the previous question but answering it all the same. "I should be getting back to the floor."

"You know about the bank loan extension that was signed the morning of the murder?"

"I heard about it."

Time for Tracy Brubaker, Little-White-Liar-At-Law. "I was at the bank looking into that and someone there told me you had been asking about bank loans." He didn't answer her. "I just ask in case Max was asking you maybe to take out a loan to help him."

"Really."

"What other reason could there be?"

Brookhouser stood up. "I should be getting back now."

"But all those moments you promised me…"

He turned and left her there. "Good," she thought. "He broke up with me before even asking me to go to bed with him." Then she started getting angry with herself for letting her contempt show. But she couldn't stand him anymore, she knew the type all too well and in most situations she could just turn and walk away. Now it may have cost her. She wouldn't be getting anymore out of him, not voluntarily anyway. She'd have to talk to Craig Marwood before Brookhouser got to him to make any comments— or threats. She quickly rose and soon found the two tailors behind the same curtain they were this morning. "Have either of you seen Sonny in the last

A Tracy Brubaker Mystery

few minutes? I had one more question for him." They both shook their heads. "Thank goodness for that," she thought. Then she said to Pollenfax. "That Sonny sure is the salesman. Did Max hire him himself?"

The tailors looked at each other. "No," Pollenfax finally said. "I think Tony's wife hired him. She worked here briefly a few years ago when Max was down a salesperson. She used to work here before she married Tony, you know."

Another piece of news that Tracy wasn't expecting; Max *did* tell her his sons wives first worked for him, something she confirmed with Roberto. But she hadn't known Donna Paganini had worked here so recently. Did it mean anything? "Craig, would you mind if we talk now? You're last on my list for today."

"Yes, ma'am; that would be fine." Marwood said nervously.

"Please call me Tracy."

"Sure—okay." Tracy moved to where she and Pollenfax had met earlier. The chairs were still there.

"Why don't we sit here, Craig?"

"Yes ma'am."

"Craig," Tracy scolded jokingly, "remember I said to call me Tracy."

Marwood blushed. "Right, sorry."

"Good. How are things around the store these days? I mean, does Max seem to be doing okay?"

"I didn't kill that man," Marwood blurted out.

Tracy gave him a stunned expression. "Craig—I don't think you killed anybody."

"Good, because I didn't."

"Okay; I think we've straightened that out now."

"And Mr. Paganini didn't kill him either."

"Well we agree on that then too." Tracy wondered, "What is this all about?"

"It's a conspiracy; you know that, don't you?"

"A conspiracy?"

"Max won't buy that cheap imported garbage so they want him out of business."

"They?"

"The Chinese."

"Kripes I'm interviewing Daffy Duck," she thought. "But Craig, didn't Randy Pepper, the victim, use the cheap stuff?"

Marwood paused a bit. "My God, you're absolutely right. It's even more twisted than I thought. They're turning on each other."

This was a joke, right? "Craig, let's please focus here. Now the Chinese did not kill Randy Pepper."

"You're wrong; and I can prove it."

"Any how can you do that, Craig?"

"The phone of course."

"The phone?"

"Mr. Paganini said he didn't call the dead guy, didn't he?"

"That's right."

"Then how is it the records show he called?"

"I'm working on that Craig."

"The Chinese have the cell phone technology to do something like that. They copied Max's phone and tricked the phone company."

"I don't think so Craig. I think someone here borrowed Max's phone and made the call pretending to be Max. I mean, come on Craig, can you see a Chinese person adopting an Italian accent to fool Randy Pepper into thinking he was Max?"

Marwood pondered Tracy's argument. Then he started nodding. "My God, I think you're right. When you put it that way the whole thing does sound absurd, doesn't it?"

"Absurd is the word, Craig. Now let's rejoin planet earth and talk about the morning of the murder last November."

"Yes."

Marwood didn't offer anything new or different from the others she had already talked to. But she was more interested in the potential partnership with Pollenfax and Brookhouser. "I hear you, Sonny, and Jeff are going to open your own shop," Tracy said flatly. "I think that's pretty exciting."

"I'm not sure if that's going to happen."

"Why not?"

"Money. I mean, none of us have it. We'll have to borrow."

"Right—from the bank."

"I don't like banks."

Sweet Sister Mary Francis. "Why is that Craig?"

"Because we owe the Chinese so much money that eventually the banks will just start giving them our cash. The government will call it a tax, and they'll just send the money right over. That's how the government steals, you know. If they want more money they just tax you. They're all

     A Tracy Brubaker Mystery

in on it; the whole political party system is a means of distraction. They all just share in the wealth while we fight over the letters d and r."

"What in the world does that mean? Max is in bigger trouble than he thought," Tracy considered silently. "I think that's all I have for now, Craig. It's been enlightening talking to you."

"Oh, that's it? That wasn't so bad. Well, goodbye then. And remember what I said, *if* you want to find out who really killed that Pepper fellow." And then Marwood trotted back to his station.

"Pay no attention to the man behind the curtain," Tracy thought as she got up from her seat. She wanted to talk to Tony Paganini pronto.

"Yes, Donna *did* hire Sonny," Tony told Tracy. They were both seated in Tony's office. "She had worked in the store before we got married as you know, so she gave Pop a hand until a replacement could be found."

"What do you think of Sonny?" Tracy asked him.

"What happened, Tracy? Did he come on to you?"

"He looked at me like I was a glass of ice water in the desert."

Tony shook his head. "I'm sorry Tracy. I didn't even think to warn you. He's actually a very good salesman but he doesn't know when enough is enough. He thinks women like to be flattered."

"He wasn't flattering me."

"I realize that. But you must have set him straight."

"What do you mean by that?"

"I was on the floor when he came back from talking with you. He was muttering to himself and shaking his head. I only see him do that after his wife's dressed him down about something over the phone."

"I like her already."

Tony laughed. "I bet you would at that."

"And what's the deal with Craig?"

Tony looked at his desk. "Oh. Craig's alright, a good tailor with quite an imagination."

"Tony," Tracy said firmly, "what are you planning on doing with the store when your father retires?"

He looked up at her. "To tell you the truth Tracy, I don't really know yet. I may have little to say in the matter if the bank decides this is our last extension."

"I see."

"Did talking to anyone today help your case?"

"Actually, a couple things did come up. They may or may not prove helpful. But I really can't go into details."

"I understand. I was just hoping you had some good news for Pop."

"I believe I might at that. But mum's the word right now."

Tony smiled warmly. "Okay Tracy. Are you leaving then?"

"Yes; going back to the office. I want to say goodbye to your dad first."

"Sure; let's go together."

Tracy looked at Tony as he pushed away from his desk. "Do you check on your father a lot during the day?"

The question caught him off guard. "I never really thought about it. I guess I like to see how he's doing during the day."

"And did you check in on him the morning of the murder maybe?"

Tony blinked. "Earlier in the day. But I didn't see him make any phone calls if that's what you're asking."

"No; I was thinking more along the lines if you saw anybody coming out of or going into his office."

"Oh. I wish I had something I could tell you."

"Okay Tony. Let me say goodbye to Max." And the two headed to Max's office.

"You think that's funny, do you?" Tracy asked Neal tersely as he started laughing. She had just recounted the interviews for the day, saving the one with Brookhouser for last.

"Not in the way you're obviously thinking," he finally answered her. "I just can't believe in this day and age someone could be so...be so...un-subtle."

"How diplomatic of you."

"Tracy, you're a beautiful woman. Guys are going to look at you. And some guys, unfortunately, are going to do more than that."

She ignored his attempt at a compliment. "I wonder what he would say or do if he found out someone treated his daughter like that at an interview. The jerk needed a drool bucket."

"Someone like that? He'd probably punch the guy's lights out."

"He just reached over and touched me, my suit I mean. Just put his hands on me, no warning. I feel violated; I feel dirty."

"Tracy," Neal said concerned, "you shouldn't let him get to you like that. He's not worth the worry. Don't give him free rent in your mind."

A Tracy Brubaker Mystery

She shook her head. "You're right of course. But I take that aspect of my life very seriously. And now part of me hopes he's the killer so he'll one day have a cellmate who reaches for *his* collar."

"Jeeze, Tracy. He really got to you. I'm so sorry."

"Oh, *I'm* sorry Neal. It's just guys like that really frost my flakes."

"I can tell."

"Anyway, about Craig Marwood, I'm not sure if he's for real or if this was some kind of act. It seemed a little over the top to me; a little pre-planned. But see if you can find out if he spent any time at some facility."

"Oh—like something for mental observation."

"Mm-hmm; and given what I learned about Sonny boy maybe take another run at him."

"Sure." Neal studied Tracy a moment. "Tracy, what else is bothering you?"

"What do you mean?"

"Come on; we've worked together long enough that I know when something's nagging at you. What is it?"

She met her associate's eyes. "Tony Paganini."

"What about him?"

"He lets Craig and Sonny work there when he knows neither is playing with a full deck. He has no real future plans for the store. Lester told me he's gone to Tony with ideas and Tony just sends Lester to Max. Basically, I don't think Tony wants to be there."

"You're not suggesting you think Tony would do something like this to his father."

She shook her head. "No, at least I don't think that right now."

"What *do* you think?"

"I think I'm working late and that I'm ready to order some dinner."

"Oh," Neal gently laughed. "Any ideas?"

"Yeah—Chinese food."

Tracy rubbed her eyes; almost 10:00 p.m. Neal and Rebecca were long gone. She leaned back in her chair, stretched her arms, and then yawned; time to go home. She looked at her notes. Sonny, Craig, and Jeff, three men in search of their own shop. Sonny was the dominate one among them, the proverbial salesman who was convinced of his own charms. She shuddered. If there was in fact something there Sonny would be the most likely suspect; smiling at Max and Tony all the time while figuring out a way to get the hell away from them. But murder Pepper and frame Max?

Lester Grossman, a man with ideas. Get rid of a tailor and a salesman he had told Max time and again. Did he know about Sonny's plans? Lester dealt with the bank. He could have learned something and is keeping his mouth shut. But what does he benefit if Max goes to prison? Another dead end.

Abe Denberg, friends with Max before coming to work for the store. Tracy liked him based on the talk she had with him. Abe didn't like Pepper for lots of reasons; Pepper's store ran Abe's old one out of business after all. But that is how business works, right? Giants swallow or smash smaller competitors all the time. Then again, not too many make it a point to gloat, to lord their success over you. Pepper deliberately made things personal. Okay, Abe kills Pepper. But then frames Max for it? No, doesn't make sense.

What about Tony? No, discontent does not a killer and framer-of-one's-own-father make. Bottom line, the motive has been carefully hidden. That's why Max was in so much trouble. Now Tracy was thinking like Craig, a conspiracy. More than one person could be involved in this; each one covering for the other.

Next she thought of Paul Iris. She hadn't reached out to him yet; he wasn't at the store that day and thus couldn't have used Max's phone. But if it were a conspiracy, then he may not have had to be at the store to play his part, if he had one. Someone on the inside had to be involved, but that doesn't mean they actually pulled the trigger. Did someone who knew Iris' situation approach him? Did someone offer him a large enough sum that made him an accomplice? If he suddenly didn't need three jobs anymore, that would certainly answer the question. She'd *have* to talk to him. But the thought of questioning this man—a man who lost a wife and now barely sees his daughter—made her uncomfortable.

Now her self-doubts were returning. "You're a lawyer not a detective; you're not your father," she said aloud. But how could she, legally speaking, get Max out of this? She could play up the health angle, even if Max wouldn't like that. She thought, "Ladies and gentlemen of the jury, my client didn't do it, but if he did, it's because he's sick and Randy Pepper was an asshole anyway so find him not guilty for any or all of the aforementioned reasons. Yeah—real fine lawyering there, Tracy. Enough; I'm going home." She shoved her laptop and notepad of letter-sized paper into her briefcase, grabbed her coat, and then locked up her office. *"Always look at the bright side of life,"* she started humming to herself on her way to the car. But it was so dark out.

The first snow of the year hit Baltimore City January 6. Only a few inches had fallen but the timing still had the city traffic backed up for hours. Fortunately Tracy managed to leave her city condo unit early enough so that she was at her office before 8:00. Rebecca and Neal had families whose activities and schedules had to be coordinated, but both were at their desks by 10:30 a.m.

"Today we're the firm of Tracy Brubaker, Archaeologist-At-Law," Tracy told Neal when he came into her office. "We have to dig, Neal—dig until our fingers are bleeding. You get me?"

"Uh, sure," Neal said with uncertainty. "Dig our heels in and all that."

"And your toes too if you have to."

"You okay, Tracy? You look frazzled."

"No scat Sherlock. We're not doing our jobs here. Two-and-a-half months left until trial and I've reached the Pink Panther theme."

"Huh?"

"You haven't heard the joke about what the Pink Panther said when he came to the end of an alley? *Dead end. Dead end. Dead end dead end dead end—"*

"Yeah yeah yeah," he cut in. "Get a grip Tracy. Take a deep breath. Your Max's lawyer not his savior."

"That's not the way I see it."

"I know, and that's part of the problem. Focus on legal strategy, not on doing the job the cops are supposed to do."

Tracy didn't feel like a lecture today. "If you haven't realized it yet, Neal, the cops think they're finished doing their job," she said tersely. "If you're not going to help me with this then go back to your office and do something officious." Neal rolled his eyes; another mistake. "And do not roll your eyes at me. I can make heads roll around here, you know? I am the boss, you know?"

Tracy rarely pulled rank, so there was no doubt in Neal's mind this case had already taken its toll on her. "Okay, Tracy; okay. I'll put on my pith helmet and get my pick and shovel." He got up to get his tools.

Tracy sighed. "Wait, Neal." She stood up. "I'm sorry. I'm sorry for taking it out on you."

He turned and gave her a smile. "It's okay Tracy; I get it. You're very worried about your client. You're a caring person and that's how you're always going to be. That's one of the reasons I love working for you so much." And then Neal left her. She didn't know whether to smile or cry. She felt like doing both. She found herself touching the cross on her necklace. Charlie Betts—the skunk—had reminded her that faith was important. She needed some kind of small miracle; it's not like she was asking for a red sea to be parted or for water to become wine—just something small. Well, back to work; God helps those who help themselves after all.

"I may have something," Neal said excitedly as he entered Tracy's office as the sun was setting. "You remember Edward Grimes, Abe Denberg's old boss?"

Tracy was in her chair at a perfect right angle. "Yeah; he closed up shop and moved to Florida I think."

"Correct. Randall Pepper sued him."

"For what?"

"Slander and all that goes along with it; Grimes was vocally blaming the close of his business on Pepper's store, and not just in the papers. Apparently he also complained to some of his customers, who took it upon themselves to stage a little protest; you know, the evil mega-corporation versus the small businessman."

Tracy was nodding like a bobblehead on speed and shaking like a poodle with bladder control issues. "Yeah, and?"

"Well the suit didn't go anywhere and at the end of the day it was probably all in the name of publicity for Pepper. But the lawyer's name who filed the suit on behalf of Pepper was Robert Shecter."

"Neal, you're *killing* me here!"

"Robert Shecter worked for the law firm that defended Pepper in some house flipping cases in the 1990s—managing partner was Leonard Ralston. Pepper wasn't convicted of anything and Shecter moved onto bigger and better things."

"Neal, for the love of—"

"Shecter now works for the very same law firm that defended Reginald Walters when he went to trial in September 2013 on murder and conspiracy charges. Shecter didn't actually work on the Walters case, at least not as reported in the press or anything else I could find. But Shecter is an employee of that firm; who knows what went on at the office."

A Tracy Brubaker Mystery

"But Pepper and Walters shared a law firm." Tracy repeated.

"Right. You wanted a connection between Walters and Pepper, and now you have one, sorta."

Without thinking Tracy sprang up from her chair, ran over to Neal, and squeezed him tight. She kissed him on the cheek and practically shouted, "Thank you Moses!"

Neal, slightly embarrassed, nevertheless laughed. "What is that, some other Monty Python reference?"

She laughed too. "No, Neal. You may have just parted the red sea; removed an obstruction to seeing what may be really going on here."

"Unfortunately, no lawyers are going to talk to us about any of this; another Pink Panther theme probably."

"True—but it's a lot easier to put the puzzle together when you have an idea of what the final picture is supposed to look like. And I think you just brought that picture into a much clearer focus."

Chapter 8

"I don't think it really proves anything," Detective Tanner said.

"Oh come on, El. This is just a coincidence?" Tracy asked, not hiding her frustration. She was in Detective Tanner's office wandering around, unwilling to take the seat he had offered her upon her arrival. "Pepper and Walters shared the same law firm; Brandice works for Walters; perfect circle."

"Sounds more like you're chasing your tail."

"I beg your pardon."

"Tracy," Tanner said with exasperation, "just because they shared a law firm doesn't suddenly prove the two knew each other. Plus, Pepper used that firm only the one time; right?"

"Maybe; I'm having Neal see if he can find any other suits filed on behalf of or against Pepper. I just found out about this today."

"Then why are you here instead of helping your associate?"

She frowned. "Because you said you'd help me unofficially. I was hoping to get some unofficial confirmation maybe."

"Tracy—"

"Don't be a Brutus, El."

"A what?"

"Can you just tell me if you know if Pepper and Walters had any kind of relationship?"

Tanner studied her a minute. He looked through his office windows and saw his conversation was being observed. Then he returned his attentions to his persistent guest. "I'm going to have to talk to Lennon about this. This is a sticky situation you're about to get yourself into if you try to pull Walters into your case."

Tracy pursed her lips. "I'm *already* in whatever this situation is, sticky as it may be, even if I don't quite yet understand it."

Tanner shook his head. "How about the other people in the store; find anything there?"

"I'm working on it."

"You're going to have to give me a chance to speak with Lennon or Roper first, like it or not."

"Not."

"Sorry Tracy."

"Can you call one of them now?"

"I'll most likely be leaving a message. Who knows how long they'll take to get back to me."

Tracy frowned and threw her arms up in the air. "Fine!" she shouted, and then turned to leave Tanner's office. People moved out of her way as she made her way to the parking lot.

Tracy was in her Audi nearing the lot's exit when a light blue Camry suddenly pulled out in front of her, forcing her to slam on her breaks to avoid a fender bender. "Goddamnit," she muttered. The offending car then pulled out into the street and had another driver skidding to avoid a collision. The noise of the other auto's horn was too little too late.

Tracy started shaking her head. "Why did I blow up at El like that?" she asked herself. "I've been hollering at people I care about too much lately. And I'm cursing more, too. A belated New Year's resolution—improve my self control." She sighed. "I'll call and apologize to El as soon as I get back to the office. That's the right thing to do."

The sun had practically vanished from the sky as she pulled into her office building's parking lot. She gave herself a quick look in the rearview mirror hoping her recent scowl-fests hadn't left permanent wrinkles.

And that's when she saw it, the light blue Camry, the same one in the BPD parking lot she almost hit, or almost hit her. At least, she thought it was the same car. It was parallel parked alongside the entrance curb, and there was someone inside. The parking lot's night lights had come on but the car was far enough away from any one of them so that she couldn't make out any details. The driver seemed, however, to be looking straight ahead, not at her. But Tracy still felt nervous. Was she being paranoid, or was this in fact the same Camry? Had he tore out of the parking lot intending to beat her here in the hopes she wouldn't realize he was following her, not realizing that by doing so she *did* notice him? Was she going to sit here all night? Should she call El? "Well," she thought, "let's see what happens."

Tracy slowly opened her car door keeping an eye on the mystery driver from both her inside and outside mirrors as she did so. He didn't move. She closed her door and then opened the driver's side backdoor to remove her coat and briefcase; still no movement on his part. She quickly closed the backdoor, pushed the auto car lock button on her key, and moved to the building walkway which led to the main entrance. And then she saw the occupant's head turn. She could swear he was looking at her; he was looking at her looking at him. But the figure remained a black silhouette. He didn't emerge from his car. Then she saw his head turn back to its previous position of facing straight ahead. When Tracy was at the main doors she was able to view the license plate. She passed through the doors and once inside quickly pulled out a small pad and pen and scribbled down the plate's characters. She took the stairs in lieu of the elevator so she'd be in her office more quickly. At least she would feel safe there; Neal and Rebecca should still be in the office.

"Hi Tracy," Rebecca greeted as her boss made her entrance. Tracy gave her a nod and immediately proceeded to her office, deposited her coat and case on the small couch, and moved toward the window, which overlooked that part of the parking lot from which she just came. The car was still there. Rebecca and Neal were shortly on either side of her.

"What is it?" Neal asked.

Tracy pointed at the source of her worry. "That blue Camry there; I think it was at BPD earlier. I almost hit him when I was leaving, and now he's here. He was just sitting in the car when I got here."

"Are you sure Tracy? There are lots of blue Camrys around."

"No, Neal; I'm not absolutely sure. But I've never noticed that car in our parking lot before."

Rebecca offered, "Maybe he's waiting for somebody. It's after 5:00 now so he could just be there to pick someone up."

"Maybe," Tracy muttered. Then she pulled her phone from her pocket and dialed Detective Tanner's cell phone.

"Yes, Tracy; what is it this time?" he answered in not the most friendly manner.

"Are you having me watched?" she asked quickly.

"What? No, I'm not. Why?"

"Do you think the feds might be?"

"Not that I'm aware of. What's going on?"

"I think someone's following me. I'm at my office now and there's a light blue Toyota Camry in the parking lot that I'm pretty sure was at your place today. I have no idea what the year is but there was somebody in the driver's seat when I got here. And he's still there. I have the license plate."

Tanner paused. "Give it to me." She did just that, and then he said, "I'm going to see if there's a patrol car near your area and ask them to swing by just to check it out. Where is the car parked exactly?" She told him that too. "Okay, just hang tight. I'll call you back."

A Tracy Brubaker Mystery

The entire staff of the office of Tracy Brubaker, Attorney-At-Law remained standing at the windows, a pseudo front row seat to what was about to occur. They were all nervous and silent. Minutes passed by; the Camry didn't move nor did anyone emerge from the car. Eventually Neal and Rebecca each placed a hand on Tracy's respective shoulder.

Rebecca spoke. "Here comes the patrol car." All eyes were now on the police vehicle that was pulling into an entranceway that was to the right and several rows away from the parked threat. They were all looking to the right when the sound of screeching wheels forced their heads to move left in unison. The Camry was pulling out of the lot with its lights remaining off. Then their heads turned back as they all simultaneously noted the blue and red lights that were now emanating from the roof of the new arrival. Next they heard the siren as the chase began. But it wasn't much of a chase for the onlookers. The unlit Camry quickly disappeared into the evening's darkness and the pursuing lit car eventually did the same.

With the show now over Tracy turned and walked slowly to her chair. She sat down, placed her elbows on the desk, and rested her forehead against her folded hands. Neal and Rebecca stared at each other briefly and then looked at Tracy. The silence was finally broken by the sound of Tracy's vibrating phone. She quickly answered.

"Hi, El."

"I'm sorry Tracy; we lost him."

"I'm not surprised. He knew I noticed him so he was probably ready to go."

"We ran the plates and we have people on their way to the owner."

"Who's the owner?"

Tanner paused. "I'd rather not say right now until I get some more details. I will tell you it's not someone related as yet to your case; it's some 78-year-old retiree in the city."

"Okay."

"Stay at the office for now. I'll call you right back when we have something; it shouldn't be too long."

She paused before commenting. "You know, El, I was feeling pretty lousy about how I treated you today. But after this, I don't think I'm the one who should be doling out apologies."

Tanner was silent a moment. "I'll get back to you. Sit tight."

Tracy placed her phone on the desk and told her employees what Tanner had said.

"Well, I'm certainly spooked," Rebecca said after the update.

"Tracy, do you want to stay with me and the family tonight?" Neal asked. "I'm told we have a very comfortable guest room."

Clearly moved by the offer, Tracy couldn't answer. She just shook her head. "No way am I pulling your family into this, Neal," she thought.

"I'll be at my desk," Rebecca said as she left Tracy and Neal. "I'm not leaving until I know what the cops are going to do about this. I don't know about you two but I've had it with this crap." Tracy and Neal had no comment to that.

The time moved slowly as Tracy waited for Tanner's return call. Then Rebecca buzzed; "Detective Tanner's here and on his way back Tracy."

Tracy stood up as he entered. "Okay Tracy here's what I can tell you," he began, dispensing with any formalities. "The car appears to have been stolen; when exactly we don't know. The owner and his wife left the area just after Christmas for their winter home in Florida. We got that info from their daughter who we tracked down and confirmed the details with. We did find the car abandoned about 10 miles from here. The lab is going over it now."

"They won't find anything," Tracy said flatly.

"I've got calls in to both Lennon and Roper. If I don't hear from either of them soon I'll start doing things on my end that will get their attention."

Tracy sat back down. She was still a little angry with Tanner for not sharing what information he had with her, but she said, "Thanks, El."

He moved closer to her. "Tracy, I'm sorry. I really am. My hands are tied in certain respects but that doesn't mean I've stopped caring about you. I promise I'll find out what I can. But I can't promise those who know more about this than I do will tell me anything."

She looked at her designated father, the one who promised his partner he would fulfill the role as protector if need be. And the need was clearly there. "I'm scared, El," she admitted. "And there are people who know what's going on who have no problem keeping secrets, even if that means others are going to get hurt."

Tanner nodded. "I've got someone going through your condo building's garage and the nearby street parking. I know the garage is private but I'll feel better if we take a look nonetheless. Are you going to go there tonight after work or would you like to stay with someone? You're welcome to stay with me and Rita."

    A Tracy Brubaker Mystery

A lump rose to her throat, another offer of protection, another guardian angel. "Thank you, El. But I have a feeling I'll be alright for the foreseeable future; whoever he was knows people will be watching."

"I thought you said you were scared."

"I am, but not in the sense that I think I'm going to be attacked or something like that. I meant that it scares me that someone or someones want Max to burn for this so badly that they're coming, in some form or another, after me now. And that there are people who are most likely aware of all of this, people who are supposed to protect the Maxes of the world, and they just don't care." Then she added, "And please don't try and tell me I can't know for sure what happened tonight isn't related to the Paganini case. Please don't."

Tanner shook his head. "No, Tracy; I won't. I believe you're right. I hope I can tell you something about all of this very soon. Are you sure you won't take me up on my offer, just for tonight? You may find you're going to want to talk to someone later if sleep proves difficult."

She came around her desk and hugged Tanner. "I think I'll be okay. But I really appreciate the offer."

"Alright then. Maybe you could leave now too and I'll follow you."

Tracy thought a moment. "Okay, that offer I'll accept."

"Good. I'll be out in the reception area when you're ready. Take your time."

Tracy packed up and sent Rebecca and Neal on their way. She locked the office doors and allowed Tanner to escort her to her car. He left her as her auto entered the private garage at her condo building, and she arrived safely at her fourth floor unit. There were no more unwelcome followers noted for the evening.

Her bedroom ceiling was something like a second office at times; she frequently stared at it working through various theories as she lay in her bed unable to secure sleep. Someone had stolen a car, one not likely to be missed until spring, to follow her. How long had she been followed? Why? Was today orchestrated to let her know she *was* being watched? Would someone have the balls to risk being caught by the police in a stolen car to accomplish that goal? One man might, based on what she heard about him, her new friend Charlie Betts. But weren't the feds watching him? Was that the reason a stolen car was used, to lose the feds for a few hours? Maybe they didn't even realize he'd been lost. Would the feds confide in Tanner at all, or just tell him to buzz off, although in less polite terms? In spite of her verbal melee with Tanner this morning he was right, a shared law firm didn't inexorably tie Pepper to Walters. But it *was* a beginning. She was now very interested in learning if Pepper and Walters shared any other firms in common, realtors and appraisal businesses especially. Pepper was a flipper and Walters liked profitable real estate transactions. Wasn't it more ridiculous to assume they *hadn't* crossed paths? There had been a silver lining to this cloudy night after all, she knew she had El completely on her side now, and that Neal, the big brother she never had, was something of a genius at finding connections that even the feds might miss, and he now had the scent. She had stolen him from a private detective agency years ago and believed it was one of the top three smartest things she'd ever done. And Rebecca, she was poised to kick ass and take names. In short, Tracy wasn't going to be alone in solving whatever it was that was going on here. She had Team Tracy at the ready, willing, and able. "Walters, you bastard," she thought. "You may have finally met your match."

A Tracy Brubaker Mystery

Chapter 9

Early the next morning in Tanner's office, the futility commenced. "What exactly do you expect of us, Ms. Brubaker?" Agent Lennon began in a most unfriendly tone. "You want us to make your defense case for you?"

Tracy tried to keep calm. She hadn't slept much and was this close to losing her temper. "You think last night wasn't the kind of thing that Walters' boy Brandice would pull? That driver wasn't some amateur, stolen car and all. And I think you know that."

"Brandice is under surveillance," Roper added.

"What kind; the kind where it looks like he's in his room or whatever so your people just sit in a car all day, waiting for him to come out the front door?" Roper just stared at her a moment. "I'm right about that, aren't I?" Tracy finally commented.

"Look," Lennon barked, "Walters is not involved in your case. Stop trying to pull him into it."

Tracy still retained her composure, although it was getting more difficult. "I know Walters and Pepper had some kind of relationship."

"How?"

She ignored Lennon's query and continued. "If you're honest with me, and I believe you're right in thinking Walters isn't involved, then I'll look elsewhere. But right now the only person connected with this case that seems capable of murder is Walters or one of his people. So that's where my focus is going to be unless you can show me otherwise."

Lennon was a bit taken aback. He wasn't used to being challenged. This lady obviously didn't know whom she was talking to or how these kinds of cases worked. "I don't have to tell you anything. I let you know some of the details earlier out of a courtesy to some people in the department. Now I'm regretting it."

Tracy wasn't ready to back down. "Why do you think Brandice came to see me if Walters isn't involved in this case?"

"Are you hard of hearing or something?" Lennon asked angrily.

"Answer my question!" Tracy barked.

"We're done here," Lennon said. "You've got no link with Walters and Pepper and I have nothing more to say to you on the matter; good morning." Lennon then exited Tanner's office and Roper quickly followed.

Tracy's face held a mix of mild shock and exasperation. She turned to Tanner. "That Lennon is a first grade ASSHOLE!" She hoped Lennon had heard her.

"Easy, Tracy; easy."

"The hell I'm going to be easy. I want to know what all of this is about!"

Tanner went to shut his door. He had an audience again. "Tracy, you need to calm down. I appreciate that you're frustrated and all of that. But the feds trump the locals most of the time. You need to understand that. *Do you understand that, Tracy?*"

"Stop treating me like I'm a child."

Tanner rolled his eyes. "I'm trying very hard not to. But you're acting — excuse me for saying so — like a bit of a brat."

Tracy was a bit stunned by his comment; she thought he was on her side, especially after last night. "I'm trying to save Max's life here."

"I understand that."

"Do you really?"

"Yes, I do. And if I had something concrete I could share with you I would. Tracy, you are just going to have to take my word for it that, while there may be some minor details that tie Walters to Pepper, there is nothing even remotely resembling damning when it comes to the murder. I won't pretend the feds are being upfront about everything; but there are some things at stake here that you're not privy to."

She turned her back on Tanner, took a deep breath, and then started again. "Can't you make me privy to these mysterious things?"

"No, Tracy; I cannot."

"El —"

"Tracy, you only know what you know because of our relationship. If we did not have such a relationship the feds never would have shown up at your office and you'd still be wondering why Charlie Betts came to your office that day."

"I am still wondering —"

"Stop that; you know what I meant." Tanner turned, his own emotions coming to the forefront. "Look Tracy, you know I love you like a daughter. And I love Max too. And if there was some way I could help you I would. Now, so we both don't say things we'll be apologizing for later, I want you to leave my office."

Tracy was near tears. She and Tanner had never had anything even remotely resembling a fight — until now, that is. She was ready to launch

A Tracy Brubaker Mystery

another verbal assault, but she decided against it. She *didn't* want to say something she'd regret later. So without another word she left Tanner's office and headed back to her own.

She recounted the blow by blow to Neal shortly after arriving at her place of business. "And then I just left. It was obvious that I hit the wall and was in danger of losing El's help for the rest of the case. Right now I just feel devastated. I can't even think straight." Tracy was looking at her lap. "The highs and lows of this case are just too much. I don't know what to do."

Neal had resisted speaking. She wasn't really seeking advice. Tracy usually had already thought of the things Neal would offer. But he couldn't recall the last time he had seen her so down, feeling so hopeless. "Tracy," he finally said. "I'm really sorry about the way you've been treated by the cops, both federal and local. I guess they think they have good reasons but that thought isn't going to make any one of us feel better. But I do know you. I think you should have yourself a good cry or whatever, take a power nap, and then recharge. I dare say maybe you could even go home for the day; you never really take vacations. Then let's meet first thing tomorrow and talk. I'll see if I can find anything in the meantime. But I hate seeing you like this." He had said his piece and hoped it helped her in some way. The silence continued for a few minutes more.

"Neal, can I ask you a question?" she finally asked, looking at her associate.

"Anything, Tracy."

"Do you think I should try to get Max to take a plea?"

"He says he's innocent."

"I know. But do you think I should try anyway?"

"Not if you believe Max is innocent."

"Do *you* think Max killed Pepper?"

He hesitated. What he thought about guilt or innocence really shouldn't enter into the case. But it mattered to her obviously. The truth was he really hadn't thought through everything enough to come to a conclusion. So he went with his gut. "No, Tracy. I think you're right about him being innocent. And so no, I don't think you should try to plead this out. Let Max have his day in court."

"But should I be the one representing him? I haven't found anything that any other decent lawyer wouldn't have found. I don't have much experience in this area. And I even have a friend at the department and that's gotten me nowhere. I suck at this."

"Tracy, that's not true. You're being too hard on yourself. But you *are* going to have to get mean."

"Huh? What does that mean?"

"You're going to have to give the jury another suspect, like that Sonny prick. Make sure it comes out what he was doing behind Max's back, and that he's a womanizer even though he's married; basically he's untrustworthy. Put Craig on the stand and show what a wacko he is with his various theories about banks, the government, and China. Tell them how Lester was tired of Max running the company into the ground financially and frustrated that no one would listen to him. Tell them how Abe's old boss was run out of business by Pepper. And make a point of brining up Max's health; that he really can't be sure about the phone being in the office so that any of the people I mentioned could have used the phone."

"Max will hate me if I do that."

"So what? He'll go home most likely. Is it more important to you that he likes you or that he goes home at the end of the day? Tracy, I've seen you go after people in depositions and civil matters. Judges and juries like you and there's no reason on this earth to think the Paganini trial will be any different. But you can't be nice about it."

"They like me because they know I believe what I'm saying because I *do* believe what I'm saying. I don't feel comfortable implying things about people I don't know to be true, even people like Sonny Brookhouser, vermin that he may be."

"And that, Tracy, is your problem. You don't want stuff to come out because you don't want to risk hurting people, people you think are as innocent as your client. But are they really so innocent? Now I'm not saying you should lie; I'm not saying to make stuff up. You know all those things I just said about Craig and Sonny and Abe are true. You just put it out there and offer theories. It's the jury that ultimately will have to decide what to believe."

"And then I will be exactly what my father loathed, someone who says anything about anybody just to get a client off, regardless of the consequences. And there would be consequences, Max would be broken-hearted, people could lose their jobs; the store could ultimately close."

Neal was getting exasperated. She had an answer for everything. "Okay, Tracy. I see what your real struggle is now. You want things to be black-and-white. But life is full of grays, and most criminal attorneys have to dress in gray, to play both the good gal and the bad gal. If you can't do

A Tracy Brubaker Mystery

that then maybe you *should* see about getting Max another attorney, because you're not prepared to defend Max to the best of your ability, only to the limits you've set up for yourself. And that's not fair to Max. I'm sorry if that sounds mean or hurtful, because I don't want to be mean or hurtful. I think you're a great person who could win this case if you really wanted to. But, in all honesty, it's not just the feds or cops or lack of solid suspects that's holding you back." Neal paused and then continued, "I'm going to leave you now. When you're ready, let me know what you want to do." Neal arose from his seat, his consultation over, and he made his way back to his office.

Tracy sat at her desk; she had never been evaluated in quite that way before. Normally she'd be angry at someone who had the presumption to tell her about herself with such seeming authority. But Neal, by and large, was correct. She had no interest in exposing potentially embarrassing or hurtful information if she didn't really believe it was germane to her case. It would just make someone look bad, and no apology after the fact would undo that. Neal was wrong though if he thought she felt this way because she wanted to be liked. No, she felt this way because, quite simply, she thought it was wrong, the equivalent of lying because she would know that her intention was to lead the jury in another direction, a direction she didn't really believe was correct. There wasn't anything honest about that as far as she was concerned. She had been raised Roman Catholic, and for the most part still practiced her faith. She went to church every Sunday and Holy Day, and tried to follow the commandments. She prayed regularly — well, sometimes. She didn't pretend that she was perfect; she knew she had done things that were against the church's teachings, willingly losing her virginity to Brian Shane being the one she thought about most often. But, for better or worse, she did try to basically do unto others what she would want done to herself. And she wouldn't want someone to imply something about her they knew was untrue, no matter what their reason was. And Neal was saying that's just what she should be doing. No, she couldn't do it. She wouldn't do it.

So now she was faced with a decision, keep or drop the case? Either way would be difficult. She sighed. She knew what she had to do, talk to Max and be as honest as she could with him without breaking any promises she may have made to people involved in the case. She would let Max decide once and for all whether she was up to the task of defending him; after that, no more pity parities, no more choruses of "Oh, poor me." So the law enforcement people didn't want to help; screw 'em. She'd go after Walters if she found something on him. And she thought there were things to find out. Why would Lennon be so gung ho on shutting her down? Maybe she could even somehow use this in her case; juries are made up of people who don't trust the government—shades of Craig Marwood—and now she didn't either, at least not Agent Lennon. She felt herself coming out of her funk, getting angry again about being treated like some annoying puppy dog that can just be shooed away. But first she would talk to Max. She picked up the phone and called him.

Max told Tracy they could meet for lunch. Tracy told Max she would stop at the deli and pickup something for the both of them. She would be there close to noon. She arrived, as promised, with nourishment for her client. But she wanted to talk to Max before she ate. Otherwise it would be a miserable dining experience for her. She told him her dilemma, she didn't want to imply another person's guilt unless she really believed it. Other attorneys would be able to do that; that was their job. She worked a little differently, and while these differences in approach had brought her success in the past, they may not be the best when defending someone accused of murder. She didn't give him many details, more like "what if" scenarios. "In hindsight, Max, maybe I was too cocky, too arrogant. I thought I could swoop in here, clear everything up with no problems, and be on my way to save the next person who asked me for help. I guess I need to dine on some humble pie. I will still defend you if that's what you want. But I wanted to be completely honest with you. If I blow it I'm not the one going to prison." She paused. "I guess that's all I have to say."

Max Paganini looked at the humbled woman who sat across from him, the not-so-little-anymore girl who once upon a time was such a carefree and happy child, one who would come into his shop singing some song she made up, or wanting to show Mr. P (she could never pronounce his last name in those years; the best she could do was Mr. Paggy) a dance routine she learned, or taught herself. He missed her when she stopped coming to the store with her father. But Peter Brubaker would just say how she was studying, or doing some extra credit project, as if she really needed it. How smart his little girl was, how she was destined for great things, how proud he was of her. Tears came to Max's eyes; there didn't seem to be much happiness in her now. "You think I'd fire you because you don't want to hurt other people?" he finally asked. She didn't answer. "Tracy, I don't want

A Tracy Brubaker Mystery

anyone else but you sitting next to me when the time comes to go to court. If I go to jail, who cares?"

"Your family will care Max," she answered quietly. "I care."

"And *that's* why I want you by my side."

"Max, did you just set me up?" Tracy asked, a slight smile returning to her face.

"I don't know what you mean. Now enough of this; let's eat." And so they ate. When she finished, she asked Max a question.

"Can I talk to Sonny before I go?"

"Sure you can. Do you want to use my office?"

"That won't be necessary," she said firmly.

Max smiled. "That's more like it."

Brookhouser was on the sales floor chatting with Denberg when he saw Tracy approaching. He managed an unenthusiastic smile. "Back again huh?" he asked.

"Can we have speaks, you and I?" When he hesitated she added, "Max said it would be okay."

The smile left Sonny's face. She seemed to have that effect on him. "You told Max you wanted to talk to me again?"

"Yes, and that's all I told him; for now, anyway." He got her point, and they found themselves back in Tony Paganini's once-again vacant office space.

"What's this, blackmail or something?" Sonny asked as soon as Tracy closed the door.

"Is that what Pepper was doing to you, Jeff, and Craig, blackmailing you guys over what he learned at the bank?"

"I don't know—"

"Yeah, you do. I can see it now, Pepper coming in here; giving you knowing winks; your ego taking one hit at a time until you'd had enough."

"Now you listen—"

"No, Sonny—*you* listen. You have one chance here, one chance only, to level with me or this all will come out in court. I don't want to play it that way but if you force my hand that's exactly how I'll deal with it. You get me?"

Sonny looked at her. He drew the correct conclusion that she wasn't bluffing. He had no reason to think that she was. "What is it that you want to know?" he finally responded.

"Did Pepper find out that you went to the bank inquiring about financing?"

Sonny turned so he wasn't facing her. "Yes."

"How did he let you know that he found out?"

"He came in the store one day. I got lucky 'cause Abe was in the back helping out with something so he didn't even know Pepper came in; nobody did."

"And what happened?"

"He offered to help."

"Help? He was going to loan you the money?"

"That's what he implied. He liked that I told him we wouldn't be opening in the city. He said he wouldn't gouge us on interest or anything if we borrowed from him. He even knew about some places that would make good sites and said he could get us a nice deal probably."

"And what did you say to all of that?"

"I said I liked the idea very much, but that I would have to talk to my potential partners about it."

"I see. And did you talk to them?"

"I talked to Craig. I didn't see Jeff having an issue with it."

"Issue — you mean taking money from Pepper?"

"Right."

"What did Craig say?"

"He said it sounded fine to him."

"Let me guess, he liked the idea because you wouldn't be borrowing from a bank."

"Huh?"

"Craig doesn't like banks."

Then Sonny started laughing. "Oh, Craig played crazy for you, did he?"

"What do you mean?"

"Craig's a pretty shrewd and angry guy. His wife really fu — , I mean, messed with him during the divorce. He started that routine of his around that time, just to mess with his ex and her lawyers. He enjoyed it so much that he's been doing it ever since. Basically though he doesn't care about anybody; not even dear old Max."

"And how do you know all of this about the real Craig?"

"He told me. I called him on it not long after meeting him. I could read him; I could tell what had happened, women are always screwing guys over, especially in divorce cases. I guess he saw me as a kindred spirit or something."

A Tracy Brubaker Mystery

"So that was it," Tracy thought. Sonny didn't love his wife but didn't want to get taken to the cleaners in a divorce, so he just came on to anything in a skirt to help him cope. Craig and Sonny, two peas in a pod; two conspirators in murder? She asked, "So did you and Craig formally accept Pepper's offer?"

"Didn't get a chance to; he was dead the next week."

"He didn't screw you over like a woman, did he? You didn't accept his offer only to have him say he was just kidding or something and that he was going to tell Max the whole the thing?"

Sonny was looking at her again. "No. Like I said—well, *I* didn't contact Pepper anyway. Maybe Craig did; maybe you should talk to him again too."

"I'll do that."

"And you might want to talk to Lester too."

"Oh yeah, why?"

"Because he sold some supplies to Pepper awhile back at a great discount and Pepper offered him a job. That's what Pepper told me anyway, that everyone who worked for Max could come work for him, even the sons if they wanted to."

"But no one ever did, did they?" Tracy challenged, not liking the serpentine smile that was now residing on Sonny's puss.

"Max didn't give anyone the chance," Sonny grinned, flashing his pearly whites, making sure she got the implication. And Tracy thought if she were a man, she'd have dislodged those pearlies right then and there—with a hammer.

"Well, don't let me keep you any longer, Sonny," Tracy finally said. "Why don't you slither on back to your sales floor now? Just make sure you don't get stepped on."

He continued smiling as he made his way to the door. Before opening it, he turned back to face Tracy. "I'd still like to bend you over that desk right there. Who knows, you may end up liking it." And now having had the last beyond-offensive word Sonny Brookhouser widened his smile, and then left the room, leaving Tracy standing there downright horrified about what he had said.

"As God is my witness," she thought to herself, "even if he's not the killer, he's going down anyway." She regained her composure and was officially back in this case. In a twisted way she needed what just happened to get her anger brewing. So now she was ready for a face-off with Craig

Marwood. An image of a dead parrot popped into her head. She didn't laugh, even though the bird bore the face of Randy Pepper.

"Craig, can we talk?" Tracy asked after pushing the curtain aside. "I just had the most *delightful* chat with Sonny." She didn't have to say anymore. Marwood put his needle and thread down, and marched toward Tony Paganini's office. He pushed the door open, went to the opposite end of the room, and turned to face her. She used her right hand to push the door closed behind her, not taking her eyes off Marwood, whose face told her he was ready for battle. "How are things in China?" she sarcastically began.

He didn't smile. "Cut the crap girlie—what do you want?"

"Was Randy Pepper blackmailing you, or did he just tell you he was going to inform Max about your little mutiny?"

"Pepper's dead, so anything that he may or may not have threatened is just mist. You can't do anything with it."

"Your comrades may not be so confident."

"They'll do what I tell them. I know how to deal with you lawyers. I've had some success in that area. So if you try anything with me missy I'll make your life miserable."

"Bullies and their threats," Tracy countered, shaking her head. "You take on one or two attorneys and you think you have it all figured out. I've been taking on fellow attorneys for more than five years now mister; I do pretty well for myself."

He blinked. "So, what are you going to do, tell Max a few of us looked into starting our own place? So what? I don't have the right to start a business?"

"Sure you do—as long as it didn't lead to murder. *Does* any of this relate to Pepper's murder?"

"How would I know that? I didn't kill that douche bag."

"Don't be offensive to douche bags, Craig. They can actually be quite useful."

And then Marwood started laughing, laughing hard. His face turned red. He pointed at her, although Tracy wasn't laughing herself. "Hey... hey...that was...pretty good," he said between gasps. "I think I'll use that sometime. 'They can useful.' That's great!"

Tracy just stared at him. Was this part of his act? "Uh, Craig—"

 A Tracy Brubaker Mystery

"I like you lady. You're pretty quick. And I bet you *are* a real ball buster in court too, aren't you?" He was regaining his composure again. "I wish you had been my divorce attorney. I could have introduced you to some more douche bags, my wife being one of them." And then he started laughing again.

She waited for him, once again, to pull himself together. "Craig, did Pepper threaten Sonny, you, or Jeff?"

He was back to his earlier position, but his face wasn't as hard. "Look, Pepper made us an offer to loan us some money. Heck maybe he would have even just flat out given us the money. But we never got a chance to accept his offer, no matter what you're thinking. Now that's all I have to say about it." He started walking toward her and stopped a few feet in front of where she continued standing, blocking his exit. "If you will excuse me, please?" he asked. She moved aside so he could continue out the door. "They can be useful—I love it," he said starting to chuckle again. Tracy followed Marwood to the door. She saw him pull aside the curtain. "Hey Jeff, what's the difference between Randy Pepper and a douche bag?" she heard him ask Pollenfax. She didn't wait to hear if Pollenfax laughed at the answer.

Lester Grossman didn't immediately respond to her question so she asked it again. "*Did* Randy Pepper offer you a job when you sold him those poor quality materials?"

He looked at her indignantly. "I don't think it was a serious offer. How on earth did you find out about that?"

"Does Max know about any of this, that you sold the stuff to Pepper and the offer?"

"Of course not; at least I don't think so." He shuffled some papers on his desk. "I don't know. Max never said anything to me if he did know."

"How exactly did you come to work here, Lester?"

"How's that?"

"You worked at a temp agency and then you landed here. Did you temp here and then get offered a permanent position? If you don't want to tell me I guess I can ask Max about it."

"No, I didn't temp here exactly. I was recommended to Max by someone I did temp for. A man named Leonard Ralston."

Tracy recognized the name—the man Robert Shecter worked for back in the 1990s; Shecter, the man who represented Pepper in a lawsuit and now worked at the firm that defended Reginald Walters. "You temped at Ralston's law firm?"

"Yes."

"Did you know Pepper used to be a client of theirs?"

"No, I can't say I recall that. I helped with bookkeeping. I didn't have any contact with the clients."

"What about clients who were late paying their bills? Who would follow up?"

"I see you don't know much about bookkeeping. The accounts receivable clerk would follow up on past due bills, not me."

Tracy let Grossman's mild jab pass. "So it's just a coincidence that Pepper and you had Ralston and Max in common?"

Grossman was visibly agitated. "Look, Ms. Brubaker, Leonard Ralston's firm specialized in real estate matters. Ralston helped Max out when Max was negotiating the purchase of his store all those years ago, and he helped Randall Pepper out with his real estate dealings. It's really not unfathomable that Max and Pepper happened to use the same firm in the same part of town for *something*."

"And then Leonard recommended you to Max?"

"Yes. Max called Leonard asking him if he knew a good employment agency and told him what he was looking for. Leonard told Max about me, that he liked my work, and that Max might want to try me out through the temp agency. If Max too liked my work too he could offer me a full time position. There's absolutely nothing sinister about any of that."

"Of course there isn't," Tracy said reassuringly. "Did you know a man by the name of Robert Shecter when you worked for Ralston?"

Grossman thought a bit. "I cannot honestly say that name is familiar to me. He may have worked there. But I wasn't involved in payroll so I didn't have reason to engage with the full time employees. I was just a temp you know."

"Oh, I see."

"Good. I'm glad that you see. Is there anything else I can do for you then?"

Tracy studied him a bit. Now she was out of favor with Lester too. "No, Lester; that's all for now I think. I just wanted to get the real story about the Pepper job offer. I don't make conclusions based on gossip, you understand."

A Tracy Brubaker Mystery

Lester smiled. Maybe all was not lost with him after all. "Well, in that context I appreciate you wanting to hear my side of things. Not everyone would do that. I apologize if I lost my composure and offended you."

"Oh, no worries Lester. You didn't offend me. I'm glad you're not mad at me."

"Certainly not; you are after all trying to help Max."

"Well, thanks again for your time. I'll be on my way."

He reached for her hand. "I wish you continued luck on the case," he said gracefully as they shook.

Tracy made her way back to Max's office but paused to lean against a wall. She was almost dizzy due to the whirlwind of interviews she just had, some yelling, some laughing, and an offensive sexual overture. All in a day's work for Tracy Brubaker, Archaeologist-At-Law. It had been a good dig. She took a breath and then went to say adios to Max for the day. She had a lot to think about.

"We're still representing, Max," Tracy told Neal shortly after her return. "I told him some of the truthful observations about me you made earlier, told him what I would or wouldn't do; bottom line is he wants us to defend him."

"Great Tracy," Neal said sincerely. "Everyone believes in you except you, apparently."

Tracy blinked. "Look, Neal, thanks for earlier today, for being cruel to be kind and all that."

"I didn't mean to be cruel."

"I meant that just as an expression. Anyway, I'm done with the self pity and am ready to get to work, in part thanks to you."

"That's the spirit."

"And do I have some things to tell you. But first I have I have riddle for you."

"Oh yeah; what's that?"

"What's the difference between Agent Lennon and a douche bag?"

Chapter 10

There wasn't anywhere else she could go. In spite of the tantalizing possibilities, Tracy ultimately could not connect the dots. Sonny Brookhouse and Craig Marwood—two misogynists who had dreams of selling their own suits—were guilty of many things, most likely. But at present murder didn't seem to be one of them. Abe Denberg? No clear motive. Lester Grossman? Zilch. Jeff Pollenfax? Not likely he would have told Tracy about the possible defection if it had anything to do with the killing. What other motive could he have? Nothing had surfaced on *that* front. Forget about the sons—Tracy refused to consider the possibility. Max would probably just as soon be convicted than find out one of his boys was involved in this. Neal hadn't turned up any known enemies in Max's life; her possible theory that Max was the real target of this wasn't working out either. And that brought her right back to Reginald Walters. But all she had there was a shared law firm. Then of course Grossman worked for Ralston, who represented Pepper in the '90s, whose employee Robert Shecter worked at Walters' law firm; vague connections at best, nothing solid. It was Friday January 30. Today was her motion to suppress the Pepper employee's testimony about the alleged Paganini phone call. She wasn't optimistic. Tracy pulled into the courthouse parking lot and sighed. It was nearly 11:00; better hurry.

"Let me get this straight," Arthur Pankow complained. "Defense counsel wants the nature of the phone call suppressed because her client killed the man who otherwise could tell us about that very phone call. That hardly seems in the spirit of the law."

"As expected, the state's representative is deliberately misrepresenting defense's position here," Tracy countered. "Our problem is that the witnesses can testify only to what was told *to* them. They cannot testify with absolute certainty as to *who* made the call. The jury is likely to take this testimony as evidence that my client made that call, when such testimony does not establish the aforementioned as fact."

Pankow responded, "Defense can make that argument to the jury if she wants to. Plus, we have the evidence regarding the call being placed by the defendant's phone."

"…Which still doesn't prove my client made the call."

"…Which, again, you can argue in court." Tracy scowled. Pankow continued. "The State also will hold that this testimony meets the future intention exception. It explains why the victim went to the defendant's store at 8:30 that night. We all know the victim isn't here to explain it."

"We're not denying that someone called the victim and told him to be at my client's store that night. The issue is *who* made that call. The victim thought it was my client because the caller told him he was my client."

"Right—so the victim's state of mind was that he thought he was being called to a meeting by Mr. Paganini with Mr. Paganini. And he just relayed these feelings to his employees. We are offering this testimony to establish the state of mind of the victim on the night of the murder."

"It's prejudicial; the jury will just assume as fact that my client made that call."

"Again, you can make your point in court."

"Alright," Judge Milton Reynolds said. "I understand your point here Ms. Brubaker but I think the State has met the hearsay exception, maybe more than one. You're free of course to cross examine the witnesses and raise the questions you've raised here. But I'm loath to deny the testimony since that testimony involves the victim. I realize your client hasn't been convicted yet. But if I disallow this I'd be effectively rewarding the elimination of a witness, who also happens to be the victim."

"Thank you, Your Honor," Pankow stated.

"I understand, Your Honor," Tracy said, not at all surprised.

"Is there anything else for us to discuss?" Reynolds asked.

"I don't believe so," Pankow answered.

"No Your Honor," Tracy added.

"Very well then; I'll see you both on March 16."

Tracy and Pankow left the courtroom and were moving side by side down the hall toward the exit. "Nice try, Tracy. But you had to know your chances were slim."

"Who knows? I may have grounds for appeal if Max is convicted. I'm on record objecting to this evidence. Today was a win-win situation for me as far as I'm concerned."

Pankow smiled. "I like your optimism, misplaced as it may be."

"Uh-huh."

"Seriously, how about five years with a chance for parole after two?"

Tracy stopped to turn and face Pankow. "For first degree murder?"

"I told you before how we could knock it down to manslaughter."

"Uh-huh. Why would you do that since your case seems so solid?"

"I'm trying to give the old guy a break here. I can't believe you're giving me grief for it."

"I think *you* don't think Max is guilty."

"That's not what the evidence says."

"I'm not talking about the evidence. I'm talking about you—as an honorable man, as a man who knows he's prosecuting the wrong guy *in spite* of what the evidence says."

Pankow looked at her a moment, deciding how to respond to her suggestion. "Look, just take the deal to Max. Okay?"

"Sure Art. But he won't accept it." Tracy turned and continued toward the exit stairs. She found herself wondering what was harder, defending a man you believed was innocent, or prosecuting a man you didn't think was guilty. She and Arthur Pankow, contrary to appearances, had a lot in common.

"Tracy, what's wrong?" Violetta asked her daughter. It was the last Saturday of January and Tracy was again in Aberdeen at her mother's abode. But Tracy's mind was elsewhere. She wasn't very good company.

"I'm sorry Mom. It's Max's case. I've run out of ideas."

"Oh, you poor child. I'm sure you'll think of something. Try not to worry so much."

"I can't help it. I'm not the one who goes to prison if I fail."

"Tracy, you need to stop such talk. You didn't put Massimo in this position; someone else did. You're trying to help. Stop being so mean to yourself."

"You're right Mom. But—"

"But nothing; you'll think of something. Now how many cards do you want?"

"Oh—uh, two." Tracy handed her mother the 10 of diamonds and queen of spades. She had the 3 of diamonds, 4 of spades, and 5 of spades in her hand. She decided she'd go for a straight. Her mother handed her the two cards, ace and 2 of hearts. Tracy's eyes widened. "I'll be darned," she thought.

"I want three," her mother announced. Violetta took her cards. "Bah," she exclaimed. "A pair of 10s."

Tracy put her hand down. "I wasted my straight on a measly pair? Gadzooks!"

A Tracy Brubaker Mystery

Violetta chuckled, more for the fact that her daughter's true personality had shown through for the first time today than her finding her daughter's quip humorous. She really didn't understand what Tracy had said.

"Mom—what's that?" Tracy asked while pointing to Violetta's discolored wrist.

"What?"

"That bruise on your wrist; how did you get it?"

"Oh, I got my hand caught in a cabinet; the door closed on me."

Tracy raised her eyebrows. "You had just hurt your elbow last November; now when did this happen?"

"I don't remember exactly. It's not important. Why do you worry so much?"

"Oh that's rich coming from you. You write how-to guides on worrying. You should have your own cable show—call it *Violetta Brubaker's Fretting and Sweating: How to Obsess Over Everything.*"

"What are you talking about now?"

Tracy grimaced. "Are you doing okay, Mom?"

"I'm fine."

"What if I ask Mrs. Raccio? Will she say you're doing fine?"

"You are being disrespectful," Violetta said tersely.

"No, I'm being a concerned daughter."

"I don't want to talk about this anymore. Do you want to play another hand?"

Tracy sighed. "It's almost 7:00. Do you mind if I head home? I have a slight headache."

"Let me get you something. I have plenty of things here for headaches." Violetta arose and shortly returned with a glass of water and two Advil. Tracy accepted.

"Thanks Mom. I'm sorry about today. Maybe I'll be feeling better next time."

"Oh my poor Tracy, stand up and let me hug you." Tracy obliged and the embrace actually made her feel better.

"Are you sure you're doing okay, Mom?"

"Worry about yourself. I'm fine."

Tracy gave her mother a skeptical look and then headed for the door. "Goodnight Mom. I love you." Her mother just nodded, so Tracy turned and closed the door behind her. Now she had something else to worry about. Something was up with her mother; what, she had no idea. Was someone hitting her? No, the bruises were too oddly placed for that. Was she just getting clumsy? Maybe; maybe too she'd risk her mother's wrath and call Mrs. Raccio sometime soon. She rubbed her temples as she approached her car door. She took a quick look around. No mysterious figures in parked cars. Then she yanked her door open and concentrated her thoughts on the comfortable bed that awaited her.

Tracy entered Derwood's Pizza around 3:00 on Sunday. She figured it wouldn't be terribly busy during that zone between lunch and dinner. She'd figured correctly. There were only two occupied tables that she could observe. Given the place seated about 40 patrons she figured they did mostly carryout business.

Tracy approached the cashier. "Hi!" she greeted. "Could I speak with Paul Iris please?"

The attendant blinked. "I'm Paul. You're that lawyer, aren't you?" he then asked, smiling.

She smiled back. "Oh, you've heard of me?"

"Sonny described you."

Tracy's cheeks reddened. "Oh."

Iris chuckled. "I know, he's a pig."

Tracy declined to comment. "Do you think I could talk to you for a few minutes?"

Iris turned his head and shouted, "Kelly, can you watch the front for five minutes?"

"Be right there," a female voice answered.

Iris turned back to Tracy. "Want something to drink?"

"Ice water would be supreme."

"I'll get that for you and be right out. Pick any table you want. We won't get busy again until about 5:00."

"Thanks, Paul."

"Sure."

Tracy took a seat at a two-person table. Pizza, one of her favorites. There was no way she'd be able to avoid ordering a slice or two. She shouldn't though; she had already eaten lunch and she had eaten too much over the recent holidays. Pizza, so basic a food — cheese, tomatoes, and bread — and yet, so delicious. And no two eateries' pizza tasted exactly the same. She had never tried Derwood's offerings; maybe just a slice of basic cheese.

A Tracy Brubaker Mystery

Iris put the water in front of her as he sat down. "You want anything to eat?" he asked.

"Ask me that when we're finished talking," Tracy grinned.

Iris grinned back. "Okay; I'll do that. I'm off at 6:00. Maybe we could have dinner."

Tracy's eyes widened. Wow, Paul Iris moved fast. "Don't you have to pick up your daughter?" she responded.

"My sister won't be bringing everyone back to her place until 8:00. That gives me two hours of 'me' time. I don't get much of that."

"Oh. Well, tonight's not really a good night for me."

"Okay; I just thought you might like some company. I know you're single."

"Just what did Sonny tell you about me?" Tracy asked sourly.

Iris sighed. "Never mind; I get it. What can I tell you?"

Now Tracy sighed. "To tell you the truth, I'm not really sure. I know you weren't at Max's the day of the murder. So I guess I'd just like to know what you've observed for the last few months, or the time before the murder."

"Nothing that can help Max, I'm afraid," Iris said, continuing to look at Tracy with his eyes fixed on hers. "Everybody likes Max; everybody's worried about Max. And that Pepper guy—good riddance."

"You knew him?"

"I knew who he was; never talked to him though. But I know Max. And if Max didn't like him, that's good enough for me."

Tracy couldn't help but smile. And when he smiled back at her, she found herself blushing again. "Is it true Max never leaves his office?" she managed to ask after taking a sip of water.

"Hmm; I guess that's true. But I'm kind of all over the place."

"You run errands."

"Yeah. Run out of printer paper? Paul will go the office supply store for you. Need the employee bathroom toilet fixed? Paul will get what you need from the hardware store and make it right. I help anyway I can."

"Gotcha. So you're a man on the move, I guess."

"That's me. And I guess you're a woman on the move; I hear you've been to the store a few times."

"Yeah; just interviews, and to see how Max is doing."

Iris leaned back in his chair. "This thing's going to trial?"

"Unless something amazing happens in the next month and a half…"

"Mm." He smiled at her again.

Tracy cleared her throat. "Iris, that's an unusual last name."

Iris chuckled. "It was originally Irish, at some point one of my ancestors dropped the 'h' for whatever reason. Are you by chance Irish? You have an Irish lass' hair."

She laughed. "I'm German on my father's side and Italian on my mother's."

"Italian? Then I insist you try something. The owners are authentic Italians."

"I'll have to take a rain check."

Iris frowned. "Well, okay."

"Say Paul, did you ever see anyone borrow Max's phone by any chance?"

He shook his head almost immediately. "I don't think so. But I really wouldn't know."

"Yeah; I guess you wouldn't. I guess those things start to look alike."

"I guess."

Tracy looked down at the checker-clothed table. "I guess it's hard to work three jobs and raise a daughter by your lonesome. I'm in awe of people who can do that."

The smile left Iris's face. "My daughter is why I do it. I'd do anything for her."

"Do you ever get to see her with all the working you do?"

"Sure, mornings, evenings, sometimes at lunch. I talk to her on the phone when I can."

Tracy nodded. "I was really sorry to learn what happened to your wife. I lost my father when I was 20. But that's not the same thing, is it?"

They were looking at each other again. "It gets lonely sometimes; I don't exactly get much of an opportunity to meet people."

She felt the warmth return to her face. Paul Iris *was* a very good looking man. "I guess I should let you get back to work."

"I guess."

"Let me leave you my card in case you think of anything…anything that might help with Max's case."

He smiled again as he accepted it, and their fingers briefly touched. "I may call you about that rain check too."

Tracy just smiled and stood. They shook hands, and then Tracy started toward the exit.

 A Tracy Brubaker Mystery

Iris said, "Sonny's a jerk but he was right about one thing."

Tracy turned. "I'm sorry?"

"You're a very beautiful woman."

Tracy just blinked; half-smiled; and then continued out the doorway, not saying another word.

Back home, she put on her pajamas and then sat on her living room sofa. Paul Iris's smiling visage was on her mind. "Two weeks until Valentine's Day," she thought, "just another lonely-heart day for Tracy Brubaker." What was it about her that Irishmen found so attractive? First Brian, and now Paul; she found her eyes were looking at her phone. Call Brian to get a status report? Call Brian to see if he's on the straight and narrow? Maybe call his sister Crystal to get an update? And if it's all bad news, she could call Paul Iris and redeem that rain check. Tracy Brubaker, Max, Neal, and now Iris had told her how beautiful she was. Brian always told her that too. Tracy Brubaker; successful career woman admired by many. But here she was, alone in her condo. She had dreams and not only for her professional life. She wanted to meet Mr. Right and fall in love again; she wanted to get married and have at least two babies, because she wanted her children to know what it was like to have a sibling, something she never had. But she *was* in love. Or maybe she wasn't. Or maybe…

"Damn you Brian!" she suddenly shouted. Then she shook her head and started chuckling. She pressed her right hand against her face. Then she made a deal with herself, get through the Paganini case, and then call Brian. And if he hasn't kept his most recent promise, then it would be time to move on—to finally, unequivocally move on. She knew of at least one person out there who wanted at least to have dinner with her, and probably more. She looked around her home one more time for the evening, stood up, and then moved toward the bedroom. She didn't want to spend the rest of her life going to bed alone. And it was time—or nearly time—to do something about it.

Chapter 11

Monday, March 16, 2015, the trial of the State of Maryland versus Massimo Paganini commenced. At approximately 9:30 a.m. Judge Milton Reynolds entered the courtroom, and shortly thereafter Arthur Pankow rose and moved toward the 12-seated men and women who held the fate of Tracy's client in their collective hands.

"Good morning," he began. "My name is Arthur Pankow and I will be the State's representative in this case. On the morning of Wednesday, November 5, the victim Randall Pepper received a phone call summoning him to a meeting that night at the clothier and tailor shop of the defendant, Massimo Paganini. The State will show that it was Massimo Paganini that made that phone call and set up the meeting. When Randall Pepper arrived he was let in the shop, and then shot at close range. He died instantly. The State will show that it was Massimo Paganini who pulled the trigger. The State will provide evidence of the long-standing feud that existed between Mr. Pepper and Mr. Paganini, which led to the killing. The State will show that there was no one else in the tailor shop, other than the defendant, at the time of the murder." Pankow paused; his eyes scanned the jury; and then he stepped back away from the box and moved toward the table where Tracy and Max were seated. He turned to face the dozen.

"Now during this trial you may come to feel sympathy for the defendant, Massimo Paganini. It is no secret he has been struggling to make ends meet and to keep his shop open. You may grow to dislike the victim, Randall Pepper, who *did* antagonize the defendant." Pankow then turned to face Max, who was looking down at his own lap. "But make no mistake, ladies and gentlemen, this was a premeditated, cold-blooded act of murder. Mr. Paganini called Randall Pepper, told him to come to his store, and then shot him dead within seconds of Mr. Pepper arriving. The State will prove all of this. So even if you do indeed feel for this man seated at the defendant's table, remember what he is guilty of, the planned execution of a man who never did him any harm other than, essentially, to bully him. We'd never tell our children that killing a bully is the right thing to do. Let's not teach that it's okay for an adult to do it. Find Massimo Paganini guilty of murder in the first degree." Arthur Pankow again studied the jurors' faces and then returned to his seat.

Tracy took a sip of water from the glass in front of her and then stood. She moved slowly toward the gathered jury. "Facts do not always tell a

A Tracy Brubaker Mystery

convincing story, in spite of what the esteemed Mr. Pankow would have you believe," she began. "And I think at the end of this trial that not only will you feel sympathy for my client, Massimo Paganini, Max to his friends, you will also like him. My name is Tracy Brubaker and I've known Max for most of my nearly 32 years on this earth. So of course, I'm biased. I love Max. But I know you won't take my word for it when I tell you Max didn't kill Randall Pepper. The State says Max called the victim to set up the crime. But we'll show you that all they can really prove is that someone called Pepper using Max's phone. The State says they can prove it was Max who called Pepper. We'll show you that the only person who really knew whom he talked to was Randy Pepper, and that Pepper only knew *that* because of what the person on the other end of the phone call told *him*. The State will introduce fingerprint evidence with respect to the gun. We'll ask you to question why the fingerprints weren't in more locations on the gun. And then there's the question of why would Max do this. The State says it's because of a 'long-standing feud.' But while we have no intention of putting the victim on trial here, we will nevertheless show that the victim had feuds with several persons other than Max Paganini. And I haven't even gotten to the rebuttal witnesses we will present who will refute the State's portrait of my client as some angry, bitter businessman. No, Max Paganini is a kind-hearted man who loves his family and his business' employees, and never harmed a single person in his life, in any way. He didn't kill Randall Pepper." Tracy turned to make her way back to her table, but stopped to add one last comment. "I may be wrong about one thing though, at the end of this trial you may more than just like Max, you may love him, almost as much I do." And then she took her seat, gave Max a smile while squeezing his hand, and wondered if anything she would say or do during the ensuing days would make any difference in saving Max from prison.

Most of the morning resembled the preliminary hearing. The arriving officer testified to Max's hearing the noise and investigating, the time of the 911 call, and Max's delay in reporting the murder. Tracy again asked if the officer thought Max acted consistently with someone who claimed to be confused. Again the officer said his experience told him Max *appeared* confused. No surprises. The coroner was then brought on to confirm the method and time of death, single gunshot between 8:00 and 9:00 that night. No surprises there either.

Next Pankow called Detective Garrison. The questions and cross examination again were essentially the same. But here Tracy was going to be bit more aggressive when covering the fingerprints. After Pankow sat down, Tracy started in first on the phone call, again pointing out the phone records only proved Max's phone was used. She also pointed out that Pepper's employees only had their employer's say so on who made the call. Now it was time to address the gun. "Detective, you stated in your testimony that the gun was unregistered."

"Yes."

"Did you determine how or when Mr. Paganini purchased or otherwise obtained the gun?"

"No."

"Well could you at least determine where the gun came from based on its markings? By that I mean, was it purchased from a certain store, or maybe reported stolen?"

Garrison cleared his throat. "It was part of a shipment of weapons that was stolen."

"Really? When was this?"

"A couple of years ago."

"From what you were able to find, was this particular weapon used in any prior crimes?"

"No; there was no match when we ran the ballistics."

"So you believe my client bought this gun two years ago and waited until this time to murder Randall Pepper?"

"Not necessarily; he could have bought it for sale on the street or by some other means at any time."

"But you weren't able to determine the alleged means?"

"Asked and answered already!" Pankow shouted.

"Withdrawn then; tell me detective, were any other guns from that stolen shipment used in crimes in this area?"

"Objection!" And Pankow was on his feet. "Relevance?"

"Because if the stolen weapons were utilized in specific crimes related to another group—for example, drug dealers—I think that would be relevant to my defense."

"The objection is overruled," Reynolds announced.

"But I cannot comment on ongoing investigations, Your Honor," Garrison told the judge.

A Tracy Brubaker Mystery

"You presently have ongoing cases involving guns stolen from the same shipment as the murder weapon in this case?" Tracy asked quickly.

Garrison looked to Pankow and then to Reynolds.

"You can answer *that*, can't you?" Reynolds asked.

"Well, I suppose."

"So, do you, detective?" Tracy asked growing impatient.

"Yes, we do."

"And are these investigations concentrated in one particular area or with one particular group of people?"

"I told you, I cannot answer that. It involves ongoing investigations."

Tracy felt excitement in every part of her. She had hit on something although what it was exactly she wasn't sure of yet. She made her way quickly to her desk, scribbled a note to herself on the first available paper she saw, and then again faced Garrison.

"Detective, you say my client's prints are on the handle and barrel of the murder weapon."

"Yes."

"But nowhere else on the gun."

"No."

"Neither on the clip nor on any of the remaining cartridges?"

"No."

"Based on your experience would you say that was an odd circumstance?"

"Perhaps unusual; but certainly not unexplainable."

"Really? What would the explanation be?"

"That he prepared the cartridges and clip earlier, perhaps while he was wearing gloves. Then he handled the gun with his hands when he actually fired it."

"Hmm," Tracy wondered aloud. "So you're saying he fired the gun with his bare hands?"

"Uh, well…" Garrison stammered.

"Isn't it true you performed a paraffin test that showed no gunshot residue on Mr. Paganini's hands?"

Garrison squirmed. "That is true, yes."

"And did you check his clothes for residue also?"

"Yes."

"Any luck with GSR there?"

"No."

"So how did Mr. Paganini manage to fire the gun?"

"He could have been wearing gloves."

Tracy stepped back a bit and made sure the jury saw the confused look on her face. "Wait a minute detective, are you saying that my client wore gloves when he loaded the gun and wore gloves or something like that when he fired the gun?"

"That's what we think, yes."

"But then how did his prints get on the handle and barrel?"

"We think he put his prints on the gun to support his story about finding the gun."

"But why touch the gun at all? Why not just say he noticed the body and not even bother with the gun?"

"We think he did that to cover himself just in case he didn't completely remove the prints."

"Ohhhh…" Tracy exaggerated. "Wow, you must think Mr. Paganini is a criminal genius to plan for *that* contingency."

Garrison squirmed some more. "Well, I don't know about that."

"Your Honor…" Pankow whined.

"So are you asking this jury to believe that Max Paganini, criminal mastermind, he who thinks to wear gloves but touch the weapon anyway just in case, calls Randy Pepper to a meeting at *his* shop where he'll be the *only* person there for the purpose of killing Pepper, essentially setting *himself* up as the murderer?"

There were some snickers from the jury box and the viewing public. Garrison turned red. "It's just one possible theory."

"It needs a lot of work," Tracy quipped quickly.

There was outright laughter this time as Pankow sprang up. "Your Honor!"

"I'm done for now," Tracy cut in returning to her seat.

Max leaned over to her. "I think they like you," he whispered. "That's good for me, right?"

"It couldn't hurt," she whispered back.

"The State calls Louis Temple to the stand," Pankow called out. After Temple was sworn in Pankow asked, "Mr. Temple, you worked for the victim Randall Pepper at his clothing store?"

"Yes."

"For how long?"

"Over five years."

"And you know the defendant, Massimo Paganini?"

"Sure."

"Were you at the Mason & Bond Store on November 5 of last year?"

"Yes."

"And did you witness Mr. Pepper have a phone conversation around 10:25 a.m. that morning?"

"Well, I can't be sure of the exact time but it sounds right."

"After the phone call ended, did your employer tell you about its nature?"

"Sure."

"Just to you?"

"No. There was me and Cheryl and Tim. We all happened to be close to his office when he came out laughing."

"Laughing?"

"Well, yeah. He said old Max was ready to sell. But it was too late for Max because Mr. Pepper had made other plans. And then he said that he couldn't wait to tell Max he wasn't interested anymore."

"And you and the other two people mentioned *all* heard this?"

"Sure."

"So you were aware of the animosity that existed between your boss and Mr. Paganini?"

"Sure."

"Did Mr. Pepper, to your knowledge, ever threaten to do physical harm to Mr. Paganini?"

"No, he never said anything like that that I heard."

Pankow returned to his seat. "Your witness, Ms. Brubaker."

She stood quickly. "Mr. Temple, you said Mr. Pepper told you he'd made other plans when talking about my client's store."

"That's right."

"Do you have any knowledge of what those other plans were?"

"No; sorry."

"Going back to the call, did you and your two associates know what time the meeting was to be held?"

"Yeah—I remember him saying he'd be leaving in time to get to Max's by 8:30 that night."

"How do you know for sure that it was Max who called Mr. Pepper and not someone acting on Max's behalf?"

"Well, I don't, I guess. I mean, Mr. Pepper was the one who said he just got off the phone with…Mr. Paganini."

"So you're basically telling this court you *think* it was Max on the phone the morning of the murder because your boss *told* you it was Max."

"That's right."

"Tell me, Mr. Temple, how often did Mr. Paganini call your boss on his cell phone or land line phone?"

Temple hesitated. "Um, I'm not really sure."

"Well, was it something like once every week, or once every two months?"

"Well, I can't really be sure."

"Okay, Mr. Temple, let me ask you this, prior to the call the morning of the murder, when was the last time you were aware that Mr. Paganini called your boss on his cell phone or any phone for that matter?"

Temple was silent. Finally he sputtered, "Well, I don't think…I mean I'm not sure that Mr. Paganini ever called Mr. Pepper before. At least, I can't remember any time."

"Well then how did you come to know the defendant? You testified that you knew him."

Temple shifted in his chair. "Well, Mr. Pepper would tell us about him."

"Wait a moment," Tracy interrupted. "Are you telling this court that the sole basis for you knowing Mr. Paganini is what Mr. Pepper *told* you about him?"

Temple shifted again. "Um, yeah; I guess I am."

"Then you never saw, talked to, or otherwise met Mr. Paganini?"

"No."

"And your boss did not regularly speak with Mr. Paganini on the phone, to your knowledge, I mean?"

"Not to my knowledge, no."

"Then how could your boss have been sure it was Max who called him?"

Pankow stood up. "Objection! How can Mr. Temple possibly answer *that* question?"

Tracy faced Reynolds. "Since Your Honor is allowing the testimony of the phone call to be offered into evidence by the State, I am curious if Mr. Pepper told the three employees on what basis he concluded it was Max who called him. Did he *think* it was Max, or did the caller actually identify himself as Max?"

A Tracy Brubaker Mystery

"I agree that to the extent the witness' knowledge as to defense's last question is based on what Randall Pepper *told* him, that he may answer that question." Temple looked confused. So Reynolds addressed him directly. "Mr. Temple, did Mr. Pepper tell you on what basis he concluded it was Max Paganini who called him to make the appointment the morning of November 5 year last?"

"Well, he said something like I just talked to old Max, or something like that. But I don't know how he knew it *was* Max."

Reynolds looked to Tracy who had an appreciative smile on her face. She turned to Temple. "Can you recall, Mr. Temple, if Mr. Pepper said anything about recognizing Max's voice?"

Temple thought a moment. "No, I don't remember him saying anything like that."

"So we don't *really* know who called Mr. Pepper that morning, do we?"

"Objection!" Pankow called out.

"Withdrawn," Tracy said a bit gleefully. "I have no more questions at this time for Mr. Temple."

Reynolds looked at the clock on the back wall. "It's just past 12:00 p.m. so I think this a good time to break for lunch. Court will resume at 2:00 p.m." Then everyone was dismissed.

Tracy quickly turned to her associate. "Neal, I can't believe I didn't think of this before."

"What are you talking about?"

"The gun, it was part of a stolen shipment. I wonder if any of the other guns in that shipment were used in local crimes."

Neal's eyes flung open. "That murder Walters was involved in maybe?"

"That's what I'm thinking. The Walters' case certainly falls under the category of ongoing investigation; no one was ever convicted for that murder. Check the court transcripts from Walters' trial — see what's there about the specific weapon used."

"Absolutely!"

"If it turns out there is a connection to Walters and the cops and feds knew it I'm gonna raise *serious* hell, ongoing investigation or not."

"I'll get on this right away, Tracy."

"Thanks Neal." And he took off like a bat outta hell.

Max approached Tracy as she was turning her cell phone back on. "How'd we do?" Max asked.

"I don't know Max. I put on a good show I think but, the police have you on record saying you're sure the phone was in your office the whole time."

"Because it was."

"I know, Max. I still haven't figured a way around that yet."

"Oh. So now what?"

"The next two witnesses will be basically a repeat of what you just saw, talking about what they know — and don't know — about the call. Soon they'll switch to focusing on your motive. But your business attorney isn't on their witness list so I guess Marty was able to dodge being a witness due to client confidentiality. Instead they plan to put some members of the bank board on the stand to get across what Pepper was trying — " Tracy looked at her phone that was now buzzing. She thought it must be Rebecca calling since her office number was on the read out. "Max, let me take this, okay?"

"Oh; sure."

"What's up Beck?" Tracy answered.

"Tracy, a Mrs. Raccio just called here," Rebecca began somberly and sounding upset. "Tracy, I'm so sorry, your mother's been taken to the hospital. Mrs. Raccio thinks she just had a stroke."

A Tracy Brubaker Mystery

The panic and fear Tracy was feeling as she entered St. Michael's Hospital were too reminiscent of learning of her father's death 12 years ago. She was feeling numb; she wanted to scream; she wanted to cry. At the reception desk she was told to go to the second floor. When she entered the waiting area she saw Mrs. Raccio seated, her face was pale and her body stiff. "Mrs. Raccio..." Tracy said as she approached her mother's best friend.

"Oh Tracy, Tracy, Tracy...you poor dear...your poor mother..." Mrs. Raccio stood up to hug Tracy but the latter wanted details.

"What happened, Mrs. Raccio? How is Mom? What have the doctors told you?"

Mrs. Raccio took a tissue from her pocketbook, wiped her eyes, blew her nose, and then sat back down. "We had just finished lunch in the city, at the Harbor; but you know about that. We were leaving, and then she suddenly felt dizzy, then she said one her legs didn't feel right, and then she fell down and hit her head and then..." But the friend couldn't finish, she started crying again.

"Okay, Mrs. Raccio, okay. What's going on now?"

There was another blow of the nose. "Well, I don't know who called the ambulance but they were there real quick. They took her back there" — she was waiving her hand toward the doors marked 'Emergency' — "and then I called you." Mrs. Raccio wiped her eyes again. "And it had been such a nice day."

Tracy took hold of the woman's hands and gave them a squeeze. "Okay, Mrs. Raccio. I'm so grateful you were there with her and called me. Thank you." Mrs. Raccio nodded. "Has the doctor been out to see you?"

"No. I told one of the nurses I called you and that you were coming right away. They said they'll talk to you as soon as they know—"

"Ms. Brubaker?" Tracy turned sharply in the voice's direction and saw a man with olive skin, probably in his 40s, standing behind her. Tracy had been so wrapped up in what Mrs. Raccio had been telling her that she didn't even realize anyone else was there. She arose.

"Yes, I'm Violetta Brubaker's daughter."

"I'm Dr. Nidra, a neurologist. Let me first say that your mother is fine and resting comfortably. She was in some pain because of injuries she sustained when she fell. But that will all heal. We're going to move her to the third floor in a few hours and I want to keep her a few days just to make sure everything is okay. But first and foremost remember your mother should not have any permanent damage from what occurred today."

Tracy breathed a heavy sigh of relief while Maria Raccio started sobbing again. "Oh thank the merciful Lord," she said between sniffles. Tracy went to hug Mrs. Raccio again, and then returned her attentions to Dr. Nidra. He started making his way to an empty chair and sat down. Tracy sat down beside him.

"Your mother had a transient ischemic attack, or TIA; a mini-stroke. Normally the symptoms, such as dizziness and numbness, the ones your mother apparently experienced, last a short time and go away. But in this case, because your mother fell down, she was brought here. Now, your mother hasn't been able to tell us that much about her history and she doesn't see a doctor affiliated with St. Michaels."

"She lives in Aberdeen. She was in the city today having lunch and accompanying her friend Mrs. Raccio."

"I see."

"What do you want to know? What can I do to help you?"

"How old is your mother?"

"59."

"Is there a family history of heart disease, high blood pressure, or similar condition, or relatives who have had strokes; is your mother a smoker?"

Tracy was shaking her head. "My paternal grandfather died of a heart attack but my mom's parents are still alive. They live in Sicily and are in their 80s. I just…" Tracy realized tears were coming down her cheeks.

"It's okay, Ms. Brubaker; something like this is never easy." He paused briefly. "How about the smoking?"

"No, neither of my parents smoked."

"Diabetes?"

"Not that I'm aware of."

The doctor nodded. "Your mother is slightly overweight so if her diet is poor that could be a contributing factor. But right now I'm thinking she suffered a blood clot which should right itself within 24 hours or so. But of course we will want to find out what happened, perhaps put her on some medication. I know this will sound odd but it may be a good thing she fell because, if she hadn't, she may not have come to see us. Mini-strokes can sometimes lead to a full-blown stroke. With her here with us now we can greatly reduce the risk of *that* happening."

Tracy was nodding and wiping her eyes, listening to every word. When Dr. Nidra had finished she said, "Thank you doctor. When can I see her?"

"Being family you can see her right now," he answered, a warm smile on his face. "She's asleep due to the pain medication and I'm not sure when she'll wake up. But please, come with me."

"Thank you. Let me just tell Mrs. Raccio what's going on."

"Take your time. I'll be right here when you're ready."

Tracy repeated most of what the doctor had told her to her mother's nervous friend. "You drove, right?"

"Yes."

"Well why don't you go home and get some rest? I'm going to stay here until she wakes up and I can talk to her a while. Then I'll call you and let you know when she can have visitors. Right now I think its family only — I mean immediate family. I certainly think of you as family, Mrs. Raccio."

"Oh Tracy, you are so sweet." The woman rose from her seat holding onto to her purse tightly. "You can call me anytime to let me know what is happening."

"I will; I promise." And then Tracy gave Mrs. Raccio another hug and watched as she made her way to the elevator, waving as the elevator door slid shut. Tracy quickly turned and followed the understanding Dr. Nidra to where her mother was resting.

Entering her mother's room, Tracy's stomach turned to knots. Violetta Brubaker had ugly looking black-and-blue bruises resembling tattoos on her right arm and right side of her head. Her eyes were closed and she was apparently resting, but her face appeared to be that of someone in great pain. Wires, tubes, and humming machinery formed a U-shape around the bed. Perhaps seeing the terror in Tracy's eyes the doctor moved close to her and started whispering. "I assure you it's not as bad as it looks. The IV tube is for food and medicine; the rest is to monitor her heart and brain, just to keep an eye on things. The bruises will, as I told you, heal. It's scary to look at; I know."

Tracy didn't initially respond but rather lowered herself into the chair right next to the bed. Finally she said, "I'll just stay here for now. That's okay, right?"

"You can stay here as long as you want. I'll be back to check on things in an hour or so. But the nurses will be keeping a close eye on your mother." Tracy nodded as the doctor exited the private quarters and exhausted, leaned back in the chair staring at her mother. It was scary looking alright. And then she covered her face with her hands and started weeping.

Tracy jerked her head up. Her mother had made a noise that woke her. When had she allowed herself to fall asleep? The chair wasn't comfortable and the room was well-lit. She quickly looked at her watch, 7:02 p.m. Tracy stood up and leaned into the bed, stroking the un-bruised side of her mother's head. "Are you okay Mom? Do you need something for the pain?"

Violetta was groggy, but she recognized her daughter's voice and forced her eyes open. "Tracy," she whispered. "Tracy you should be in school. I meant at work."

"Work's done for the day Mom. Rebecca from my office called El for me, and he explained everything to Art Pankow, the State's Attorney. They suspended the trial for the rest of the afternoon. I told them I'd be back tomorrow at 9:30 a.m. sharp unless they hear differently. But enough about that; can I get you anything?"

There was a brief pause. "How about some cheese?"

And Tracy stared laughing as the tears returned. "Oh Mom, you're such a kidder," she told her. But her mother wasn't a kidder. And yet, Tracy hadn't heard wrong. They were interrupted as a nurse invaded their bonding time.

"How are we feeling Mrs. Brubaker? How is your pain?"

"It's still there."

"I can give you something at 7:30 p.m., okay?"

"Tell that to my head and arm," Violetta said sternly. Tracy stifled a giggle. *This* was the Violetta she remembered.

The nurse asked, "Are you hungry dear?" Tracy looked at the nurse's name pin, Wanda Rawlins.

"Mom, Nurse Rawlins wants to know if you want something to eat."

"I don't think so."

"The sooner you start eating orally the sooner we can get you home," Nurse Rawlins said.

"What, and leave this?" Tracy had to stifle another giggle. She hadn't heard her mother talk to anyone like this since the days she'd admonish Tracy's father for something or other. And then Tracy realized some of her

A Tracy Brubaker Mystery

smart aleck tendencies came not just from her dad. "Just come back at 7:30. I'll be fine."

Nurse Rawlins gave a smile that Tracy would have termed patronizing. "Very well; but you'll have to eat something for breakfast tomorrow." And then the nurse turned and left.

Now Violetta Brubaker was fully awake and a bit grumpy thanks to her uncomfortable bed and bruised body. "Tracy, stop rubbing my head; you'll take the skin off."

Tracy laughed. "Sorry Mom. I was trying to slowly get it to match the other side."

"Bah," her mother croaked as Tracy returned to her seat.

"Do you want me to turn the TV on, maybe look for a game show? I know you like those."

"No. I'll just wait for my medicine; then I'll go back to sleep."

Tracy nodded. "Okay. The doctor said you're going to be fine. They may have to put you on medication but after a few days you'll be able to go home."

"They know best," her mother said unconvincingly.

"I should call Mrs. Raccio and let her know how you are. She's worried about you."

"Let her worry."

"*Mom!*" Tracy shouted.

"It was her idea to come down here."

"Mom, location had nothing to do with it. You should be thanking her instead of blaming her. If you had been alone…" But Tracy decided not finish that thought.

"I don't want to talk to anyone right now. You can call her and let her know I'm alive after you leave."

"Leave?"

"You're not going to stay here all night are you?"

"I was thinking about it," Tracy answered quietly.

"Oh dear child, that would be foolish. What can you do that these hospital people can't?"

"I'm your daughter."

Violetta looked at the young lady sitting in the chair across from her, now staring at her own hands. "Oh Tracy, I will be fine. You need to get your rest so you can get Mr. Paganini out of the mess he's in. If the beds are this bad I can guess what the chairs are like."

Tracy looked at her mother and started laughing again. "Yep; your mind seems to be working just as well as ever."

"You never thought it was working too well before."

"Oh Mom, stop that."

"I want you to go eat and get your rest, Tracy. I know I'm in good hands here. And when you talk to Mrs. Raccio tell her I'm fine and thank her for all her help. Maybe I'll feel like seeing her tomorrow."

Tracy nodded. "Okay Mom. I'm just glad you're okay." And Tracy started tearing again.

Moved by her daughter's concern, Violetta said, "Come here and give me a nice goodbye hug. You come and see me at lunchtime tomorrow maybe. Say some prayers for me." Then she paused and said, "You're a fine daughter and I love you." Tracy wiped her own eyes, arose from the chair, and then leaned in and embraced her mother.

"I love you, too Mom. I'm so happy you're my mother."

And there was quiet until a voice called out, "It's 7:30." But Tracy ignored the nurse's announcement and continued the intimate moment. Finally her mother patted Tracy's back, and when Tracy pulled away both women wiped the water from their eyes.

"This is my daughter Tracy and she's a lawyer," Violetta started telling Nurse Rawlins. "So you better take good care of me, or else."

Tracy started laughing, and even the nurse joined briefly. "See you tomorrow Mom." Then Tracy put her hand on Rawlins's shoulder. "Good luck, you're going to need it."

"Bah," Tracy heard her mother say as she started to leave the hospital room. Then Tracy reconsidered.

"I think I'll stay until you fall back asleep, Mom."

"Well, okay. It's not like I can stop you. And you never listen to me."

It wasn't long after Nurse Rawlins administered the pain-killing drugs that Violetta drifted back to sleep. Tracy arose, kissed her mother on the forehead, and made her way to the door, all the while smiling. She kept the smile on her face as she headed down the hall, to the elevator, and ultimately to her car. She took out her phone, called Mrs. Raccio to keep her promise to update her, and then noticed there were several voicemail messages. Neal, Rebecca, Tony Paganini, Martin Nestle, and even Paul Iris called to see how Tracy and her mother were doing. There were other calls from clients too, wanting to know the same thing. She found emotion overwhelming her again so she sat in the car until she thought she could make it home without having to pull over. No matter what the doctor had told her and regardless of what the statistics may be, Tracy was feeling scared and worried and helpless. She was feeling, she thought, like Max Paganini.

Arriving at her condo, Tracy commenced with the return calls, first to Neal and Rebecca, and then to Tony. The others would have to wait until tomorrow for their callbacks. She was tired and hungry, although she really didn't feel like eating. But an image of her mother's disapproving face suddenly popped into her head, and in no time at all Tracy was dumping the contents of a can of hearty soup into a saucepan. The warmed up repast was gone almost as quickly as it had been transferred into a bowl. In bed, she did as her mother asked, prayed that everything would be okay and that her mother would be home soon. She suddenly felt incredibly tired; perhaps a drain of adrenaline was the cause. She closed her eyes and hoped sleep would provide a haven from the nightmare this day had been.

Tracy was at her office before 7:00 the next day. Court would resume at 9:30 a.m., so she had some time to clean out her inbox and send a status update to those who inquired about her situation via electronic means. She heard Rebecca unlock the front door about 7:15. Rebecca didn't wait long before deciding to get a status update and see how her employer was coping.

"How's your mother, Tracy?" she asked sympathetically as she entered. "How are *you* doing?"

Tracy sighed. She essentially repeated what she had told Rebecca over the phone last night. "Mom's fine. The doctor said the stroke was minor but of course they want to keep her for observation and all that. She got some bruises when she fell but no broken bones thankfully. But it seems the bruises are bothering her most of all so she's being given something for her pain. I know I should be thankful but..." she trailed off as she looked down at her desk.

"I understand, Tracy. I am *so* sorry. I won't pretend to know how you feel since both my parents are still around and feisty as ever. But I can imagine how hard on you this has been."

Tracy looked back up, a slight smile on her face. "I can't lose her now, Beck, not when I have so much to make up for."

Rebecca gave her a confused look. "What do you mean, Tracy?"

Tracy sighed. "Well, Mom did all the work around the house, you know; took care of me 24/7. She cooked and cleaned; did the laundry; all of that. And she was the one who always had to calm down the hyper daughter who always seemed to be in the way. So I gravitated toward my father. Every time he was home I was by his side. What I mean is, he probably got most of my affection because he was always the *fun* one. I think I hurt my mother's feelings by doing that. She did everything for me and I paid her back by looking forward to when my father got home and then wanting to be with him."

Rebecca was nodding. "I don't think it's unusual for a child to gravitate toward the parent they see the least."

"Yeah, I can see that. And that of course is why I was so close to my father. I could joke around with him; we would tease each other, sometimes mercilessly, especially as I got older; it was just a great all around relationship. I had nothing like that with Mom. She just didn't understand it." Tracy stood up and moved toward her window, and was now staring at nothing in particular in the parking lot. "After Dad died, I realized I wanted that kind of relationship with Mom, the closeness, the playfulness, the affection. So for more than 10 years now I've tried kidding around with her, treating her more like a pal than a mother. But I just seem to frustrate her." Tracy paused, and her voice cracked as she said, "And now she's in a hospital bed." She wiped some tears from her eyes.

Rebecca rose and went to put her arm around Tracy. "I bet she understands what you're trying to do Tracy, after watching you and your dad together for all of those years. I bet deep inside she appreciates it even if she doesn't quite know how to express it."

Tracy looked at her. "Do you really think so? I can't help but think that all the worry about me and this case is what caused the stroke."

Rebecca pondered a bit. "I'm not an expert of course but I do have a daughter. And I can tell you I will be worrying about her for the rest of my life. Your mother would be worrying about you if you taught pre-schoolers in the most heavily protected school in the world. I can also tell you as a mother it's difficult to find a balance between being a disciplinarian and being a friend, because you want your kid to love you but you know you sometimes have to do and say things they won't like, things they may hate you for and not hesitate in sharing that feeling. You are who you are, Tracy, and she is who she is. And I don't think either of you are going to change, nor should you. So keep joking around with her, and seeing her like you do. I suspect that's all your mother really wants." Rebecca gave Tracy a comforting squeeze, rubbed her back, and then headed for the doorway.

A Tracy Brubaker Mystery

"Beck, you are awesome beyond words. Thank you."

Rebecca smiled. "I am awesome, aren't I?" Then she gave Tracy a wink and returned to her desk to continue being awesome. Not long after Rebecca sat down at her desk, the main desk phone rang. Normally she wouldn't start answering until around 8:30, half-an-hour before the office doors officially opened. But given the last day's activities, she decided to take the call. "Office of Tracy Brubaker, Attorney-At-Law."

"Rebecca, its Elias Tanner."

"Hi Detective—I'll put you right through."

Rebecca announced the caller holding on line one. Tracy grabbed the receiver immediately. "Oh, El. I cannot believe I didn't call you already. I am so sorry."

"Tracy, don't apologize. How is your mother?"

"She's fine, El. I mean, she's going to be fine."

"Do you think she'll be up for visitors today? Rita wants to see her."

"That's not up to me to decide, El."

"Right. Of course."

"I think they're going to move her today if they didn't already. She just wanted to sleep last night."

"How are you holding up, Tracy?"

"I'm doing okay. I'll be fine."

"Can I do anything for you or your mother?"

"No, El. I think right now we just need to wait and see what the doctor finds or doesn't find. But if I need anything I'll let you know."

"You don't feel like talking right now, do you?" Tanner stated.

"Is it that obvious? I'm sorry El."

"Stop apologizing. Let me know if you need anything."

Tracy paused. "Actually, I do need something."

"Name it."

"Could you tell me if the gun used to kill Randy Pepper came from a shipment that also supplied the gun involved in the Walters murder trial?"

"Wait—what? That's not what I was talking about."

"You said, 'name it'."

"Tracy—"

"You said if I needed any unofficial help with the case to ask you; so I am asking you, unofficially."

"Tracy, this is not fair."

"And what you and the feds are doing to Max is fair?"

Tanner paused. "Tracy, you are going below the belt here. I told you earlier, I'm not privy to all the details of Max's case."

"El, if you tell me yes, then at least I know I'm on the right track. And I can get my verification through other means."

"Good Lord, Tracy. Do you know what you're asking?"

"Probably not. But El, I need to do what I can to help Max." Then, without planning it, she blurted out angrily, "*I have to help somebody, damn it!*"

Tanner was quiet. "Okay Tracy. Let me see what I can find out."

"Thank you El," she said quietly.

"Sure Tracy. I'll talk to you soon."

"Goodbye, El."

Tracy was at the courthouse by 9:15 a.m. She called the hospital to talk to her mother, needing to hear her voice before the day got away from her. Unfortunately Violetta Brubaker was currently out of her room for tests, and the nurse's station couldn't be sure when she'd be back.

"Please let her know that I called," Tracy told the nurse. "And please tell her I will call when court breaks for lunch and try to see her then."

"Sure Ms. Brubaker. I will give her your message right away."

"Thank you." Tracy then set her phone to vibrate. She wouldn't be turning it completely off for the rest of the trial.

Arthur Pankow was now preparing his table. After he saw Tracy end her phone call, he went over to her. "Tracy, are you okay? We could ask for another day if you need it."

"I'm fine, Art. Thanks." Then she suddenly laughed. "Oh look what I did there, fine art."

Pankow chuckled. "Yeah, you *are* okay, aren't you?" Then he returned to his seat.

Moments later Max, Gloria, and the Paganini sons entered and asked the same questions Tracy was finally getting tired of answering. Max took his place beside Tracy as Neal arrived, one minute before court was supposed to start. He looked at her, and she gave him a "thumbs up". He smiled in return and gave her a quick nod. They had no time for a pre-court conference.

Tracy felt a hand on her shoulder, Martin Nestle. She felt her cheeks flush. "Oh Marty, I'm sorry for not calling you back."

"Hey, don't worry about it," he said sincerely. "It's good to see you here. I guess that means your mother is going to be alright."

 A Tracy Brubaker Mystery

She smiled and nodded and Nestle gave her a quick rub of the shoulder. Then he took his seat. Tracy took a deep breath. Then Judge Reynolds entered the court, and day two began. "Will counsel approach?" Reynolds asked. Pankow and Tracy obliged. "Are you okay to continue, Ms. Brubaker?"

"I'm ready, Your Honor."

"Okay." And then he leaned back in his chair and the two attorneys took their seats.

The morning went as Tracy expected. Pankow called the other two Pepper employees—Cheryl Fazik and Tim Carlisle—who Pepper made aware of his meet with Max. And each of their testimony was not too much different than Temple's the previous morning.

"The State calls Lester Grossman to the stand." Max Paganini's bookkeeper walked to the stand and was sworn in.

"Mr. Grossman," Pankow began, "you are employed as Mr. Paganini's bookkeeper?"

"Yes."

"For how long, sir?"

"More than 15 years."

"On the morning of November 5th, last year, you were at Mr. Paganini's place of business?"

"Yes."

"That morning, you were directed to write a check for a bank loan extension?"

"Yes."

"Had you been directed to write bank loan extension checks before?"

"Yes, a few times."

"Was there anything different about this particular request for such a check?"

"Well, Mr. Paganini wanted it in a hurry."

"Do you know why?"

"His lawyer was going to pick up the signed extension form and check that afternoon."

"And how was this different?"

"Usually they get picked up the next day so I have the whole day to take care of it. But this time they wanted it that same day."

"Do you know why it was so urgent?"

"No."

"Mr. Paganini didn't give you any hint about it when he told you to hurry the check?"

"Objection!" Tracy called out. "Ask and answered. Mr. Pankow should save the hints for Heloise."

Pankow gave her a what-the-hell look, and there were some scattered chuckles throughout the room. "You can object without the commentary, Ms. Brubaker. But the objection is sustained."

Pankow shook his head. "Mr. Grossman, about what time that morning did Mr. Paganini tell you that he wanted the check to be ready later that same day?"

"Around 10:15, or maybe 10:20; something like that."

"Are you aware that Mr. Paganini's attorney called him at 10:15 a.m. that morning?"

Tracy arose. "Sidebar, Your Honor." Reynolds nodded and Pankow and Tracy were back in front of Reyonolds.

"What is it Ms. Brubaker?"

"What is Mr. Pankow trying to accomplish with this seeming end run around the reason for the expediency of the check?" Tracy asked.

"It is the State's position that the call from Mr. Paganini's attorney is what motivated Mr. Paganini shortly thereafter to set up the meeting with Pepper," Pankow offered.

"Then why not call Nestle to the stand?" Tracy asked.

"Because Nestle contends the phone call falls under privileged communication and will not testify to its specific contents unless directed to by his client."

"Which Mr. Paganini of course refuses to do," Reynolds stated.

"At the advice of his present counsel no doubt." Pankow gave Tracy a quick scowl.

Tracy scowled right back. "If Mr. Pankow wants to enter into the evidence the fact that Mr. Nestle called Mr. Paganini, that's one thing. But to go any further than that is guesswork and innuendo, and not evidence."

"She has a point, Mr. Pankow," Reynolds agreed.

"Your Honor, we know Mr. Pepper recently was admitted to the bank's board and recommended a curb in extending loans," Pankow continued.

"So what?" Tracy countered. "Can you prove that my client *knew* this?"

"He probably did. That's why getting the paperwork in became important."

     A Tracy Brubaker Mystery

"First of all," Tracy scolded, "the extension had already been approved by the bank. Second, 'probably' knew isn't good enough."

"The bank representative hadn't signed the extension yet because they didn't have the check yet."

"But the extension did ultimately go through, didn't it?" Tracy challenged.

"Yes; it did. But Paganini wouldn't have known for sure on that Wednesday."

"Alright," Reynolds said. "I've heard enough. Mr. Pankow, you're going to have to bring me something a little more solid than 'probably' to claim Mr. Paganini knew about Pepper and his policy change recommendations. Now let's move along, shall we?"

After returning to his table, Pankow announced he had no more questions for Grossman. Having established the rushed check was unusual would have to suffice for now.

"Mr. Grossman," Tracy began, "I want to be clear on the reason for the quick turnaround for the check. Is it true to your personal knowledge that the reason was because Mr. Paganini's attorney wanted to pick it up that afternoon?"

"Yes; that's all I can say for certain."

"Thank you, Mr. Grossman. That's all I have for now."

At the lunch break, Tracy went to Martin Nestle. "Marty, can I ask a favor?"

"Sure Tracy; anything."

"Can you get a hold of some financial reports for me, income statements, budgets, the stuff you might pull together if you were going to apply for a loan extension? Oh, and maybe some payroll records too."

"Okay; I'll see what I can do. What are your lunch plans, by the way?"

"I was going to check on my mother."

"Of course; I'll let you know when I have everything together."

"Thanks Marty."

"Sure." He gave her a smile and then turned and left the room. Neal approached Tracy.

"Don't you want to talk about what I found out about the gun?"

"Oh—right. Actually I asked El to look into it, thinking he'd get the answer quicker. *Did* you find anything?"

"I went through the Walters' trial transcript most of yesterday and last night. Now Garrison said that the shipment was stolen a couple of years ago and that lines up with what was in the transcripts—at that time the stolen shipment would have been about a year prior. Tanner could probably confirm it, but I think you're right Tracy, the gun that killed Pepper came from the same source as the one that killed Donaldson, the man Walters' was supposed to have had murdered."

Tracy was shaking her head. "They lied to my face, Neal. They've known about the gun all along. But now I *really* have a connection to Walters and Pepper that I can use."

"Even though Walters wasn't convicted?"

"It doesn't matter. I have a legitimate reason for adding Walters to my witness list. His reputation and the coincidence of the source of the guns should be enough for the jury to make the connection."

Neal nodded. "The feds aren't going to like that. And there remains the problem with the phone call. We still don't have much."

"We have Abe Denberg. He knew Pepper via his former boss Ed Grimes. All that business is public record."

"You think it's Denberg, then?"

"I'm not sure. But he's the most likely at this point." Tracy checked her watch. "Neal, I want to go to St. Michael's now and check up on my mother. If I'm a little late, can you cover for me?"

"Sure Tracy. You bet."

"Call Beck and see if she can set up a meeting with Walters for me tonight, say after 5:30. We'll talk after court's done for the day." And then she was off to St. Michael's.

At the hospital, Tracy's mother seemed to be resting comfortably. Tracy entered the room out of breath. "Sorry Mom. I wanted to be here sooner. I can't stay too long. I have to be back in court by 2:00."

"Why don't you breathe a little bit before they have to put *you* on one of these machines," Violetta scolded.

"Uh-huh," was all Tracy said as she sat down. "Mom, I think it's time we talked."

"We always talk."

"Okay; I'll be blunt. I think it's time you were honest with me."

"What are you talking about?"

"Those earlier bruises of yours, how did you get them?"

"I told you already."

A Tracy Brubaker Mystery

"I think you told me some fibs."

"I don't understand you."

"Mom, I think you hurt yourself those times pretty much the same way you were hurt yesterday. You felt dizzy, lost your balance, and banged against something." Her mother turned her head. "Why didn't you tell me?"

Violetta could still not look at her daughter. "I didn't want you to worry."

"Guess what, it didn't work."

"I felt better real quick."

"Mom, those other times were probably mini-strokes too. You're lucky this last one wasn't worse. The doctor says these small strokes can lead to bigger, much more serious ones." No response. "Mom, are you listening to me?" Tracy was getting upset; the stubborn woman in the bed versus the stubborn woman in the chair. Who'd win?

"Tracy, what does it matter? I'm old."

"First, you're not that old. 59 is *not* old by today's standards. Second, what the hell does that mean, anyway?"

"Don't raise your voice," Violetta said sternly.

"I'm going to raise my voice until you start listening to me. What is it with you and Max, saying you're old, implying that that means you're not worth as much or something?"

"Well, it's true."

"It is NOT true! I never want you to die!" Tracy's tongue came to a screeching halt. She hadn't meant to say what she said — acknowledging the truth that her mother wouldn't be around forever but that she couldn't do anything about it. Now Tracy was crying again, and her mother wouldn't even look at her. Tracy wiped the tears from her eyes. "Listen you stubborn woman, you better realize this. I love you and you are important to me in ways you cannot possibly understand. So you better get well and take the medicine they tell you to take when you leave here. Or I'm going to drag you to my place where *I'll* take care of you. Is that what you want?"

Violetta shook her head, but was still looking in the opposite direction. Then she turned to face her daughter, tears in her eyes, and Tracy bent over to hug her. For a while neither said anything. Tracy made the move to break away, but not because she wanted to. "I have to head back to court Mom," Tracy said wiping her eyes.

"Okay."

"I'll be back tonight."

"You should go home and sleep."

Tracy ignored the implication. "I'll see you tonight." She gave her mother another quick hug and then left the room. She hurried to the car, and pulled her door shut with more force than was needed. She was suddenly pounding the steering wheel with both hands. "That foolish, obstinate woman!" she shouted. Finally she sat back in her seat; she glared at the windshield. Then she jammed her key into the ignition switch and pulled out of the lot. Court would be a chore this afternoon. But there was one thing that might brighten her spirits. "Please let them call Sonny Brookhouser to the stand this afternoon," she thought. Now she was grinning. "If misery loves company, Sonny, I'm going to invite you to my party."

A Tracy Brubaker Mystery

"The State calls William Brookhouser to the stand," Pankow announced shortly after court was officially back in session. Brookhouser was sworn in.

Pankow moved toward his witness. "Mr. Brookhouser, you are an employee of the defendant, Massimo Paganini?"

"Yes."

"How long have you worked at his clothier and tailor store?"

"Three years or so."

"You knew the victim, Randall Pepper?"

"Not really, no."

"But you knew who he was, by sight I mean."

"Yes."

"Did he visit Mr. Paganini's store on occasion?"

"Yes, every once in a while."

"Why?"

"Objection!" Tracy interrupted. "The witness cannot know the reason for Randall Pepper's visits, especially after just testifying that he didn't really know Pepper."

"Sustained," Reynolds nodded.

"Mr. Brookhouser," Pankow continued, "when Mr. Pepper would visit the shop, what behavior did you personally observe?"

Brookhouser cleared his throat. "Well, he'd come in and look around. He'd say stuff like how sad and lonely the place looked; that the store was probably not gonna make it much longer. Stuff like that."

"And you personally witnessed this?"

"Yup. I'm on the sales floor so I deal with the customers and anyone else who comes in."

"And how often would you say that Mr. Pepper visited the store in the three years you worked there?"

"Oh, I guess one a month, or once every month and a half."

"I see." Pankow turned to face the jury. "And how did Mr. Paganini feel about this?"

"Objection!" Tracy called out again. "I doubt Mr. Brookhouser knew my client's innermost feelings."

"I'll rephrase, then," Pankow said quickly. "What behavior did you personally observe of the defendant when he saw Mr. Pepper in the store or learned that Mr. Pepper had been in the store?"

"He'd get mad. His face would get red. He'd start speaking Italian. That's how I learned the Italian word *asino* means jackass." There were chuckles throughout the courtroom. "Yeah old Max would get real steamed."

"Would Mr. Paganini ask Mr. Pepper to leave if he was on the showroom floor when Mr. Pepper came in?"

"That only happened once when I was there that I remember. As soon as Pepper saw Max was there he turned and left."

"I see." Pankow returned to his chair. "I have no more questions; defense's witness." Pankow sat down.

Tracy remained in her chair. She stared at Brookhouser. He looked at her. Then she smiled at him. Pankow looked over at her. Judge Reynolds was about to speak when Tracy stood up. "Mr. Brookhouser," she began as she moved out from behind the table, "did you ever hear my client threaten Mr. Pepper with any kind of violence?"

Brookhouser gulped. "No."

"Did you ever hear my client threaten *anyone* with violence?"

"No."

"Did you ever witness my client get angry with anyone other than Mr. Pepper?"

"Sure."

"Give us just one example based solely on your own personal observation."

"Okay; last year we got the wrong the order on some materials. The next time the driver came in to drop off materials Max started going off on the guy saying how he screwed up last time and would have to wait until Max looked things over."

"I see. Did he call the driver any names, by chance?"

Brookhouser paused. "I think he called him an idiot." Another chorus of chuckles filled the air.

"And, to your knowledge, is the idiot driver still among the living?"

"Your Honor…" Pankow complained.

"Fine," Tracy snorted. "Tell us Mr. Brookhouser, were there other similar incidents with other people that you witnessed?"

A Tracy Brubaker Mystery

"Sure."

"How about you, did my client ever get mad at you?"

Brookhouser cleared his throat. "Yeah, at least when I just started; he thought I was a little too aggressive with the customers; too in-your-face. But mostly we got along just fine."

"To your knowledge did Mr. Paganini ever hurt a person he got angry with?"

"No. Max got mad, blew off his steam, and then went on like nothing happened. That's just how he was. You'd get used to it."

"I see." Tracy paused. She wanted the jury to know what kind of person Sonny Brookhouser was, and she was mulling over what question she could ask to start down that path. But he had actually been a better witness for her than for Pankow. She loathed him; but she wasn't going to bring her personal feelings into her cross examination, as much as she wanted to. "I have no further questions for Mr. Brookhouser." She gave him another smile and returned to her seat.

Pankow called Abe Denberg and Jeff Pollenfax to fill out the rest of the day. Like Brookhouser, they testified to Max's feelings about Pepper. Like Brookhouser, they never heard Max threaten him or anyone else. At the end of the day Tracy thought the employees' testimony and subsequent cross could be called a draw. Tomorrow would no doubt see Craig Marwood on the stand, and, more importantly, Tony Paganini. Tony seemed okay with respect to testifying. But practicing how you'll respond to the State's Attorney can be prepare you only so much for the actual questioning. Tracy phoned Rebecca. "Did you have any luck with Walters?"

"I left a message with his secretary; nothing yet."

"I can't say I'm surprised. Make a note to call again first thing tomorrow for me please."

"You bet. Tracy, how's your mother?"

"I think she's depressed, feeling sorry for herself. That's probably normal though."

"I take it you're headed there tonight."

"Yes; then I'll be in the office later tonight, or very early tomorrow."

"Okay. Tell her I asked about her. I've talked to her on the phone enough; I think she knows who I am."

Tracy laughed gently. "I think she'll remember you, yeah. Thanks as always, Beck."

"Sure Tracy; goodnight."

Tracy turned to Neal. "I want to see my mother. Can you talk to Tony and make sure he's okay about tomorrow? I think it's going to be rough."

"Sure Tracy."

"Thanks Neal; I'm going to St. Michael's then. I'll call El later and see if he can give us any further info on the gun. Hopefully I can wait until Monday to start my defense; that would give us a few days."

"Gotcha."

"Well, I guess I'm outta here. See you tomorrow Neal."

"Give your mother my best."

Tracy smiled and nodded as she hurried out the door to her car. Hopefully tonight would be a much less stressful visit than earlier today.

"So far everything looks fine," Dr. Nidra told Tracy. She was outside her mother's hospital room; she had been fortunate that the doctor was working a later shift this evening and was available. "There doesn't seem to be any kind of damage to her brain that I can see. There are still some more things I want to look at, of course. And we want to make sure she continues to improve as she has been doing. But I think, if nothing changes, she'll be able to go home this weekend."

Tracy was so relieved she almost slunk to the floor. Dr. Nidra smiled at her as if he had just read her mind. "Thank you so much doctor."

"I know it's difficult; but try not to worry. Your mother is doing very well." He lightly touched her arm, smiled again, and then started moving toward the nurses' station. Tracy pushed her mother's door open.

"Hi Mom; how's tricks?"

"What?"

"How are you feeling?"

"I'm fine."

"You could be on fire and you'd say, 'I'm fine'. Are you hungry? Do you need anything?"

"No. I ate at 6:00."

"Oh good; that's certainly a good sign."

"You're a doctor now?"

Tracy sighed. "I'm not going to argue with you tonight, so stop trying to push my buttons."

Violetta paused and then said, "Rita Tanner was here today."

"Hey, that's great. What did you two do?"

"We talked. She brought cards so we played for a while."

"It's lonely here, huh?"

"It's fine."

Argh. "Are the cards still here? If not I bet the gift shop has some. I can check."

"Rita left them in the drawer. But I don't feel like playing."

"Okay. Let me know if you do." Tracy looked around the room. "Dr. Nidra thinks you'll be able to come home this weekend. That's good news."

"If you say so."

"Mom, please stop. Look, I'm sorry for losing it earlier today. I was upset; I don't like seeing you like this and I don't like the fact you don't think I care about you."

Violetta waved her hand. "I know you care, Tracy."

"Alright then, I don't like the idea that *you* don't care."

"I don't like it here."

Tracy nodded. "I'm sorry you're here too. But I doubt many people *do* like being here. And when you leave, if you do what they tell you do, you won't have to come back for a long time." Tracy moved closer to the bed. "Mom, would you like to come live with me, or at least stay with me for a while?"

"We've talked about this."

"That was before this happened."

"I like it where I am."

"Sure; okay." Tracy moved back in her seat. Violetta remained quiet. Tracy again moved forward and took her mother's hand and started rubbing it. Violetta turned and smiled, and then she put her other hand on top of Tracy's. The silence continued. Eventually Violetta drifted off to sleep. Tracy stayed a while longer, but at 9:00 she decided it was time to go. She leaned over and kissed her mother's forehead, whispered "I love you" into her ear, and then made her way to her car.

She called Detective Tanner as soon as she closed the door. "Hi Tracy," he answered.

"Hello, El. I hear your missus visited Mom today."

"Yes. Rita said she thought your mother was doing well, if a little down."

"I concur with that diagnosis."

"So, I guess you're calling about the gun."

Crossed Stitch

151

Tracy sighed. "Neal looked at the transcripts from the Walters trial. I know the weapons in both cases came from the same source. But I'd rather have something official."

"Tracy, I'm afraid you're not going to able to get something official."

"You can't help me?"

"No; they're part of an ongoing—"

"Investigation," she finished. "I get it."

"I *am* sorry."

"I know."

"So we're good, right?"

"Always."

"I'm glad to hear you say that. And I'm sorry this is playing out like it is. I'll let you go then."

"Goodnight El. See you soon."

"Bye, Tracy."

Tracy sat in her vehicle. She had handled that disappointment rather well, she thought, a good beginning to the months-old New Year's resolution she had made. The truth was she was tired of yelling at people. She had been doing too much of that lately, at people she loved, no less. Nor did she feel like crying; she just wanted to go home and put her head on her pillow. She'd make sure she got into the office early. This day was done.

Tracy was preparing to leave her condo Wednesday morning when her cell phone started vibrating. There was a moment of panic that it might be the hospital so she answered immediately. "Tracy—it's Arthur Pankow."

"Good morning Art," she answered relieved.

"Can you come to my office first thing before court? Those two feds you've been doing the tango with want to see you."

"Uh, well, okay." She paused a moment and then said, "I'm in trouble, aren't I?"

"They didn't give me any details. But it was Roper who called; he seems like the calmer one."

"Agreed. Okay Art, I'm on my way."

"See you shortly then."

When Tracy entered Arthur Pankow's office, she found agents Lennon and Roper already there waiting for her. Tanner was present too. She suddenly felt like the naughty student who's been summoned to the principal's office for a parent conference. "And how is everyone doing today?" she asked after putting her case and coat on an empty chair.

A Tracy Brubaker Mystery

"The agents would like to talk to you for a few minutes," Pankow answered.

"Sure; okay."

Lennon started. "I hear your secretary called yesterday trying to set up an appointment with Reginald Walters. I thought I told you he's not involved in the case."

Tracy frowned. "Yes, she did, and yes you did. But I think we all know he's connected to the murder of Randy Pepper."

"How so?" Lennon challenged.

"You're kidding me, right? I know about the gun, Agent Lennon."

"The gun?"

"The gun used to kill Pepper came from the same stolen case that the murder weapon in the Walters trial came from."

Lennon blinked. "You can't *know* that."

"Sure I can; my associate when through the transcripts. And before this trial is over I plan on getting very specific about it in open court. You get me?"

There was more stunned silence from Lennon. "You won't get any official testimony on that, young lady. That missing case of firearms is part of an ongoing investigation and no law enforcement officer can testify to anything related thereto. Do *you* get *me*?"

"I get that you've *lied* to me since the beginning. You knew Walters and Pepper had business together. You knew about the gun. And you certainly knew about Carlton Brandice coming to see me. You knew all these things and you had the gall to say to my face that Walters had nothing to do with the murder. Now I know I'm just some local mouthpiece to you. But you had no right to treat me like you did. Being a federal employee *you* work for *me*, smart guy."

Lennon's face looked like it had spent a day in direct sunlight, so Roper jumped in. "Brandice hasn't bothered you since that one time."

"I don't think that's true either. I'm sure he was the man in the car a couple months ago, in spite of your so-called surveillance. But even if you won't agree with me on *that*, you have to admit it's too big a coincidence that Brandice shows up to see the person who's representing another person in a case where Brandice is an associate of yet another person who knew the victim."

Lennon said tersely, "Look; it's like this, I don't want you bothering Walters."

"Why?"

"Because I don't want him thinking he's a target of a murder investigation right now, no matter who's doing the investigating."

"Sorry agent; that's not good enough. I'm doing this for my client, not because I'm trying to annoy law enforcement. The latter's just a fringe benefit."

"I don't want you bothering him!" Lennon repeated, raising his voice.

Tracy looked around the room. Tanner and Pankow were looking at her. Suddenly she felt like everyone else knew something she didn't. And she didn't like *that* at all. "What is going on here? Why shouldn't I talk to Walters? And I'm *not* leaving until someone answers me."

There was more silence. She looked to the two agents who were exchanging glances. Then an idea came to her. "Pepper was working for you guys, wasn't he?" She stared at Lennon until he met her eyes.

"Ms. Brubaker, I don't know you. But your friends here say you can be trusted. So yes, Pepper was working for us."

"And how did that come about?"

Roper said, "During the Walters trial Pepper got arrested for a house flipping scam in Prince George's County that had been going on a while. He helped arrange phony appraisals on numerous homes and shared in the proceeds when the homes were sold at the greatly inflated prices. When we got involved and learned of his connection with Walters, we made him an offer."

Lennon gave Roper a brief scowl and then turned his attention back to Tracy. "The bottom line is, we don't know if Walters knew about Pepper's deal with us and had him killed. I'm just being cautious on the chance that your client wasn't involved after all."

Tracy thought a bit. "Wait a minute. Since Pepper is dead why would you care if Walters found out or not?" Again she looked around the room and again she felt like she was being kept out of the loop. Then she had another thought. "Unless you have someone *else* in Pepper's group—maybe an actual undercover agent—and you're afraid he's in danger." The exchanged glances seemed to confirm her guess.

"Pankow told me you were quick," Lennon said flatly.

"Don't patronize me," Tracy snapped.

"I wasn't. At least now you can understand our problem."

Tracy was losing her patience. "Listen, I think all of you know in your heart of hearts that Walters had Pepper killed, and the most likely reason is that he found out what you just told me. Pepper was an amateur at un-

A Tracy Brubaker Mystery

dercover work so he probably gave himself away. In short, your guy may be in trouble anyway."

"Right now he's fine," Lennon stated.

"But for how long?"

"Who knows? Probably at least until the trial's over and things get back to something resembling normal."

Tracy moved closer to Lennon, her anger and contempt barely contained. "Oh, so that's it. You hope your guy might magically find something while Max is on trial for a crime you damn well *know* he isn't guilty of on the *chance* that Walters, who probably is being extra cautious right now, will nevertheless slip up."

"You're oversimplifying things," Lennon said with hostility.

"And you're knowingly letting an innocent man be persecuted."

"I don't *know* that he's innocent."

"Your nose is growing, Pinocchio."

Lennon's face started changing colors again. "You seem to be under the misapprehension that this is some kind of discussion or negotiation. It is not. Stay away from Walters."

"I will do no such thing."

Roper interjected, with a much calmer tone. "Ms. Brubaker, aren't you being a bit hypocritical here? Our agent's life may be in danger here. And he has a family too. If you go after Walters he may get hurt, or much worse. Are you willing to risk his life for your client's? Because if you are right that Pepper was killed because he was found out, that is exactly what could happen."

Tracy thought a moment. "No, I'm not the hypocrite here," she answered firmly. "You have options; you can pull your guy out right now if you really think he's in danger. Max doesn't have that choice."

Lennon jumped back in. "Are you serious? Ruin a months-long investigation just for Paganini? I've invested too much in this—"

"*You've* invested?" Tracy interrupted. "*You're* the one putting his life on the line day in and day out, taking all the chances surrounding yourself with thugs and killers? No, the lives of the people involved in this mean *nothing* to you. This is all about your career and advancement isn't it? It would be quite the feather if you get Walters, wouldn't it?"

Lennon turned from her, looked at Roper for some help, which he didn't receive, and then turned back to the young woman who wasn't the game player he was hoping for. "Stay away from Walters!" he shouted.

Tracy turned from him, grabbed her belongings, and started out the door. Before leaving she told Lennon, "If you really actually care about your undercover agent you may want to start planning his evacuation. I'm Max Paganini's lawyer and will defend him with every means at my disposal. Don't bother me again." And then she turned and marched out the doorway.

Lennon turned to Pankow. "I thought you said she'd be reasonable, that she was smart."

"Asking her to ignore a possible means of clearing her client probably didn't sound reasonable or smart to her," Pankow responded. "And if you know anything else about this case that you haven't told us you better do it right now, because I'm tired of you. Now get out of my office."

"So you're going to screw around with me too now? Do you really want to do that Mr. Pankow? I could end your career."

Pankow shook his head. "I doubt it. You see, I'm not a politician, and good State's Attorneys aren't easy to come by. But be my guest if you want to have a go at it. I sense that there is something else going on here that you aren't telling me. And I think that at the end of the day *you're* going to be the one seeking employment elsewhere if trying to intimidate everyone around you is the best you have." Pankow sat behind his desk and Tanner took a seat in front of it. Roper made a move toward the exit. Eventually Lennon followed. He had nothing else to say.

"You really think he's hiding something Arthur?" Tanner asked.

"Every time I've worked, or tried to work, with the feds they've never been 100% upfront about everything. And Roper remaining mostly silent during the whole thing just adds to my suspicions."

Tanner nodded. "What about Tracy? If Brandice *was* the one in the car and she starts after Walters, I worry what might happen."

Pankow looked at Tanner sympathetically. "I hear you. But Tracy's going to do what Tracy's going to do. And now that Lennon's practically dared her to bring Walters into this thing, well…I guess we'll just have to wait and see, unfortunately." Tanner shook his head. In his experience the wait and see approach rarely ended well. Instead, he was more likely than not to be launching a new homicide investigation.

A Tracy Brubaker Mystery

Tracy was sitting in her auto plotting her next move while waiting for her blood pressure to decrease. She looked at her watch, 8:18 a.m. She dialed Neal's cell phone number. "Hi Tracy," Neal answered.

"Hey Neal. I have a new research project for you."

"Sure. What is it?"

"Randy Pepper got arrested during Walters' trial for house flipping in PG County. I'm not at liberty to reveal my sources, but just take my word for it that he did. It wouldn't have made the papers though because Pepper ended up making a deal. I need you to take another look at him for me, concentrating on whom he was working with before and during the Walters' trial. Maybe with this narrower window to look through, we can find a familiar name connected with *our* case."

"Oh, okay. I'll get on that post haste. Anything else?"

She hesitated. "Has Walters or any representative of his returned Rebecca's calls yet?"

"Not that I'm aware of. But it's early in the day."

"Okay. I figured as much."

"Martin Nestle called; he tried your cell but you must have had it off. Anyway he said he had those reports you asked him for."

"Oh good. I'll give him a call. I'll be going then."

"Are you okay Tracy? I mean, you seem a little perturbed."

"I'll have to tell you about all of that later, Neal."

"Alright."

Tracy started fuming again. "Screw it. Neal, I want you to get the paperwork together for a subpoena."

"For whom, Walters?"

"Yes. I'm tired of this. I'm going on the offensive no matter whom I offend. You get me?"

"Yes boss. I'm on my way to the courthouse after we hang up."

"Thanks Neal. I'll be in touch. Goodbye."

"Bye, Tracy."

Next up, call Nestle. He picked up on the second ring. "Martin Nestle."

"Marty, it's Tracy."

"Hi! Tracy, how's your mother?"

"She's going to be fine, they tell me. They're doing tests but I think everything will be okay. Thanks for asking Marty."

"Sure. Well, I am glad to hear its good news, relatively speaking. Look, I have those reports you wanted."

"Great! I'm in the parking lot of the State Attorney's office. Where are you?"

"I'm just leaving a client in the city so I'm probably not too far from you."

"Want to meet at our favorite coffee shop?"

He chuckled. "Sure. I'll meet you there."

"Thanks bunches, Marty. I need to be back in time for court at 9:30 so it'll be a quick one. See you soon." The two rang off and then Tracy made her way to her impromptu meeting. She beat Marty there so she grabbed seats for them and ordered two waters while she waited. Five minutes later he came in with his trusty briefcase and saw Tracy seated; he started making his way to the friendly face in the crowd.

"Hi Tracy," he said offering her his hand. She stood up to shake, and then the two sat down.

"Hungry?" she asked him.

"Not really. But I guess I should order something."

"Get something to go. I think I'm getting a grilled cheese on a bagel."

He smiled at her. "Hey, that sounds pretty good." Two orders of grilled cheese on a bagel were placed shortly thereafter. Nestle then started removing papers from his case, handing them across the table. "Here are the payroll reports from the payroll service for the last few years. And here are the reports showing budget-versus-actual expenses that were given to the bank for the last few periods that they requested. Last we have some income figures for the past few years. Oh, and here's a balance sheet dated December 31, 2014."

Tracy commenced surveying the papers. "This is perfect, Marty; thanks."

"No problem. Not that I minded getting this stuff for you, but why didn't you just ask Lester?"

"Lester's kind of sensitive and I'm an outsider. I just thought it would be easier this way. Make sure you send *me*, not Max, the bill for your time."

"Okay. Looking for anything in particular?"

She shook her head. "I'm trying to get a better handle on the financial aspects of a small tailor shop. My associate is very good at statistics, and comparisons, and all that kind of stuff. He might find something if there's something going on with the numbers, although I'm sure everything's fine. I'm also getting interested in the appraisal business and how one comes up with valuations. I'm curious what Max's shop's true value may be. But truthfully I don't have anything specific in mind. It's just that during Lester's testimony yesterday I started wondering what kind of information of Max's Randy Pepper would have access to if he was mulling around the bank. I know he has or had an appraisal business. And he may have been looking into places outside the city where one could set up a tailor's shop."

"I see. How do you think the case is going? I haven't been able to see too much of it." He put his head down.

Before Tracy could answer, their food arrived, so there was a brief pause while the diners sampled their purchases. Tracy continued, "Well, right now I'm trying to argue Max was framed of course. There's the victim's connection with Reginald Walters, which I think cannot be ignored. Quite frankly, I think Walters had Pepper killed. He used somebody at the shop to borrow the phone and set the meeting. Who that was I'm not sure yet. I can't believe it to be any of his sons, so that leaves me with Lester, Jeff, Craig, Sonny, and Abe, the only other people in the office when the call was made."

"Okay, so one of them makes the call, and then, what, kills Pepper himself?"

"Max believes the store was all locked up so the killer had to have a key."

"Oh, I see."

"And then *I* get a visit from a thug. He doesn't threaten me or anything, but he makes it a point to engage in some personal small talk. I think the implication is pretty clear, he wants to make sure I know he knows about me."

Nestle nodded. "There's just one thing I'm not quite sure I understand," Nestle said.

"What's that?"

"If your theory is right, why not just threaten Max directly instead of going through you? Why not say to Max, 'Confess to this murder or we'll hurt your family'? See what I mean?"

Tracy put her sandwich down and nodded. "I wondered that myself, and my guess is that they knew Max wouldn't be able to follow through on it."

"What do you mean?"

"Max wouldn't have been able to look his wife and sons in the eye and say he was a killer when he wasn't. And when he eventually told them the truth there's no way his sons would have let him follow through on it no matter what the threat. They would have gone on the offensive. The way it's playing out now, the Paganini family is on the *defensive*."

Nestle nodded. Then he stopped and looked at Tracy. "If you're right then the person who did this has to know Max pretty well."

She looked at him. "Yes, Marty. That's why I insist that one of the people in the office when the call was made *has* to be the killer, or at least the one that used Max's phone. But Max won't hear of it."

Nestle shook his head and looked at his plate. "It's my fault, isn't it?"

Tracy stiffened. "What do you mean?"

"I shouldn't have said anything about the loan extension being scrutinized. I gave the police their motive."

Tracy shook her head. "No, Marty; you shouldn't think like that. I think the police got that info by speaking to some people at the bank and just assuming you told Max about Pepper being on the board. The police *think* they know what happened but can't really prove it. Besides, you can't hold yourself to blame for someone else's evil."

Nestle jerked his head up. He was surprised by her use of the word evil. He looked back down at his plate. Then he turned his head to the side and observed a young couple seated at a booth near the restaurant's window. "Look at that," he told her.

"Look at what?"

"Those two over there; they should be having a nice breakfast and a nice chat but they're both staring down at their smart phones or whatever."

Tracy followed Nestle's stare and saw the people he was talking about. Then she shook her head. "A couple of weeks ago I was at a dinner meeting with a client, and this family of four comes into the restaurant, parents and their two teenaged kids. The whole time up until their food came, all four of them were doing the exact same thing, playing or whatever on their electronic gizmos. They didn't say a word to each other. They didn't even look up to thank the waiter for the food when he brought it. They just kept on texting away as he put their plates down. I mean, that was just downright rude."

Nestle nodded. "Technology has its good and bad points. It always has."

A Tracy Brubaker Mystery

"It's more than that, Marty. People just aren't as nice and courteous as they used to be. I see it all the time. People come into the grocery store yacking on their phones and barely look at the cashier. I remember when you'd at least exchange some pleasantries; make the cashier's day a little easier. Maryland can pass all the laws it wants but I still see people on their hand-held phones in the car, barely paying attention to the road, and then beep at *you* if they almost hit you. Look at the kind of language politicians are using in the public forum. Anyone can come up with a screen name anywhere and say whatever they want any way they want whenever they want without fear of being called on it. It was bad enough in my day with the bullying but today young people take to social sites and continue spewing their vitriol at all hours. And then the bullies' own parents defend their behavior. It's sick. But then again, look at the examples the kids have." Tracy felt herself getting angrier and angrier and decided she better calm down. She blew out a sigh, and looked back at Marty. "Anyway, that's why I don't yet have one of those smart phone things. My associate does though. I'll probably have to get my own eventually." She paused again and then she smiled at her companion. "Sorry Marty; didn't mean to go on one of my self-righteous rants."

"Hey, no problem. And I can't say I disagree with you about any of it." Nestle looked at her. "Tracy, can I ask you something off topic?"

"Sure Marty."

"Are you seeing anybody?"

His question caught her off guard, although it shouldn't have. She had sensed that he liked her. She felt herself blushing anyway. First Paul Iris and now Nestle. Maybe she should be handing out numbers like they do at the deli. Then she smiled. "Well, I don't quite know how to answer that. I guess I'm in a holding pattern right now. It's complicated."

Nestle started nodding. "Hey, you don't owe me any explanation. I know I'm not much to look at."

Tracy straightened up. She knew *those* feelings, believing you're unattractive and that people would pass you by because of it. She really hadn't blossomed until she was a senior in high school. As a result, much of those early teen years had been hard for her. Of course, that's when she really developed her sense of humor, which helped some. She wondered if Nestle went through the same thing. "Marty, that has nothing to do with it and you shouldn't think that. You're a good looking guy. I was telling you the truth. Maybe if things were different…"

He nodded and smiled at her. "Stop being so nice," he laughed.

She returned his smile and laughed herself. "So we're still friends right? You're not mad at me?"

"Of course not. I just have never met anyone like you before. And I mean that as a compliment."

They both looked down at their respective food remains and finished them off. Then Tracy found herself smiling. "Marty…"

"Yeah?"

"I think you just made my day."

He smiled. "Stop being so nice, I told you." And they departed the eatery with barely another word spoken between them.

Tracy's day became unmade when she decided to call the office after lunch during the afternoon court recess. The morning testimony of Jeff Pollenfax had been a repeat of his co-workers. The phone company representative had authenticated the phone bill proving the phone call was made from Max's phone the morning of the murder. Now Rebecca had a message to relay to Tracy. "Arthur Pankow called during the lunch break and said you should come to his office again before court resumes. Those FBI agents want to have yet another meeting and your attendance is…highly recommended."

She felt the temperature of her blood starting to rise. "I really don't have time to waste with those clowns," Tracy said.

"Should I call Arthur and say you're on your way?" Rebecca asked sympathetically.

Tracy pursed her lips. "Yeah Beck. And tell Art to tell the male model wannabes that if they're not there when I get there they'll have to come and see *me* at *my* convenience."

"Righto."

Tracy said adios and began her journey to what she was sure to be an unpleasant experience, her second of the day. When she arrived at Pankow's office, everyone was waiting for her again, Pankow, Tanner, Roper, and the visibly irritated Lennon. "Déjà vu," she thought. Lennon didn't even say hello.

"We need to talk to you," he began.

"No kidding," she responded tersely. "I'm not here because I thought I won a vacation or something." Tracy liked most people. Most people had

A Tracy Brubaker Mystery

something to like about them. But for the life of her she couldn't figure out what that might be in the case of Agent Lennon.

Lennon glared at her. "Listen, I thought I was clear this morning, you've got to stay away from Reginald Walters. I hear you're associate was at the courthouse filling out subpoenas; I can guess who for."

Tracy glared back. "Walters is tied up in my case somehow. And he won't return my calls."

"I don't care."

"I don't care that you don't care; my client's life is on the line."

"You're being melodramatic."

"I am not. Max's health is poor. If he goes to jail he will die there."

"Look, there are bigger things at stake here. You're being naïve."

"And you're being an arrogant, insensitive ass."

Roper started coughing. Tanner and Pankow looked to the floor.

Lennon took a few steps closer to her. She didn't back away. "Ya know, I really don't like you Ms. Brubaker."

"Oh, that's too bad. I was really hoping we'd make some babies together when this was all over."

Roper started coughing again. Pankow snorted. Tanner practically left the room. But Tracy met Lennon's stare. There was no amusement in her face. Then Lennon stepped back a bit and sat on the corner of Pankow's desk. He smiled at her. "You think you're pretty entertaining, don't you? You think *you're* right and everybody else is wrong, is that it? Well let me tell you something, if you screw with my case I'm going to make things unpleasant for you and people you may care about. You're friends with a lot of cops around here, aren't you? Are you confident that their records could handle federal scrutiny?"

Pankow jumped in the ring. "There's no call for that at all, Agent Lennon."

"Then you tell little miss mouth here how things are going to be going forward." Lennon stood up again and moved closer to Tracy. "You want to be an entertainer, save it for the courtroom. Keep it out of the real world and stay away from Walters. Do we understand each other?" Tracy continued to meet Lennon's eyes a while longer. Then she turned to leave the room. Lennon stared through the doorway as she exited, while the remaining occupants exchanged slightly embarrassed glances. Lennon started to turn toward Roper when Tracy came back into the office, and then Lennon felt something lukewarm hit him in the face. Coffee started dripping from his nose and he looked down in time to see a Styrofoam cup hit the floor. He quickly wiped his face with a bare hand and looked up to see Tracy already leaving. "That…" he started to say. And Lennon swore he heard Tanner mumble, "That *was* pretty entertaining."

Tracy Brubaker had had it. She had never done anything like that before; she regretted only that the coffee wasn't steaming hot. She didn't like being this person, this angry, hostile, impatient mutant that she felt herself becoming. Then she saw an opportunity to revert to her kindly nature, she slowed down to let someone escape from the parking lot that seemed to be holding him captive. She wasn't going to try to beat the yellow light, so why not let this fellow in front of her? He pulled out and up to the light. And Tracy waited for the friendly thank you hand wave. And when it didn't come she was taken over by the mutant again. Her act of kindness had backfired.

Tracy pulled open her office door with as much fury as her five-foot-five frame could muster. A solid granite scowl was on her face as she barreled toward her station in the back. Rebecca had seen Tracy like this before, and decided silence was the best option here. Things had been bubbling under the surface for the last few days and now it had come to a boil. What straw had broken Tracy's back was unclear. Rebecca thought she'd wait a while before asking any questions. Suddenly Neal came through the very same door with a soda can in his hand, just having returned from down the hall where the vending machines were located. "Did I just see Tracy come in?" he asked. But he did not wait for an answer.

"Neal I wouldn't…" Rebecca started. But Neal continued on, not realizing what he was in for.

"Hey Tracy…" he started.

"WHAT?" she snapped, cutting him off. She was slamming her briefcase about her desk while trying to unlatch it, all the while mumbling to herself in a language Neal couldn't quite decipher.

"Tracy, what is it?"

She looked up at him. "What the hell is it with people today, Neal?"

"I don't know what—"

"I mean, where has common courtesy gone? Huh, Neal?"

"I'm not—"

A Tracy Brubaker Mystery

"I mean, I *deserved* the wave, Neal. That wasn't too much to expect, was it?"

"Tracy, I'm not sure—"

"I could have made that yellow light. I had plenty of time. And in this business, Neal, time IS money. You get me?"

"I agree that—"

"But no, I try to be nice. Try to show that that asshole Lennon didn't get to me. I see this poor guy waiting to turn right, and the traffic is already piling up behind me, so, out of the goodness of my heart, I slow down to let him in, making him first in line when the light turns green. I mean, I could have been here three or four minutes ago, you know?"

"I see but—"

"So I'm sitting there Neal for what, a minute or two, at least 60 frickin' seconds. And I'm waiting for the wave. But guess what, no wave. I *deserved* the wave, Neal. Know what I'm saying?"

"Sure I do…"

"But there's no wave. No damn wave. Where are peoples' manners today?"

"Tracy, I think you should try and calm—"

"I mean, I remember once asking my father, 'Daddy, why do you wave at other cars sometimes?' And he said, 'Because if a driver does something kind for you, you should acknowledge it. And since you can't say 'thank you' you wave. You should always acknowledge an act of kindness Tracy, even in the car.' That's what he told me."

"He's right of course but—"

"Or maybe it's a guy thing. Is it a guy thing, Neal? Do guys only give other guys the wave?"

"Hey, I wave all the time at—"

"I know how men are always making cracks about women drivers. You bunch of goddamned *sexists!*"

"Look I really don't—"

"It's just like those idiots that spend 20 minutes backing into a parking space, holding up everyone else in the parking lot so *they* can park like that." She brought up her hands and started moving them from side to side saying, "They go in and out and in and out and in and out until they're satisfied, meanwhile the rest of us just have to wait there. I mean, you can't go around them 'cause you might hit the car coming the other way. And if you try to sneak past them they may hit you coming back out, and then blame *you* for it for not having any *goddamned patience!*"

"Jesus Tracy will you please—"

"And you want to know the best part of this—the thing that *really* makes me laugh?"

"O-kay…"

"They spend 20 minutes lining up their car thinking that will get them out sooner when they're ready to leave. But in reality had they just parked front in, they'd have ultimately wasted *less* time because somebody would have let them back out in no time at all when they left." Then she stopped and slapped her forehead. "Oh, wait a minute. How stupid of me! There's no common courtesy anymore. So how could these time suckers expect someone to let them out? Do you know *why* they don't expect to be let out, Neal?"

"No," he answered, looking at his shoes.

"Because I bet they're the very same people who don't give the *freaking wave!*"

She was standing there now, breathing heavily, red-faced, apparently done. Neal looked at her a moment. He would have to choose his next words *very* carefully. "Look, I can see you're in a huff. So I'll be back in a minute and a huff," and he immediately turned and left.

"You're no Groucho Marx!" she shouted as he left.

"You're right!" he called back. "*I'm* not the grouch around here!"

She plopped herself down in her chair. "He set me up—and I walked right into it," she thought while shaking her head. She folded her arms. She looked at her watch; time to get back to court. Why did she stop here again? Right—to talk to Neal. She didn't have time for that now; so much for her resolution. Neal wouldn't be in court for the afternoon so he could continue looking into their latest lead. She'd have to follow up with him later.

The afternoon wasn't going to be any easier than the first part of the day had been. Arthur Pankow called Antonio Paganini to the stand. "Mr. Paganini, for the record, you are the defendant's oldest son?" he asked, standing, from behind his table.

"Yes."

"And you are presently, let's say, the second-in-command at the store?"

"Yes."

A Tracy Brubaker Mystery

"You will eventually run things when your father retires?"

Tony hesitated. "That's the plan right now."

"Mr. Paganini, are you close to your father?"

"Yes. My father is an extraordinary man."

"Of course you feel that way; you *should* feel that way." Pankow moved toward the witness. "I want to ask you some questions about the night of the murder. Do you think you will be able to answer them given how you feel about your father?"

"I'll tell the truth, if that's what you mean."

"Good answer," Tracy thought.

Pankow continued. "Tell this court what happened the night of November 5th last, starting with when you arrived at the store to pick up your father."

Tony shifted in his chair. "I got to the store about 9:30 that night."

"Is that normal; I mean do you pick your father up every night at that time?"

"No — only on the nights that my mother is having some of her friends over. Pop stays late on those nights."

"And that was the case on the night of November 5."

"Yes."

"Please continue."

"Well, I unlocked the front door and went in and went to my father's office. He wasn't there so I started calling out for him. I finally heard his voice coming from the back storeroom."

"The storeroom where the body was found?"

"Yes. I found Pop sitting on a chair. He said there was somebody on the floor; he thought it was Pepper."

"He thought?"

"Well it was dark in the room. Pop didn't turn on any lights. But I recognized the cologne when I went over to the body."

"So you were familiar with Randall Pepper yourself?"

"Sure. He'd come into the store and I'd encourage him to leave. He always wore the same cologne."

"I see. So you went over to the body, confirmed it was Randall Pepper, and then what?"

"I went back to my father. He pointed to something on the floor. I could tell it was a gun."

"Did you ask your father what happened?"

"Yes."

"What did he say?"

"That he didn't know what happened. That he heard a noise, went to see what it was, and found the body. He knew I'd be coming so he just sat down and waited for me."

"Did he tell you if he picked up the gun?"

"I don't really remember. I…I just don't remember."

"Okay Mr. Paganini. Had your father called the police at this point?"

Tony shook his head. "No. Like I said, he was waiting for me. So I called them soon after I got there."

"Now, you're aware of your father's long-standing dislike of the victim, correct?"

"Sure."

"You were a witness several times over to your father's anger when the victim entered his store."

"Yes."

"Previous witnesses have said they couldn't understand your father when he started speaking Italian. Do you speak Italian? Or more importantly, do you understand it?"

"Yes, I speak and understand Italian."

"Did your father, when speaking Italian, ever threaten to harm Randall Pepper?"

"No, not really."

Tracy felt the blood drain from her face. Pankow moved closer to Tony. "What does that mean, 'not really'?

"Pop would say anything when he was mad. It never meant anything."

"What did your father say that didn't mean anything?"

"*Fare un tiro mancino.*"

"What does that mean?"

"It means that Pepper was always up to something, something hurtful."

"So?"

"Well Pop said someday the same would happen to Pepper."

"You mean, that someone would do something hurtful to Pepper someday."

"Oh, Tony," Tracy thought.

"Yeah," Tony answered Pankow.

"It must have been rather difficult you just now admitting that."

 A Tracy Brubaker Mystery

"I…My father didn't kill that man."

"Were you a witness to the murder, Mr. Paganini?"

"No."

"Then you really can't testify as to who did or didn't kill Randall Pepper, can you?" When Tony didn't answer, Pankow turned him over to Tracy. She moved quickly.

"Did your father say *he* was the one who would do the hurting with respect to Randall Pepper?"

"No."

"Other than what you just told this court did your father ever threaten physical harm to Randall Pepper?"

"No."

"Ever vocally wish Pepper harm, again, to your knowledge?"

"No."

"Does your father, to your knowledge, own a gun?"

"No."

"Have you ever seen your father fire a gun?"

"No."

"Have you, before the night of the murder, ever seen a gun anywhere in the store?"

"No."

"Being second-in-command as was previously testified to, you have access to any and all rooms, drawers, cabinets, shelves, and the like, correct?"

"Sure."

"And you never saw a gun in the store while accessing said rooms, drawers, cabinets, shelves, and the like, correct?"

"Right."

"To your knowledge, did *anyone* in the store own a firearm?"

"I'm…I'm not sure."

"But no one ever admitted to having one in your presence?"

"No; not that I can remember."

"Any idea then how the gun got into the store?"

"Objection!" Pankow shouted.

"Withdrawn. I have no further questions for Mr. Paganini." Tracy sat down trying to put on a brave front. In all the times she talked to Tony he never brought up what he had just said in court today. She wasn't sure whether to be mad at him or feel incredibly sorry for him.

It wasn't long after Tony left the stand that the trial was ended for the day. Tony immediately approached Tracy. "I am so sorry Tracy. When he asked that question, what Pop said just came to me. I mean, I just—"

"It's okay Tony; try not to worry about it. Actually you helped lay some groundwork for me."

"What do you mean?"

"You never saw a gun in the store. The police think that your father got mad at Pepper because of that early phone call from Marty about the loan extension and that got things rolling. But how did Max manage to leave the store that day after the call and get a gun? He wasn't alone until 7:00 that evening. Would he have been able to find a dealer and purchase one between the 7:00 and 8:30 window? Not likely. Why would he have brought a gun with him that day, from home for example, since he wouldn't have known about the call he'd get from Marty? You see what I mean? If a gun was in the store prior to the day of the murder, you probably would have seen it. And your father wouldn't have known that morning to bring one with him because he wouldn't have known about the loan extension issue beforehand."

"Yeah, I see. But I could be lying, right? The jury could just think that I was lying about not seeing a gun."

"But you told them, were honest with them, about the mini-threat, for lack of a better term. I think they believed you, especially after you admitted to what your dad said. *That's* why I said I think you may have actually helped me. I wasn't just blowing smoke."

Tony smiled. "Well, I still feel like I hurt Pop."

Tracy said firmly, "Tony, let's be clear, the only person that hurt your dad—is hurting your dad—is the one who framed him." She didn't air her feelings on those who she felt were helping with the cover up. "So don't you assign any blame to yourself. Okay?"

"Sure Tracy. Thanks." Tony turned to his father. "Ready Pop?"

"Yeah. Let's go. I'll see you tomorrow Tracy."

"You bet Max." She watched as Tony helped his father down the center floor. She felt a surge of pity for them. But she wasn't going to give up; not when she truly felt she was so close to the answer.

Her cell phone started buzzing. She answered quickly. The caller said, "Hi Tracy, it's Paul Iris."

"Oh Paul! I'm so sorry for not calling you back."

A Tracy Brubaker Mystery

Pleasantly he said, "You can make it up to me by cashing that rain check. How about dinner tonight?"

Tracy smiled. "That's awfully sweet of you Paul, but between Max's case and my mother, I really don't have any 'me' time right now."

"I understand. So you how is your mother doing?"

"She's doing well."

"Great then. I guess I should let you go, huh?"

"I appreciate your concern, Paul—especially since you hardly know me."

There were a few moments of silence before he said, "I know enough. Good luck with everything and I'll talk to you later."

"Okay, Paul. Bye." Tracy closed her phone. If only she had some "me" time…

It was about 5:30 and Neal was in his office looking into home sales in PG County. Tracy returned to the office and put her belongings on her desk. She then came to Neal's doorway, looked down, and started digging the toe of her shoe into the carpet, twisting her foot. "I'm sorry for earlier, Neal. I'm sorry for calling you a…sexist."

Neal swung his chair to look at her. He had already forgiven Tracy of course. He knew she had the Paganini case, her mother's stroke, and the meddlesome feds all pulling at her. Up until lunchtime she had been handling it all pretty well, he thought. Finally she had needed to blow off some steam in her own…unique way. He wasn't going to be a jerk about it.

"It's okay Tracy. We're good. I guess your meeting with the feds that Rebecca told me about didn't go too well huh."

She came into his office and sat down. "No. They know, the cops know—they *all* know that Walters is somehow connected with the Pepper murder. But they want me to stay away because the life of Mr. Paganini doesn't mean squat in their world view. How can people be so cold? They've been lying to me—to my face—since the first meeting we had. They disgust me."

Neal nodded. "I understand. I wish I could come up with something witty to say to make it all better. But if Walters *is* involved, and he used Brandice to set Max up somehow, I don't think you'd have any luck with Walters anyway. He'd have his lawyers fighting the subpoena and Max's trial would be over before it all got worked out. That's what I think anyway."

Tracy was nodding as he spoke. "You're probably right. But I can't just ignore it, Neal. I can't do that." She looked at her associate who had a sympathetic expression on his face. "I'm really sorry I blew up at you."

"Tracy, it's alright; really. Don't worry about it. I get yelled at by my teenage daughter all the time."

Tracy laughed. "Oh, you poor man."

"No, I'm pretty rich actually."

She looked at him briefly, and then, yet again today, found herself blushing. "Any luck on what we talked about this morning?"

"I'm trying to follow some of the deals Pepper's appraisal company was involved with through the system. You can search property records on the Maryland Department of Assessments and Taxation website. You get a brief history of owners, the prices paid for the property, and other info. I figure if I can find some unusual price increases I can start looking into prior owners, who they used for the sale, etcetera. I've got some potential names already."

Tracy smiled. "That's supreme Neal. That's great work. You know, I wonder from whom Sonny bought his home when he moved here." Tracy and Neal's conversation was interrupted.

"Tracy, there's a Dr. Strong on line one for you," Rebecca began. "He says it's about your mother."

"I have to take this Neal," Tracy said while picking up the receiver. Neal gave her an understanding nod. "Thanks Beck, I got it." When Rebecca hanged up Tracy pushed the pound and one keys. "Dr. Strong, this is Tracy Brubaker. Is everything okay?"

"Everything's fine," he responded.

Tracy breathed a sigh of relief. "Oh, thank God. I thought something was wrong. What can I do for you doctor?"

There was a brief pause. "You can get that old man to take a plea."

What he said threw her, confused her. "What did you say?" she finally asked.

"I said, you should get that old man to take a plea. He's not doing too well, is he? Bad eyes, bad legs…bad everything else; I mean, how much longer does he really have left, anyway?"

Tracy felt uneasiness come over her. But her words were angry. She stood up when she demanded, "Who is this?" Neal got out of his chair, and because of the look on Tracy's face, went to tell Rebecca to call the police.

A Tracy Brubaker Mystery

This may have just been another crank call, but the fact that whoever the caller was knew about Tracy's mother set off warning bells in Neal's brain and he wasn't going to wait to find out what was being said.

The voice on the other end was self-assured, self-amused, and obviously taking great delight in his vicious tease routine. He chuckled slightly when he said, "Oh, I think you know who this is. I sure do remember your sweet face. The pretty little lady lawyer with the *dead* cop father and sick old mother in the hospital. Lots of accidents can happen to sick old mothers you know. They can fall down the stairs; slip in the tub…all *kinds* of exciting possibilities. So you get that old man to take a plea and you shut this thing down *right* now…because if you don't, I'm going to make you an orphan. And then, just for fun…then I'll make you a martyr too. *Goodbye* Tracy. *Pray* you don't see me soon." And then he was gone.

Tracy stood there stone faced. Fear and rage were competing for her attention. Rebecca and Neal were now in Neal's office, looking at her. Tracy finally put down the receiver, at which point Rebecca went over to her and put her arm around her. "I called Detective Tanner and he's on his way." Tracy didn't respond. "Tracy, what did he say? What just happened?"

Tracy slowly turned her head to answer. "They just threatened to kill me and my mother if I don't get Max to agree to a plea."

"Dear God," Neal blurted out, as Rebecca helped Tracy back into the chair. Neal then pulled out his phone, called Tanner at his mobile number, and relayed to him what Tracy had just told them.

"Tell her I'm having someone check on her mother yesterday. And I'm already on my way to Tracy's office." Tanner ended the call without saying goodbye.

"They threatened *my family*, El!" Tracy was yelling as she was pacing. But neither Tanner, nor Rebecca, nor Neal were about to tell her to calm down. That, as hard as it was to conceive, would have just made her angrier.

"That's how they work, Tracy," Tanner finally said. "They threaten and intimidate."

"And…so what? That's supposed to make me feel *better*!?"

"Your mother is fine Tracy," Tanner tried to reassure her. "I'll have someone with her 24/7 for the foreseeable future."

Tracy stopped to look at Tanner, a look of panic on her face. "She can't know what's going on."

"We'll do our best to keep this quiet Tracy. But you know I can't promise that your mother won't catch on something's wrong. She's a lot sharper than we tend to give her credit for."

Tracy resumed her pacing, shaking her head. "Oh God, this is bad," she said aloud to no one in particular. "This is *really* bad."

Tanner's phone started buzzing. "Yeah, what is it?" he answered gruffly. He was starting to lose his ability to disengage. The widow of a fallen partner had just been threatened; and so had his daughter, people Tanner had promised to watch over and protect. They were a second family to him. Sure, only threats had been made at this point. But if Tracy didn't do what they asked…

"There's no Dr. Strong on staff at the hospital. No surprise there of course. And the call to Tracy's office came from a prepaid cell, Detective," the voice said. "Sorry."

Tanner nodded and ended the call. He looked at Tracy and told her the news.

"Ain't technology just *grand*? Those damned prepaid phones, perfect for the criminal on the run." She was in full sarcasm mode.

Tanner asked, "How sure are you that the caller was Carlton Brandice?"

"I *know* it was him. He saw my father's picture and the cross I wear when he was here. He made of point of talking to me about them."

"So?"

"So he knew Dad gave me this cross and he knew I'd completely understand what he meant by 'martyr'."

Tanner nodded slowly. "But you can't be 100% sure?"

Tracy again looked at Tanner. "No, I can't. Betts or whatever his name is turned on the charm when he came to see me. The voice on the phone was…was evil. I don't know how else to describe it. But I can't honestly say I recognized the voice." She turned away and then continued. "But it doesn't matter even if I *were* sure. The feds wouldn't let anything happen to *compromise* their case." She made no attempt to mask her contempt. "It's funny, isn't it? I make a point that Pepper couldn't have known for sure who his caller was when he answered the phone that morning. And now I am in the exact same situation."

"We're not going to let anything happen to you or your mother," Tanner finally said. "I promise you that."

She turned to him, some of her fight having left her. "What am I going to do, El?"

A Tracy Brubaker Mystery

He put his hands on her shoulders and looked at her. "I can't tell you what to do, Tracy."

She nodded. "I can't try and talk Max into accepting any plea bargain; he'll die in prison. If I don't continue defending him…"

After a brief moment, Tanner said, "Well, at least this should remove any doubt on the feds part that Randy Pepper's death had some connection with Walters."

"They *already* know that, El. I don't care what they say or how many meetings we have. They've known it from the start, as soon as the murder weapon was traced to that missing shipment."

"But Lennon still maintains that Walters, Brandice, and everyone else known to work for Walters was under surveillance when Pepper was killed. The feds are their alibis, if you can believe that."

"I realize that. And I bet the Walters crew knew they were being watched. So they must have had someone else do their dirty work for them; someone on the inside who had access to Max's phone."

"You've been saying that pretty much from the beginning but there's really no proof of that," Tanner said, slightly agitated.

Suddenly Tracy's head jerked up. She looked at Tanner, but she had a look on her face he couldn't quite define. Finally she said, "Bad eyes."

Tanner raised his eyebrows, confused. "What about my eyes?"

Tracy shook her head. "No; the caller knew that Max had bad eyes. He specifically mentioned Max's eyes."

"So?"

"So not too many people know about that; his family, his employees, that's about it. I guess though there's probably mention of it in some of the police reports."

"Are you saying a cop made that call?" Tanner asked defensively.

"No, El—that is not what I'm saying *at all*. Don't you understand? Brandice called and made the appointment with me the day *before* the murder happened. How could he have known that Max would allegedly make an impromptu call the next day summoning Pepper to his rendezvous? How did Brandice even know about me, that if Max were accused of murder that I would be the one he'd turn to? And how could Brandice, who supposedly doesn't know Max at all, know about the eyes?"

Tanner looked at her. He started nodding.

"I don't care *what* BPD and the feds say or believe. Max was set up by someone close enough to him to know about his health and have access to his phone; someone who was at the office that day the time of the call, 10:25 a.m."

"But we *did* check those employee's bank records and didn't find anything even remotely resembling a payoff," Tanner offered.

"Then there was some other consideration given," Tracy said sharply. Then she gulped. "Or maybe someone just threatened their family, telling them to help frame Max, or else."

Tanner started stroking his chin. "If you *are* right about that Tracy, then I don't see anyone admitting to what they've done."

Tracy nodded slowly. "As long as Brandice is running around and Walters is out and about that's true."

Tanner now had a slightly panicked look on his face. "What are you planning, Tracy? What are thinking of doing?"

"I need to talk to Art." She paced a bit more and then continued. "And I want it made known that I'm still Max's attorney. No pleas; court resumes tomorrow."

Tanner stared at her. "Tracy…"

"They've backed me into a corner, El, the feds, the cops, and now Walters and Brandice. I don't *like* corners, El."

"Oh dear Lord…"

"I want to talk to Art. I'm coming out of my corner swinging."

A Tracy Brubaker Mystery

At 8:15 a.m. Thursday Arthur Pankow emerged from one of the interview rooms at BPD shaking his head. Tracy and Tanner followed in quick succession. "I'm sorry Tracy, but a threat on your mother doesn't mean your client is innocent. Anybody can call and make a threat. Who's to say Max didn't kill Pepper because someone threatened *his* family?"

"Then why wouldn't Max just admit to the crime if his family were threatened? Why fight it and risk his family getting hurt? Your position on this is absurd." Tracy was raising her voice as she moved through the hallway. Tanner looked around and noticed they were being observed by curious passersby.

"Tracy," Pankow snapped, "I can't just stop a case midtrial because you get a call. Don't you think *I've* been threatened before? Hell, judges have been threatened. Maybe one of Max's own kids made that call. Did you consider that? You're not even completely sure who the caller was."

Tracy grabbed Pankow's arm. "Quit being an ass. You obviously believe that threat was legit because you've got my mother being watched."

Pankow stared at her a bit. "Yeah, well…about that…"

Tracy stiffened. "What about *that*?"

Pankow turned his head to the side so he wouldn't have to face her. "I'm afraid we're going to have to pull that surveillance. We can't afford to be doing that."

Tanner was looking at Tracy and saw the expression on her face, it was a powder keg ready to explode. "Let's continue any discussion about this in my office." Tanner turned and started toward his station. Tracy followed close behind. Pankow served as the caboose, trying to get Tracy's attention. But she was too busy trying to do the same with Tanner.

"El, you can't let this happen!"

Tanner turned abruptly in front of his door. "Tracy, I have NO say in this. Do you think I'm happy about it? Don't you think *I* tried?" He was raising his voice now. Heads in the office turned to see what the drama was. "Don't you think *I* care what happens to you and your mother?"

"They'll *kill* her!" Tracy yelled, crying.

"No they won't, Tracy," Pankow interjected. "Just empty threats; I'm sure of it. You don't have anything to worry about. This is just how Walters and his crew operate; if it even is them, I mean. Like I said, you're not even sure who called you. " But Pankow sounded like he didn't believe what he had just told her.

"The both of you can go to hell!" she shouted. Her face was flushed. She was looking at them. "If this city can't afford to keep just one officer on duty to watch one of their own, then I guess I'll have to do it."

"And then your mother will know something's wrong," Tanner said quietly.

"Something *is* wrong El, with this whole goddamned department! Its Lennon isn't it? This is his revenge for me telling him off. He put pressure on someone to stop the protection for my mother. "

"Tracy, look," Pankow started. "You have to see it from our perspective. The fact that your mother was threatened is bound to make its way to the jury eventually. They find out about that then they may leap to conclusions—the wrong kind. Besides, this is your first murder trial. You're an unknown quantity when it comes to murder trials."

"What the *hell* does that mean Art?" she spit back.

"Some people in my office think this may be some kind of stunt. You know, leak that your mom's in danger because you're defending this guy; might make him look innocent."

"That's Lennon talking. You *know* that's not true," she said through tears. "You know *me*! You know I'm not like that!"

"Tracy, look, I know. And I know you came to me for help. But…"

She turned to Tanner while cutting Pankow off. "El, can't *you* convince people? They may not know me but they certainly know about *your* character."

Tanner shook his head. "I'm afraid that since the woman in question is the widow of my partner my word holds little weight in their eyes."

"Maybe I can reach out to Roper, the one you didn't piss off, and the feds can spare someone, Tracy," Pankow said gently.

"Screw the feds! It's because of *them* this thing has gotten so out of control." She turned back to Tanner. "This is a betrayal, El. This is the *ultimate* betrayal. You've betrayed my father and his family. All that garbage about 'we protect our own'…" She wiped her eyes and straightened herself up. "If something happens to Mom I'll NEVER forgive you. Either of you. EVER!"

"You and I have to be back in court in an hour," Pankow told her sternly. "I suggest you calm down and get ready for *that*." But Tracy just turned

 A Tracy Brubaker Mystery

without saying another word and left Pankow and Tanner to stare at each other and shake their heads.

Tracy was at the courtroom's defense table, a twisted knot of nervous energy. She had never felt so powerless. What was she supposed to do now, just wait until Brandice tried something? Maybe the threats were bluffs and she was worried over nothing. But who was she kidding? Neal was there with her. "Tracy, what can I do?" he asked her worriedly.

"I'm going nuts here. Certifiable. I have no idea what to do. My theories about this case are crap."

"What do you mean by that?"

"I was thinking that either Walters had nothing to do with Pepper's death and sent Brandice in to make sure I didn't learn about his relationship with Walters, or that Walters is involved with the death and sent Brandice in for pretty much the same reason."

"I thought those were strong possibilities," he said reassuringly.

"But they're not, because if Walters doesn't want to be connected with the murder then *why* would he send in Brandice *knowing* that the odds were good that I'd find out who Brandice was, and therefore link Walters to the murder. See what I mean?"

Neal nodded. "Yeah, I do see what you mean."

"It's some kind of sick mind game I keep playing and I always lose..." Tracy trailed off. Then an idea occurred to her. "I wonder if that's the point."

"Care to share?"

"The cops have Max to go after. The feds know neither Brandice nor Walters are directly responsible because they have the feds as alibis. That left me."

"I see what you're saying. They somehow knew about you and that you'd come to Max's aid, believing he was innocent."

"Right. So Brandice meets with me knowing he's being tailed, counts on his true identity eventually being learned, and figures I'd start thinking Walters was behind the whole thing. When I started looking into things the cops and feds would shut me down. And around and around we go."

"Okay. But why would he want to implicate his boss?"

"That's my problem with *that*. Unless..."

"Unless what?"

"…Unless there were problems between Brandice and Walters."

"That's quite a leap there. Anyway, how would we even find out if you're suspicion is correct?"

Tracy looked at Neal for a moment. "I might have one way." She went over to her briefcase, rummaged through a stack of business cards, and then pulled out the one she was looking for. Next she pulled out her phone and dialed the cell number listed. "Agent Roper? This is Tracy Brubaker."

There was silence on the other end. "Just a moment," he finally said. After a few more quiet seconds he asked, "What is it Ms. Brubaker? I'm surprised to hear from you."

"Can we meet, just the two of us?"

"Why?"

"I want to talk to you. Truthfully, I need some help here and I think you might be the person to talk to."

"I didn't think you were a fan."

"Not of your partner, no."

There was another pause. "When and where did you want to meet?" She gave him the name of a deli near the courthouse and said she'd meet him when court recessed for lunch. "Well, okay."

"Thank you so much, Agent Roper. I'll see you as soon as we break here. I'll call you back." And then Tracy closed her phone hoping that she hadn't burned all of her bridges with law enforcement.

Shortly thereafter Max arrived for the fourth day of the trial. He was moving slowly, holding his son Antonio's arm. Tracy looked at him and became alarmed; she quickly went over to Max.

"Max, is everything okay?"

"I need to talk to you," he said quietly.

"Sure Max. There's a room across the hall; we can go there to talk." Max nodded and then father, son, and Tracy left the courtroom. Tony helped his father sit down and then left him and Tracy alone, closing the door on his way out. "What is it Max?"

"Do you think that plea offer is still available?"

"I don't know. Why?"

"I'm thinking maybe I should take it."

"Max…"

"I'm old. Maybe I did kill that *asino* and just forgot."

Tracy gave Max a skeptical look. "You *forgot*?"

"Yeah, I could have."

A Tracy Brubaker Mystery

"You forgot prowling the streets and buying an illegal gun? You forgot calling Pepper and setting up the meeting? You forgot opening the door for him? You forgot shooting him? You forgot all of that?"

"Why not? I'm old. I'm an old man that's become a bother to everyone…"

"Max, stop it!" She paused. "What is this really about?"

Max looked at his folded hands that were resting on the table. "I just told you."

"I don't think you're being completely honest with me, Max. Don't you think I deserve your trust?"

He looked at her. "You think I don't know what's going on?"

"What are you talking about, Max?"

Max's voice cracked. "I know they threatened you and your mother."

Tracy couldn't hide the shock that was now registering on her face. "*Who* told you that?" she demanded.

"What does that matter? Are you going to deny it?"

Tracy thought a bit. "Did somebody call you Max? Did somebody *tell* you to take a plea or they would hurt me and Mom?"

He looked back at his hands, and started weeping gently. "If anything happens to you or your mother because of me I'll never be able to forgive myself."

Tracy gulped. Then the fury began to build again, the sick, evil bastards are pulling out all the stops now. She had finally managed to drag Walters into this and now people were getting nervous, the cops, the feds, the thugs. "Max, look at me," she finally said. He shook his head, so she repeated her command. "Max, please look at me." This time he complied, and then Tracy placed her hands on his. "Max, remember that first meeting we had all those months ago after you were arrested." He nodded. "And do you remember how I told you right then and there that I knew you were innocent?" Another nod. "Do you remember what you said?" He looked at her a bit confused. "You said, 'there's the faith.' Do you remember saying that?" Third nod. "I had faith in you then and I have faith in you now. But I need *you* to have faith in *me*. Do you understand?"

"You might get hurt," he said pleadingly.

"Max, I think I'm close to solving this. That's why all of a sudden, this late in the case, people are making these threats. I need you to believe and trust in me, Max. Okay?"

"I don't know what to say to you," he said looking back at his hands. There was a knock on the door.

"Yes?" Tracy called out. Neal entered.

"They're about to start," Neal announced.

"Okay—we'll be right there," Tracy answered. She turned to Max. "Right Max?" Neal closed the door, as the lawyer and client arose. Then Max put his arms around Tracy and kissed her cheek. And after a few moments of silence, the two exited the conference room.

Carlton Brandice's phone vibrated. He answered. "You're lucky, Mr. C," he said to the person on the other end. "I was about to junk this phone. I've had it too long."

"I told you not to call me that."

"Aw, did I hurt your feelings Mr. C?"

"Listen, that Brubaker woman is not pleading this out," the caller said. "She's back in court this morning, still acting like she has a chance to solve this thing."

"Give her time to come to her senses."

"I don't *have* time. You said if I did this for you you'd have my back."

"What, the money wasn't good enough?"

"It's not the money that concerns me. What were you thinking giving me a gun that could be traced back to Walters?"

"You better watch your tone with me, Mr. C. Besides, there's no way she can prove anything."

"I'm not so sure anymore. She's tenacious. She makes me nervous. If she isn't making pleas then maybe she's found something. I want—no, I *need* her focus redirected."

Brandice paused a moment. "Then what is it you want me to do exactly, Mr. C?"

"Just what you told her you'd do."

Brandice started chuckling. "You sick bastard. You want me to off the old lady?"

"That would suddenly be a problem for you?"

More chuckling; "I'm not prejudiced. But there are cops watching over her."

"That was your fault. Why didn't you tell her not to go to the police?"

"What would be the point of that? She would have anyway. Her father was a cop. That black cop was her father's partner, right? Besides, it's a lot more fun this way."

A Tracy Brubaker Mystery

"*Fun?* Good Lord. Well, the point is moot anyway. The cops won't be around much longer."

"What the hell are you talking about?" Brandice asked tersely.

"The powers that be don't like using cops as babysitters. They think you were just making empty threats. Basically they think you were a crank caller."

"How do you know this?" Brandice asked skeptically.

"I have my sources. It seems that Brubaker bitch isn't the big deal she thought she was. Some think she made the threat up as part of her defense, a stunt or something."

Brandice paused again. "You don't think the mother's death would make the cops think twice about their current theory?"

"Not if you made it look like an accident, one medical in nature. Strokes can be so unpredictable."

Brandice resumed his chuckling. "You are one cold SOB, Mr. C."

"It's not my fault the bitch wouldn't listen to your advice. And for the last time stop with that Mr. C crap."

"Let me think about it for a day."

There was a brief silence on the other end. "I told you, I don't *have* a day. The prosecutor is probably going to rest today, which means *she* starts tomorrow. Besides, I've no doubt that bitch will be raising a stink any chance she gets for the rest of the day; the cops may change their minds and put someone back on watch. I'm not sure how much time we really have here."

"*We* have?" Brandice chortled. "I don't like this," Brandice then added coldly.

"Look, you show up at the hospital; you check things out. If you think something's not right, you leave. Simple."

"Simple, huh? Now you're an expert on what I do, huh?"

"Are you going to do this or not? Because if you're not, I need to make alternate arrangements."

More silence. "Are you *threatening* me with something, Mr. C?"

"If anything happens to *me* in the near future, Mr. B, it won't be long before the cops figure out what really happened. We shouldn't be threatening each other. We should be looking out for each other's interests."

Brandice considered Mr. C's words of wisdom; a grin crept across his lips. "Okay, Mr. C. Like you said, no harm in taking a look."

"Good. If she's busy planning a funeral then she won't have the time to focus on the case and this thing will be done and over with. Everyone else wants the tailor in jail. Even he might want to go if he blames himself for that old woman's death. So, make that attorney go away, and Max goes away too. Now, goodbye." And then the caller was gone.

Brandice started chuckling to himself. "And they say *I'm* crazy," he thought. He finished his coffee and left the small shop he had been patronizing. "God I hate hospitals," he said to himself. He had some research to do. He'd also have to shake those feds who were on his tail. He'd done it before with no problems, and he'd been so well behaved they wouldn't see it coming. Yeah, this might be fun after all.

Brandice went back to his apartment, sure that he had been followed there. He turned his television on, helpfully passing by an apartment window while doing so. He then sat in his chair, looked at his watch, and waited an hour before stealthily leaving his apartment building by the rear entrance, just as he had done before when the need had arisen. Those stupid feds had gotten lazy. They expected nothing to happen so they were probably just sitting there, assuming he was still watching the tube, sucking back beer. He chuckled to himself. He walked briskly to the other apartment he kept, one that the feds as yet didn't seem to know about. Dress up time. And then there would be a quick trip to a doctor he knew, and maybe a call to the hospital to get his target's room number. Suddenly he felt something like nostalgia, it being a dangerous thing of course. "This will be just like the old days," he thought. "Yes indeed; just like the old days."

"I really appreciate you seeing me," Tracy began as she and Agent Roper took their seats. A waitress quickly brought over glasses of ice water, which Tracy helped herself to almost immediately.

"I'll be right back to take your order," the server said, and then hurried away.

"I don't know why you think I can help you, Ms. Brubaker," Roper began.

"Please call me Tracy."

"Okay, Tracy. You've already been told more than we had intended, though."

"I realize that. I saw on your business card that your first name is Kyle. Can I call you Kyle, at least for this meeting?"

He looked at her curiously. "Well, okay."

While she sipped her water, their waitress returned only to be disappointed that all each wanted was a bagel. "Be back in a flash, dears."

      A Tracy Brubaker Mystery

"Look Kyle, I realize you're just trying to do your job. But Agent Lennon's whole attitude just rubs me the wrong way. He's just so self important and superior; like he has something to prove. He must have a penis the size of a mustard seed."

Roper had been drinking from his glass while Tracy was speaking, and he started gagging to the point he had to employ his napkin to remove the water that was now on the table and his tie.

"Oh dear; I did just say that out loud, didn't I?" All Roper could do was nod. Tracy looked down at the table. "I have to stop doing that. I really haven't made a very good impression, have I Kyle? You must think I'm a real bitch."

Roper looked at her sympathetically. After he finished cleaning himself up, he told her, "No, I wouldn't say that. I think you're frustrated that you keep running into roadblocks. I think you really care about your client and that you fear he's not going to get out of this." Roper leaned back in the booth as the server dropped off the food. Then he said, "I feel for you; I really do. I hope you believe that."

"I'm really a nice person most of the time. At least, I try to be. But you're right, this case has really gotten to me. And now my mother…" she trailed off.

Roper facial expression told Tracy he seemed moved by her plight. "I'm really sorry about that too."

"Well then can I just talk to you for a few minutes, please?"

"What is it exactly that you want?"

"I think my whole theory about this case is flat out wrong. In both scenarios I have Brandice coming into the picture on the one hand, but then have Walters trying to avoid being connected with the case on the other. It's a contradiction; there's just no sense to it." Roper smiled a bit. "Why are you smiling?" she asked him.

"Because Lennon pointed out that very problem to all of us, meant as a put down to you of course."

"Oh," was all she said. She didn't want to talk about Lennon. "Anyway, I have a new theory, but for it to have any merit I need to know something, something that few people would know."

"And that is?"

"Was there bad blood between Brandice and Walters; a rift of some kind, maybe? The kind of thing where Brandice might have no problem making it appear Walters was involved, for the purpose of distraction, I mean?" Tracy was looking at Roper square in the eyes. Something told her she had struck the proverbial nerve.

Roper studied her. Perhaps it was her unquestionable sincerity that moved him. After a long pause, Roper said, "Well, speaking hypothetically…"

"I love hypotheticals." Tracy said excitedly. "Some of my BFFs are hypotheticals. I adore hypotheticals…"

"Okay, okay," Roper said chuckling. "Let's say, hypothetically, that there are two long-time business associates. And let's say, hypothetically, that one of them has gotten cocky and a little sloppy over the years with his work product, including starting his own sideline of stealing firearm shipments, hypothetically. And then let's say, hypothetically, that this sloppiness gets the other one put on trial for multiple crimes, and that, even though there are no convictions, a rift, as you put it, has started." Tracy had a hard time keeping quiet when Roper paused to finish his water. "Now, let's also throw in the possibility that during the trial the sloppy partner was approached to make a deal, which he at first seemed curious in, but ultimately turned down."

"Brandice was never put on trial was he?" Tracy interrupted.

"No, he wasn't. Pepper said he had info on Walters, not Brandice."

"Okay, so now these hypothetical fellows aren't so tight anymore."

"Right." Then Roper looked again at the eager—and pretty—face before him and said, "You know what? The hell with this. Okay, after the trial Brandice has to think he's on thin ice. And one night he makes the mistake of having a few drinks with Randy Pepper."

Tracy's eyes widened. "So Brandice didn't know Pepper was working with you?"

"Not at that point. Anyway Pepper contacts Lennon and tells him that Brandice said he regretted not taking the deal. So Lennon pulls Brandice in to make him an offer. Brandice tells Lennon to go do something to himself that's physically impossible, and now Brandice knows Pepper's with us; who else but Pepper could have let us know what Brandice was thinking?"

"Oh no. Lennon really screwed up, didn't he?"

"In a word, royally. Look, Lennon was a real good agent at one time; in many ways he still is. But he's let himself become personally involved in this Walters thing; it's compromised his judgment."

Tracy didn't care about Lennon's resume. "And how long after that sit down with Brandice was Pepper killed?"

A Tracy Brubaker Mystery

"A little more than a week."

Tracy rolled her eyes. "Oh my God, Brandice had Pepper killed before what he said got back to Walters."

"That was the first thought I had until your client ended up seeming like the killer."

"I don't believe this," Tracy said angrily although not directed at Roper.

"Lennon wanted to give Brandice a few more days to think the offer over. How could we have known how far gone Brandice was? I mean, we had eyes on him that night. He was right there for all to see; he was by a window where we observed him playing cards with his buddies at the time of the murder."

"He knew you were watching him. He used you as his alibi."

"Maybe."

"Maybe nothing."

Roper pursed his lips then shook his head. "If Brandice wasn't such a weasel I'd almost feel sorry for him. The guy's losing it. I think he had a health scare a few years ago, was going to the hospital on a regular basis for a while, and he's been something of a loose cannon since; hence the problems with Walters. And maybe that's why he entertained, at least for a while, the idea of turning on Walters. So your new theory may be right if Brandice's new motto is every man for himself."

"And of course you have no idea if they know about your other insider."

"No, we don't. That's why Lennon is gangbusters about leaving Walters alone. We *don't* know if Walters knows the truth about Pepper's murder. We *don't* know if Brandice is playing dumb for Walters or if he told Walters why Pepper had to be killed. I mean, Walters would ask Brandice how he knew Pepper was with us and what would Brandice tell him? But we have to err on the side of caution here and assume our other man is in danger."

"And Brandice is taking advantage of all of this; it's just a sick game to him. Brandice must have been the one who gave the gun to the killer. And he must have known there was a risk it could be traced back to Walters' crew, right? Or maybe he didn't care."

Roper nodded. "I suppose you could be right about that. Look Tracy, everyone is basically in a holding pattern until after this trial is over. If Paganini is convicted then Pepper's death isn't going on Walters' — or Brandice's — list of crimes."

Tracy was confused. "You'd think Lennon would want it to though, at least try to tie it to Brandice."

"And admit he helped get Pepper killed because he moved too hastily on Pepper's bad info?"

"Oh, I see. If it's Max who's responsible then what Lennon did doesn't come back to bite him in the tuckus."

"Uh, yeah."

"Do you think Walters will have Brandice, how shall I put it, taken care of?"

"That's hard to say. It wouldn't surprise me if Brandice has some kind of insurance though, an audio recording, a videotape—something incriminating against Walters. Walters would want to be sure of anything like that before severing their partnership."

"Okay. So you think my feeling that Brandice reached out to someone is a possibility given what you know."

"Tracy, we've looked into everyone who was there, the same eight names you did. If one of them is whom Brandice used we couldn't find evidence of it. But as I said, Lennon really doesn't want this to come back to Brandice or Walters. So he probably hasn't explored every avenue at his disposal." Roper looked around. "I think I've said more than enough on the matter."

Tracy put her briefcase on her lap. "Kyle, how can I thank you?"

"By pretending we never had this conversation."

"What conversation? I just wanted some confirmation that my new and improved theory had merit and you told me it did, the details of which I seem to have forgotten." Tracy reached into her briefcase, pulled out her wallet, and withdrew a $10 bill which she placed on the table. "Thanks again, Kyle," she said as the two left the diner. Their bagels had not been touched.

While in her car driving back to the courthouse Tracy kept recycling the newly learned ugly facts in the case. Poor Massimo Paganini, an honorable man double crossed by someone close to him, thanks to one thug double crossing another, evil men in sick games where there are no prizes because there never is an end to such men's greed. Max, a man who never harmed anyone—a man who went out of his way to help people—was now a player in something he had no interest in playing. She found herself getting angry again, probably not a good idea while she was behind the wheel. But she was now more determined than ever that Max come out of

A Tracy Brubaker Mystery

this so he could spend what time he had left with his loved ones. And as far as she was concerned, Lennon and his face-saving tactics could go to hell too — idiotic, it's-all-about-me politician posing as a federal agent. "Tracy Brubaker, Janitor-At-Law," she thought to herself. *Lennon* was responsible for this mess, a mess Tracy was more than willing to clean up.

Chapter 16

It had been quite a few years since Carlton Brandice had donned his doctor's garb, a simple white coat, green shoe coverings, the quintessential stethoscope around his neck. He was wearing a wig and glasses to complete his simple disguise. At 4:37 p.m. Brandice pushed through the revolving door at the main entrance of St. Michael's Hospital and made his way to the chapel, succeeding in bypassing what security the hospital had, one guard at a desk reading something or other. He would wait here a while, in the peace and quiet. There weren't too many other people there right now, a woman who looked to be in her 40s was seated a few pews ahead of him on the opposite side of his row. There was a rather large individual two pews ahead on the same side. But he was kneeling so Brandice couldn't get a good look at him.

"Go ahead," Brandice thought. "Pray to your God. See what it gets you." And then Brandice pulled his own kneeler down and assumed the position. After all, when in Rome…

5:05 p.m., someone came through the chapel doors. It was a uniformed officer. Brandice continued kneeling, but he brought his folded hands to his forehead so his face for all intents and purposes was hidden. But his heart started beating faster. Better not move. Better stay calm. The officer then genuflected and knelt down one pew across and up one from where Brandice was positioned. He made the sign of the cross and then pulled out a rosary. "Had a cop just come in badly hurt or something?" Brandice wondered. Better wait here a bit more. There's no hurry.

5:12 p.m., another uniform entered the chapel. But he was not so reverent. He tapped his comrade on the shoulder. "Come on man, we gotta go."

The other office nodded, signed again, and then arose, shaking his head. He genuflected and started following his partner. "This ain't right, man."

"I know," his friend responded. "Let's go buy each other a beer." And then the two exited the chapel.

Brandice lowered his hands; time to take a look around. He was curious to see where the cops who just left were headed. He arose and exited the calm and quiet and made his way back toward the hospital entrance. The two officers were leaving the building. Other than the useless security guard at the lobby desk, there wasn't a cop in sight. "Okay," he thought, "time to look upstairs." Brandice made his way to the elevators, and then pulled a small piece of paper from his coat. The number 314 was written on it, the number he had been given when he called earlier. He pressed the upward arrow and awaited his ride. *Here we go.* When the doors finally opened he quickly entered and pressed the '2' button. When the ascent began he removed the surgical gloves he was carrying in his left pocket and put them on. He then tapped his right side coat pocket, reconfirming the presence of the syringe. He smiled. The elevator doors opened.

As was his custom, Carlton Brandice would now survey the floors above and below the one where his future victim lay in wait. He would start on the second floor, and then use the staircase to move toward the fourth floor, and then, once satisfied, move to his target, floor three. So that's what he did. He moved leisurely through the halls, which were active because of the shift change and because dinner had started being served. *Anyone here could be a cop for all he knew.* So he paid close attention for any tell-tale signs, figures that seemed to be doing nothing but reading a newspaper or medical report; people who seemed to be doing their own observing, scanning their environment with any regularity; and for anyone who had unusual bulges beneath their medical robes or clothing. Innocuous-looking janitorial staff received extra scrutiny.

But there was nothing; nothing alarming on the second floor and nothing similar on the fourth. Just people, employees, visitors, and patients. Other than an occasional smile, Brandice made no contact with anyone. And no one seemed to know or care who he was or what he was doing there. It was thus now time to move to the third floor. It was time for Carlton Brandice to introduce himself to Violetta Brubaker.

Brandice exited the staircase and immediately tossed the small paper bearing the room number in the trash. *No need to hold on to that. Where was room 314?* He didn't want to look like he didn't know where he was going, so he grabbed someone's medical chart that happened to be lying on an empty gurney. He pretended to be studying the chart as he made his way through the halls. *No cops in sight here either.* He moved toward the nurses' station. The woman there was talking with an orderly, young guy, scrubs covering tennis shoes, Brandice noted. *A cop in disguise? Not likely. Those aren't cop shoes he's wearing.* Brandice moved away. He looked around. Nothing *seemed* out of the ordinary. Brandice made his way to room 314. *All seemed clear.*

He arrived outside the door of Violetta Brubaker's room. He put his ear to the door. Quiet. No sound of chatting with a visitor or staff. No sounds of a television set. No sound at all. He stepped back. He moved further down the hall and took another look around, nurses, orderlies, patients in robes pushing IV stands—no boys or girls in blue. He moved back to Violetta's door. Alright then; let's get this over with.

Brandice pushed in the door slowly. It was a three-bed room—all the beds on the left side. The first two were unoccupied. But he could see that someone was in the third bed. He let the door close behind him. He stood there for a moment; more peace and quiet. He placed the medical chart on the empty bed closest to him. He took a few more steps toward the back. He removed the syringe from his right pocket, brought it to his mouth and pulled off the cover with his teeth. Then he spat the cover into his left hand and placed the sheath in his pocket. A few more steps—then he turned around and looked toward the door. Then he started feeling it, the excitement, the beating heart, the dry mouth. He closed his eyes and took a deep breath. Onward…

Brandice approached the bed where the elderly woman rested. "Her daughter looks quite a bit like her," he thought. Too bad; why couldn't she have just gotten the old guy to plead this out? He had given her several chances, the initial visit he knew would lead her to Walters; spooking her with the car he, ahem, borrowed; and the phone call where he dispensed with any and all subtlety; sad, really. This shouldn't have been necessary. But that's what happens when you're dealing with newbies—people who think they know everything but know very little about the real world. After today, Tracy Brubaker would no longer be so naïve.

Brandice shook his head and took another look around. The portable table was all the way over on the right. There was a closet next to the nightstand. Brandice was now right beside the bed. He looked up at and through the large windows. The sun was going down. It certainly was. He prepared his syringe; get those air bubbles out. Where was the IV? Hmm… the IV was on the other side of the bed, which was in the corner and against the wall. Brandice frowned and thought, "Now how in the hell is someone supposed to get to the IV with the bed against—oh *SHIT*!"

"Positive ID—take him," the voice said through the earpiece. And Officer Locke emerged.

Brandice turned toward the closet just as Locke materialized from behind its door. He brought the syringe down into one of Locke's arms while at the same time he threw all his weight against the over six-foot tall police-

A Tracy Brubaker Mystery

man. Locke went down and Brandice started his sprint toward the door. All of this was observed by the team housed across the street, viewing events through their high-powered scopes. "Locke's down! Everybody in, *NOW!*"

Brandice was moving with full speed down the third floor hall, pushing aside or knocking down the occasional obstacle. He pushed open the exit staircase door and started his descent, removing his doctor's garb, glasses, and hairpiece while he navigated the stairs. He pulled open the second floor door and tossed his items into a laundry carrier he had noted during his early survey. He pulled a comb from his back pocket and ran it quickly through his hair, and then he tossed *that* into a trash receptacle. He had taken the precaution of donning a priest's outfit before putting on his doctor's coat. The last touch was to move the ring he was wearing from his left ring finger to his right one. He joined several people boarding the elevator to the first floor. The car's doors opened at their destination and Brandice made a sharp right so he could exit through a side entrance. And then he was out on the street.

But when Brandice emerged from the side street he saw he had nowhere to go. A mass of vehicles were providing a blue-and-red light show that stretched as far as he could see. A quick look to the right and left provided him little hope. He took a few steps back so he could perhaps retreat through the side street from where he had just emerged. But that was blocked off too.

"You dumb, stupid, idiotic, brainless, moronic sucker," he thought. "How could you have let yourself fall for this? You're supposed to be a professional, and you got taken by amateurs. Mr. C, yeah, his sources—gossip mongers and water cooler yackers. And that Brubaker lady, using her own mother as bait? Who would have guessed she'd have the balls to do *that*? Carl, you are officially the biggest idiot to ever walk this earth." Brandice thought he'd be safer in the hospital. But uniformed threats started moving in his direction; his disguise hadn't fooled them at all. There wasn't time to make it to the door without calling attention to himself. What he needed right now was a hostage. He'd have to head back toward the main entrance. And that's just what he started to do.

"That's him, sir," Officer Lister told her superior. Lister was observing the street with the same lens she had being using to watch Violetta Brubaker's room from across the street. "He's dressed as a priest. But I'm sure that's him."

Lieutenant Roarke relayed Lister's information to the ground commander. "It looks like he's heading back in. We want him alive so do what you can but get him. Repeat, we *need* this guy alive."

The information was relayed amongst those watching the roads. When they saw their target, they started moving slowly in his direction, and when Brandice saw that a circle of uniforms were gathering around him, he pulled out the gun he had tucked under his shirt.

"There's no where you can go, Brandice!" a voice called out to him. "Put the gun down now!"

Lieutenant Roarke was shouting through the radios. "Take him alive! We need this guy alive!"

"Oh, man," Brandice thought, still not believing he'd been such a sucker. He looked around again, and that's when he saw two figures moving to the front of the parade; he recognized the female. "So she came to see the show," he thought. "How nice of her."

Tanner grabbed Tracy before she could move any closer. She didn't resist. She saw Brandice and then she realized he had seen her. Their eyes met, and stayed locked on each other, as Brandice slowly started to raise his arms, gun in his right hand. And then he smiled at her. And then he gave Tracy a wink. And then Carlton Brandice put his own gun against his temple and pulled the trigger. Tracy turned away, pressing her head against Tanner's shoulder. *That* was something she wished she had never seen.

Shortly thereafter, several persons with authentic medical credentials suddenly pushed through the assembly and made their way to the body that lay just in front of the hospital. The simultaneous shaking of heads told the crowd what they already suspected; so long, Charlie.

"Oops," Roarke said shaking his own head. But what was done, was done.

Tracy looked at Tanner. "I want to see my mother," she said forcefully. Tanner nodded, took Tracy by the arm, and started escorting her toward St. Michael's.

"I'm bringing up the daughter," Tanner called into his radio. "Where is the woman now?"

"We put her in 317," was the answer. "She slept through the whole damn thing Detective. She's *still* asleep."

"We had given her something for her pain," Dr. Nidra started telling Tanner. "Her bruises were bothering her. But I assure you she's fine."

A Tracy Brubaker Mystery

"Thank you very much doctor."

"Surely. I'll check on her again in an hour or two." Then Dr. Nidra left room 317.

Tracy was looking at her mother. Tanner stood behind her, and put his hands on her shoulders. "You heard the doctor, Tracy. She's fine."

Tracy nodded and then turned to hug Tanner. "Thank you El. Thank you for everything—you *and* Art."

"Hey, I told you I wouldn't let anything happen to her...or you." And she embraced him harder. She then pulled back, wiping the water from her eyes.

"You know, El. She'll be able to see the crime scene tape through her doorway. You might want to move her elsewhere."

"Tracy, she's going to find out what happened eventually. You know she will. You should start thinking about how you're going to talk to her about it."

Tracy nodded. "I guess you're right." She paused. "I think I'm going to be in *big* trouble though." Tanner started laughing and pulled Tracy toward him while rubbing her shoulder.

"I'm not sorry he's dead, El," she told him after a few moments. "I wish it hadn't played out like it did—and that I hadn't seen what I saw. But I don't feel the least bit of remorse. And I don't like that I don't."

Tanner squeezed her shoulder. "Try not to think about that right now. When this is all over, and you start feeling like your old self again, you may indeed feel remorse and regret."

"Maybe," Tracy whispered. "Maybe."

Later that evening, Tanner was standing in Pankow's office. Agent Lennon had just arrived after demanding to meet them. It was clear he was furious. Agent Roper was absent. Did they really think Lennon wouldn't have something to say about this?

"18 months!" Lennon shouted, "18 months down the drain! All that work, all the risks taken...Meaningless now. And for what? For *WHAT*!?"

"He was trying to kill someone," Tanner said in a matter-of-fact manner.

"That's because you assholes set him UP!"

"I don't know what you're talking about," Tanner responded.

Lennon moved his head quickly from side to side looking at his stone-faced audience of two. "Oh, don't you *dare* try to insult my intelligence,"

Crossed Stitch

Lennon fired back. "Brandice wouldn't have tried to kill *anyone* if you hadn't practically invited him to do so!"

"I still don't know what you mean," Tanner said. "It was *your* agents that lost him."

Lennon took a couple of steps back before continuing his rant. "Bullshit! I heard about that scene you two and the Brubaker woman had. A very nicely staged scene so that someone was bound to get the rumor mill started. And I have to believe *she* knew about everything too."

Pankow shook his head. "Well why don't you ask her then? I'm sure she'd just *love* to talk to you." Lennon stared at the both of them again.

Tanner said, "Are you saying that Brandice fell for what should have been such an obvious sting? That a seasoned vet like that just walked into a trap? I mean, do you think Brandice was getting sloppy?"

Lennon glared at Tanner, moving toward him so that he was practically in the detective's face. "And it just so happened that you had a man in the room, apparently hiding in a *closet*?"

"I'm sure you heard wrong," Tanner said. "He was just visiting when Brandice showed up. He came back from the bathroom and found Brandice in the room. What did you want him to do?"

"And the surveillance across the street? And the fact that nearly every police officer in the *goddamned state* was outside the hospital to take Brandice down?"

"You greatly exaggerate," Pankow said. "The surveillance was in connection with a series of muggings in the area. We just got lucky."

Lennon looked at them in disbelief. Clearly they thought he was an idiot. "I'll make sure jobs are lost for this," he finally snarled.

"You know what Arthur?" Tanner asked while turning to Pankow.

"No, Elias," Pankow responded.

"When my mother was feeling down, she always made herself a sunny-side-up egg."

"No kidding?"

"Nope. She loved them. She loved the way they looked, a bright yellow sun in the middle of a white sky — made her smile. She loved the way they crackled as they cooked. And she loved dipping a piece of her warm, homemade bread in the yolk after it started running."

"Sounds great, Elias."

"But there was one thing about it."

A Tracy Brubaker Mystery

"What was that Elias?"

"The yolk had to be perfect. I mean, it had to be nearly centered. And the yolk could not, under any circumstances, be broken."

"Really?"

"Yes. So if the yolk got broken at any point while the egg was still cooking in the frying pan, my mother would quickly add a dash of milk, and get her spatula and transform the pan's contents into a scrambled egg."

"You don't say."

"It was still an egg after all. I mean, she still got to eat her egg. She still got the same nutritional content. An egg is an egg, right?" Pankow continued nodding as Tanner spoke. Then Tanner turned to Lennon again. "Of course, whatever way she'd eat it, she'd still have to be careful not get any on her face. It was just that the appearance had been altered, you see."

Lennon just stared at the two of them. Finally he moved toward the office doors, turned to give a last look of contempt, and then left Pankow and Tanner alone. The former looked at the latter. "When did you start speaking in food metaphors, Elias?" Tanner just shrugged. So Pankow said, "You've been hanging around Tracy too long."

Tanner smiled and then turned to look at Pankow. "What *do* you think will happen here Arthur?"

Pankow shook his head. "I'm not sure. But I doubt it will be anything serious. Think of the bad spin that would be out there if we let the media know the feds were upset that an elderly woman's life was saved—a hero cop's widow no less." Tanner nodded, but wasn't completely convinced. "Still," Pankow continued. "It wouldn't hurt to find another way to get Walters since Brandice is no longer an option. *That's* who they really want. Like you said, same end result, different presentation."

"And what about Paganini?" Tanner asked.

Pankow shook his head again. "We rested today. So it's up to Tracy now. I've already got the judge to delay until Monday, given all that's happened."

"I see."

"Sorry Elias. I know you and Tracy look at Max as family. But unless one of you can find someone else who admits to using Paganini's phone, or someone who's either involved with Walters or had some other motive we don't yet know about, I really can't do anything except keep the trial moving ahead."

"I see," Tanner said again quietly.

"But I'll be honest with you. Given everything that's happened since Pepper's body was found, everything that people I like have been through, I really wouldn't mind if I end up having some egg on *my* face when all is said and done."

Tracy had spent the evening hours of 6:00 to 9:00 with her mother, trying to act as if everything was okay. She wasn't sure if her mother believed her. She had spoken to Pankow who informed her that court would resume Monday. So Tracy had no hesitation in spending her time at St. Michaels. And there had been good news. Her mother would be going home tomorrow, Friday. Tracy could pick her up at 10:00 a.m. The problem of course was that preparing her defense would mean she couldn't really spend too much time with the elder Brubaker. But Tracy did promise she'd take some time off after the Paganini case. Now it was almost 10:00 p.m. Tracy, Neal, and Rebecca, were all still in the office, the latter two wanting to be there for their employer if she needed them. Neal and Rebecca knew that Tracy was on the edge like she never had been before. They didn't want to leave her alone. Rebecca was at her desk when she heard a knock on the glass entrance doors. She looked up to see Tanner, and immediately went to let him in. "Go on back Detective. It's just Tracy and Neal back there. Can I bring you something?"

"No thanks, Rebecca." And then Tanner went to see the boss.

"El, what's up?" she asked. "I just got here a few minutes ago myself. I left Mom at the hospital and stopped to grab sustenance on the way here."

"Well, as you can imagine, Lennon's out for blood. And he suspects the truth about our… disagreement, let's call it."

Tracy couldn't help but smile. "I wish I could have joined you. I'd have brought a freshly brewed cup of coffee with me."

"It would have gone well with the egg," Tanner said chuckling.

"What?" she asked in an amused tone. Tanner told her, and she started laughing, as did Neal. "Oh, El, that's *supreme!* I *really* wish I'd been there now."

"I also have some news to share. We found, among Brandice's meager possessions, a couple of prepaid cell phones. One of them was used to make the call the night you were threatened. He's also been calling one other prepaid cell rather regularly. We're doing our damndest to trace it."

A Tracy Brubaker Mystery

"He gave his partner the gun and a prepaid cell, El. Can there be any doubt about that now?"

Tanner pursed his lips and then cleared his throat. "What are you going to do next Tracy?"

"Well Art got us the day off tomorrow, so my defense starts Monday." She moved toward the dry erase board that was still in her office, the events of Wednesday morning November 5 there for all to see. She pointed at the list of eight names toward the bottom. "It's one of them El, one of those people got Max's phone and made the call that morning. And since I can't believe one of his sons would do this, it has to be one of the other five."

Tanner looked as directed. "Two tailors, two salesmen, or a bookkeeper?"

"Has to be," Tracy stated.

"What would the motive be?"

"At this point all I can think is money. I have it on good authority that Brandice and Walters were on the outs. Brandice thus might not have had any muscle to back up a bodily threat. I know some people who needed money to start their own business. And everyone else knew the tailor shop's days are numbered if Max continues running things as he has been. A lot of these people have been with Max a long time, and might not have the energy to start all over again. So I think Brandice—from Pepper—learned about the staff, and then used that knowledge to pick and payoff someone. I don't have all of the details worked out yet. But I'll keep at it until I do."

Tanner just nodded.

"Want some fries Detective?" Neal asked.

Tanner smiled. "No thanks. Rita has something waiting for me. In fact I should really get home. But I almost forgot what I came here for."

"What El?"

"Listen, Tracy," he began. "I don't think Walters will try anything. But I'm going to have some people keeping an eye on both you and your mother for now. Your team is outside the office right now. And when your mother's home I'm going to have some people nearby there too."

She smiled. "Thanks El."

"I promised I'd take care of you two and I meant it."

Tracy, the perpetual hugger, decided Tanner deserved one for playing guardian angel times two. Then she grabbed a French fry and suddenly turned studious. Tanner noticed the change in expression. "What is it Tracy?" Tanner asked.

"Well, I think our killer may be more cunning than I gave him credit for."

"What do you mean?"

"This thing today with Brandice, why would Brandice do something like this on his own? He probably wasn't the trigger man and thus no one had anything on him. And do you really think the order came from Walters? What would he care since I can't get near him?"

"What about your calls to Walters and your subpoena?"

"Calls that haven't been returned? A subpoena that hasn't been served thanks to the feds?"

"Oh, I see, you think the alleged inside man put in the request."

"Alleged?"

Tanner grinned. "If you can't take it then don't dish it out."

"Don't be smart," she scolded. "But yeah, my very *genuine* inside man probably did the asking. He's not the professional like Brandice and Walters. He's the amateur. He's the nervous one. But that also makes him a threat if he decides he's likely to be exposed; let's make a deal and all that. So Brandice is going to want to keep him happy; at least in the short term. I mean, that was my thinking the whole time when improvising today's agenda."

"Uh-huh."

"But now I realize that this was really a win-win for Pepper's killer."

"How so?"

"If Brandice is successful, then I'm basically done as Max's lawyer. Even I have my limits. If this was a set-up, as of course it was, then the killer could be reasonably sure Brandice wouldn't make it out alive. And there goes the only other likely person to know the whole truth."

"If that's your thinking then didn't you just sabotage your own case?"

She shook her head. "Of course not. Today wasn't about my case, El. It was about saving my mother. I couldn't risk that something would be done to her. And I knew she was close to being discharged. And I thought it was more dangerous for her to be back at her apartment than to be in the hospital. I had to force Brandice's or whoever's hand, to see if they were serious. I did what I had to do, no regrets."

Tanner nodded. "I see. Thank God it worked out. They thought it was Brandice in the chapel but they couldn't be sure, neither of the officers. I couldn't risk taking him down there and being wrong about it."

"I understand El. I hope you know how grateful I am to you and Art for helping me, for setting everything up." Tanner nodded. "We gave everyone quite a show, didn't we?"

A Tracy Brubaker Mystery

Tanner laughed. "Award–caliber; well, I'm off. Goodnight Tracy. Goodnight Neal." And the two echoed Tanner's sentiments.

Neal began. "Okay Tracy—you need to see this. I started with Prince George's County and did a search for property sales for the time period you asked me about. I couldn't do it in one fell swoop because I got a 'Too Many Results' message; so I had to use smaller windows. Then I looked for sales where the previous owner listed was Randall Pepper. No luck there. So I looked for sales where the previous owner was a business and didn't hold the property for long. Some of those businesses were owned by other businesses. But ultimately I did come up with a list where the ultimate owner, after following all the holding companies, was none other than Randy Pepper."

"Neal..." Tracy said beaming.

He beamed back. "Next I picked some sales where the price paid by the new buyer was sharply higher than the price paid by Pepper's company just a few months earlier. Then I made some calls; some owners said they had already talked to the police about it. Then I remembered that you told me that Pepper was quietly arrested, so I figured I had to have been on the right track. I got the name of the appraisal companies they used; they were all the same, Robins Appraisers and Advisors LLC. Again I followed the ownership."

"And Randy Pepper was the ultimate owner?" Tracy asked, still smiling.

"Yup. But I haven't told you the best part."

"Don't toy with me Bennett!"

"I asked the buyers how they decided on what appraisal company to use. And they all had the same answer. The same person advised them."

When Neal said the name Tracy's smile was immediately replaced with a look of rage. "The cops and feds had to know this too," she growled. "God Neal they've known this whole time."

"Maybe; but Pepper may not have implicated him." Neal looked at the board. "Unfortunately none of this proves someone other than Max made that call."

Tracy stared at the board twisting the fry in her hand, leaning against her desk. She shook her head. "What am I missing Neal? What am I not seeing?"

Neal came to the desk and leaned next to her. "I don't know Tracy. We've been through it so many times...I think my brain's as fried as that potato your holding." Tracy gently laughed as the two continued to look at the board. "You know," he resumed, "maybe Max is right in thinking the phone never left his office."

Tracy, intrigued, asked, "What do you mean Neal?"

"Well maybe the killer switched Max's phone with a lookalike, instead of just borrowing it, after the lawyer called him. Then they go someplace in the store and make the call. They could replace the phone at some point when they came back to the office, maybe around lunchtime."

Tracy appeared to ponder the idea. "Interesting; a very good thought Neal. But to tell you the truth I had that idea as well. The risk is that the decoy phone starts ringing and Max answers. Or someone calls Max's phone and it's not where Max can answer because the other person still has it. On the other hand it's true that few people called Max on his cell, so maybe that's not much of a risk. Someone close to Max would know that. But I still wonder if the killer would want to take that chance."

"Yeah, that's true," Neal said, feeling a little disappointed his idea wasn't more enthusiastically received. "I'm trying to think outside the box."

Sensing his disappointment, she responded, "Oh, Neal I appreciate your ideas. We need to be thinking outside the box at this point. Please, keep doing it." She smiled at him. Then she turned back to the board. She looked at the list of eight names. She looked to the left; she looked to the right, stretching her neck. And then she stood up straight. Her eyes widened. Her pulse quickened. And then she went around the desk and picked up the phone.

"Beck, can you please check our call log from Tuesday November 4 of last year and tell me *exactly* what time Charlie Betts called to make his appointment with me?"

"I'm on it."

"Thanks Beck. Ring me right back when you have the answer please."

"Tracy, what is it?" Neal asked.

She didn't answer. She instead went to a table where volumes of paper connected to the Paganini case were stacked. Neal asked another question. "What are you looking for?"

"Copies of Max's phone bills."

"For the day of the murder?"

"No—for the day before the murder, the Tuesday." She continued rummaging until she removed what she was looking for. "Here it is," she started to say. Just then Rebecca buzzed and gave Tracy the information she requested.

A Tracy Brubaker Mystery

"I've got him calling at 11:25 a.m. Tracy," Rebecca said over the speaker.

And Tracy smiled. "Thanks Beck."

Neal was getting impatient. "What is it Tracy?"

She was looking at the board again. "The first appointment was made at 11:16 a.m. and then nine minutes later Brandice calls here to schedule his interview with me."

Neal gave her a confused look. "So what does that all mean?"

She looked at him. "It means I think I know who killed Randy Pepper." Then she looked back at the board. "But I'll be darned if I know exactly how he set Max up, much less how to prove it. But I'm starting to get an idea." She was still smiling when she turned back to face Neal. "Are you up for a working weekend? I doubt we can do all this tomorrow."

Neal gave her a big smile in return. "Are you kidding me? I *live* for the homestretch."

"I'm all in, too," Rebecca called through the speaker. Tracy hadn't realized Rebecca stayed on the line.

"You guys are amazing." She felt like an emotional wave was about to wash over her so she quickly added, "You guys are fired for the rest of the night. Go home to your families and rest up. I'm picking Mom up at 10:00 tomorrow, so let's meet here between 1:00 and 1:30."

"You're going home too, right Tracy?" Neal asked.

"No. I want to start working this thing out. I see ahead two days of phone calls, experiments, exhibit assembly…I want to have a clear game plan when you guys show up tomorrow. I don't want to waste your time. If I need sleep tonight I have my trusty couch here. I'll be fine."

"Okay Tracy," Rebecca announced. "I'll see you tomorrow then."

Neal started to leave. "I really would like to stay and help Tracy. It might be beneficial if you had someone to bounce ideas off of. I didn't tell the wife a time when I'd be home. She understands how difficult things have been for us, for you."

"Neal…" she started.

"Don't argue. You can give me Tuesday off since we'll no doubt have this thing all wrapped up Monday. Right?"

She looked at the floor, and then looked back at him. "Deal."

"Great!" And Neal sat himself down in front of her desk. As Tracy made her way to her chair Neal added, "But before we start anything, Tracy, tell me, who is it you think killed Pepper?"

It was Sunday afternoon so Tanner assumed he'd find Tracy home. But she wasn't there. Her office? She did sometimes go there after mass. So he made his way to her office building. Her door was unlocked and he saw the light coming from her back office. "Hello?" he called out.

"Back here El," Tracy answered. Tanner found Tracy at her desk with, what looked like, phone bills spread out in front of her. She was making notes. When she looked up at him he observed how tired she looked. But, as bad as he felt for her he couldn't help smiling. Tracy moved forward in her seat. "What is it El? Why are you so happy? Can I have some of it?"

"Are you here by yourself?"

"Neal's out getting some exhibits made for tomorrow. Now tell me why you're so jolly."

"We got him, Tracy."

Tracy immediately stood up. "Who? Pepper's killer?"

"No. Walters."

"What? How?"

"Brandice."

"Don't you DARE tell me he really survived and made some secret deal!?"

Tanner shook his head as he moved toward her. "No, Tracy. Brandice kept a journal."

Tracy asked with surprise, "Where'd they find *that*?"

"He had a safe deposit box he kept at a local bank—not Max's bank, in case you're wondering. Wanna take a *gamble* at the name he used at the bank?"

She thought a bit, and then smiled. "I'll roll the Bran*dice* and place my *Betts*."

"Bingo." Then Tanner started moving about, excited. "This thing had almost everything in it, going back some 20 years, names, dates, places, and dollars exchanged…Just everything. I mean, the only thing I can think of is that Brandice thought Walters was going to have *him* offed at some point, and decided that when he went, everyone else would go down as well. He must have kept this as some kind of insurance policy. That's *my* guess."

Tracy's eyes widened. "What about the Pepper murder?"

Tanner stopped, and the smile suddenly left his face. "I'm sorry Tracy. It looks like Brandice stopped making entries not too long after the feds start-

A Tracy Brubaker Mystery

ed watching him. He must have known they were watching after all, or at least suspected, and didn't want to risk them getting curious about regular visits to the bank. So there was nothing about Pepper in there other than some evidence of payoffs, his share of the proceeds for flipping deals he helped with. Pepper helped Walters make some quick money on flipping, and everybody got a share of the proceeds, including Brandice. I doubt Pepper though ever dealt directly with Walters. That's where Brandice comes in, acting as a middle man. And if you *are* right about some inside man, I'm pretty sure Walters wouldn't even know who Brandice used. Like you alluded to earlier, Walters would want to be as hands off as possible."

"What about the fed's other inside guy?"

"He's fine Tracy."

"Could I maybe sneak a peek at the journal? The killer's name could still be listed there, from some earlier contact."

"Sorry, Tracy. The feds have it. We're on thin ice with them already so we didn't argue when they asked for it. Besides, I did look through the names; I didn't recognize any other names connected to this case."

Tracy sat back down, leaned back in her chair and closed her eyes. "Figures," she uttered. "I guess Walters won't be on my witness list after all; not that I really need him at this point."

"But this is still *very* good news Tracy. Walters and his crew are going to spend the rest of their lives in prison, at least the ones who aren't willing to make deals with the feds. And you helped bring them down. I know that doesn't really help Max at this point. But I think you deserve some thanks here and I want to make sure you get it, even if it is unofficial."

Tracy opened her eyes. "You really want to thank me El?"

Tanner put his hands on his hips. "What do you mean?"

"Be in court tomorrow. And tell Art to let me do my thing."

"Huh?"

"You may not know who killed Randy Pepper but now I do. And after tomorrow everyone else will know too."

Chapter 17

Ten o'clock in the morning Monday, court was back in session. Tracy and Neal had arranged their defense table with the various exhibits they intended to present. Tracy had also arranged for a dry erase board to be at her beck and call. When Judge Reynolds entered, he first asked both Tracy and Pankow to approach his bench. "Are we okay to proceed here?" he asked both of them. "There are all kinds of tales being told out of school about this case, if you catch my drift."

Tracy answered first. "I want to proceed with my defense, Your Honor." And when Pankow nodded in agreement the attorneys were told to return to their places.

"Is the defense ready to proceed with its case?" Reynolds formally asked.

"We are, Your Honor," Tracy announced.

"Then call your first witness."

"Defense recalls Detective Adam Garrison." Garrison quickly moved to the witness stand and took his place. Tracy rose and approached as the bailiff reminded Garrison of his oath. "Detective Garrison," Tracy began, "I want to very briefly summarize the events that took place on Wednesday, November 5, the day Randall Pepper was shot and killed." Tracy then moved to the side of the court room opposite the jury in which stood the large dry erase board. She pulled it, squeaky wheels and all, toward the center of the room, so that is was viewable by Garrison, Judge Reynolds, Pankow, and the jurors. "Detective, before I begin, I'd like to ask you one question." Tracy paused. "Would you say, as one of the investigating detectives on this case, that the telephone call Mr. Paganini allegedly made the morning of the fifth was one of the key pieces of evidence that led to his arrest?"

"Yes, I would."

"If it were learned that Mr. Paganini did in fact *not* make that call, would he ever have been arrested in the first place?"

"Objection," Pankow said while coming to his feet. "The detective does not possess a crystal ball, and this case doesn't revolve around *just* the phone call."

"I'll withdraw the question then," she said giving Pankow a glare.

"What does she expect me to do," he thought. "Just sit hit here with my thumb up my keister?"

Tracy picked up a marker and started making a timeline on the board. In the center and about halfway down she wrote 10:25 a.m.; above that she wrote 10:15 a.m. "Detective, just to remind the jury, the telephone call placed from my client's cell phone to the victim's cell phone took place at 10:25 a.m. the morning of the murder. And this call was verified with phone records for both my client and the victim."

"Yes," Garrison nodded.

"And it is the police department's belief that the call was prompted by an earlier call, the one at 10:15 a.m., from Mr. Paganini's business attorney."

"Yes."

Tracy moved back to the board, and listed, just below the later time entry, the names of the eight other people present at the tailor shop the day of the crime. She then read the names aloud. "Detective, the names I just read, were all of these people at Mr. Paganini's establishment the morning of the fifth?"

He answered, "Yes, as far as we could tell."

"Thank you Detective. I have just one additional question." Tracy moved back toward the board and pointed at the earlier time. "Going back to this earlier entry, when Mr. Nestle called my client, thus supposedly starting the murder in motion, what exactly was the nature of Mr. Nestle's call?"

Garrison squirmed a bit. "I'm afraid I can't fully answer that. It was a privileged communication and Mr. Nestle was reluctant to share any specific details."

"Oh that's right," Tracy said. "Then I have no more questions for this witness."

"No questions," Pankow called out.

Tracy returned to her table. "Given Detective Garrison's testimony I would like to call Martin Nestle to the stand." Nestle arose and was seated, after which, Tracy made her way back to the dry erase board. "Mr. Nestle, you are my client's business attorney?"

"Yes," he answered nodding.

"For how long have you been engaged as such?"

"Not counting the time when I didn't have my own practice?"

"Correct."

"It's more than three and half years."

"You visited Mr. Paganini the morning of the fifth?"

"Yes, I did."

"Why?"

"I had some loan extension documents to drop off. They needed his signature."

"I see. And about what time was this?"

Nestle hesitated. "Well, I think it was around 9:00. Max is usually there at that hour and I pass by his office on the way to mine." Tracy nodded and then moved back toward the board, writing 9:00 a.m. to the left of the already listed times. She returned her attentions to Nestle. "And then you returned later that same day to retrieve the documents, now with the required signatures, along with the extension check?"

"That's correct."

"And what time was that?"

Nestle sat back in the chair. "It was after lunch. I'd say it was close to 2:00 p.m." Tracy noted the time on the right side of the board.

"And you dropped off the paperwork and check at the bank that Wednesday afternoon?"

"Yes; I think so."

"Actually, Mr. Nestle, according to the image scan of the canceled check, the check was deposited on Thursday."

"Alright; I guess it was Thursday then."

She then turned and looked at the jury. They were definitely curious based on the looks on their faces. She turned to face Nestle. "Thank you, Mr. Nestle." Tracy now moved back to her table. "Mr. Nestle, when did you set up the Wednesday morning appointment with Mr. Paganini?"

Nestle blinked a few times. "Um, I think on Tuesday."

"Tuesday the fourth, the day before the murder?"

"Right."

"Do you recall the time?"

Nestle looked at her quizzically. "I'm not really sure."

Tracy picked up a piece of paper from her table. "I have here a copy of my client's mobile phone bill from December of last year which shows a call made from your cell phone, Mr. Nestle, to Mr. Paganini's on Tuesday, November 4 at 11:16 a.m. It lasted about two minutes. Does that sound right?"

Nestle nodded. "Yeah, I guess."

"I'd like this entered in as defense exhibit one." She moved from the desk to pass the paper around to the relevant parties so the bill could find its way to the exhibit table. Tracy then returned to her table and stood as

A Tracy Brubaker Mystery

straight and tall as she could. "Mr. Nestle, do you know a man by the name of Carlton Brandice?"

The question caused Arthur Pankow to sit up straight in his chair. Part of him wanted to object to the question, but instead he sat there. He remembered Tracy's message to him via Tanner. For now then, he'd let her do her thing. Meanwhile, Nestle just looked at her. He met her eyes. Finally he said, "No."

"No?" Tracy echoed. "His name's been in the papers quite a bit recently."

Nestle continued to meet her stare. "You asked if I knew him, not if I had heard of him."

Tracy smiled. "You're absolutely right, Mr. Nestle; touché." Tracy turned to Pankow. She said nothing, but darn it if she didn't have a "don't mess with me" look on her face. She then picked up a second piece of paper. "This is my office call log from the morning of Tuesday, November 4 of year last. Mr. Brandice, using the name Charles Betts called my office at 11:25 a.m., nine minutes after your call to my client, to set up an appointment with me the following Wednesday, the 12th. I'd like this entered as defense exhibit two." And so it was done.

Tracy moved toward Nestle. "Brandice, as you may know, worked for Reginald Walters, who had some dealings with the victim, Randall Pepper."

Tracy quickly turned to face Pankow. Was she daring him to object? He should be objecting, but instead he thought, "…the hell with it."

Tracy returned to face Nestle. "Did you call Mr. Brandice after speaking with Mr. Paganini that morning?"

Nestle scowled at her. "I told you already I never knew him."

"How about Reginald Walters, did you know him?"

Pankow couldn't let this go on. "Objection. Where is all of this going?"

But before the judge could rule Tracy barked out, "Withdrawn. Mr. Nestle, how well did you know the victim Randall Pepper?"

"Hardly at all," he answered quickly.

"But you recommended his appraisal company to some of your clients."

"I…"

"Don't you do some charitable work where you provide counsel to low income families?"

"Yes I do; lots of lawyers do that. *You* do that."

"And didn't you advise some of these families to get their appraisals using Robins Appraisers and Advisors?"

"Yes, I may have."

"And didn't you know this company was owned by Randall Pepper?"

"No I did not!" he answered emphatically.

Then Tracy quickly moved to the board. "Mr. Nestle, as someone who was at Mr. Paganini's shop the Wednesday of the murder I'd like to draw your attention to these names listed here, the eight people known to have been present. Can you please look at this list and confirm for the court that you remember these people being there that day?"

Nestle relaxed a little. "Not all of them were there the first time I was there. But I'm fairly certain they were all there later in the afternoon."

"When you picked up the signed documents and check?"

"Right."

Tracy scratched her chin. "Why did you pick up the documents that same Wednesday? Why not just pick them up the next day, Thursday, on your way to work, like Lester Grossman had testified previously was your normal routine?"

"I…" Nestle began. "I wanted to get them over to the bank."

"But you didn't do that until Thursday anyway. We established that earlier; remember?"

Nestle again just looked at her. "Things just came up."

"Never mind all that then. I want to go back to the phone call you made to my client on Wednesday; the one you made at 10:15 a.m. from your office." She then moved back to her table. "The State previously entered into evidence your phone call to Mr. Paganini that morning in order to establish that his cell phone was in his possession 10 minutes before the call to the victim." Tracy now moved from the table back to the board. "Now if someone other than my client made that call, it would presumably have to be one of these eight people." She first pointed to the list of names, and then drew a box around it. "But, what if, for a moment, we think outside the box?" She turned to give Neal a quick smile. Then she returned yet again to the table. "I'm looking at this phone record here regarding that 10:15 a.m. call and I see you called Mr. Paganini from your land line."

"So what?" Nestle interjected.

"Well why did you call him from your land line?"

"What's that supposed to mean? Because I was there at my office and the phone was right there."

A Tracy Brubaker Mystery

Tracy took a few steps toward the witness box. "But Mr. Nestle, I spent all day yesterday reviewing Mr. Paganini's cell phone bills going back nearly three years and you always called him from your cell phone; every single call. The first and only time you *ever* called him from your land line was the morning of the murder. Why was that?"

Nestle felt a flush in his cheeks. "I just told you."

Tracy quickly changed course. "Mr. Nestle, when did you first learn about me and my relationship with the defendant?"

"Huh?"

"When did you learn that I knew the defendant?"

"I don't…What's that got to do with anything?"

"Didn't you tell me in one of our early encounters that you didn't learn that I knew Mr. Paganini until *after* he was arrested, and that otherwise you would have contacted me sooner regarding the murder?"

"I may have; I don't remember."

"But isn't it true that Mr. Paganini bragged that he knew my father, considered him a dear friend, when my name was mentioned in newspaper reports last year regarding the Shane case, and that he jokingly said he now knew whom he could turn to if he ever needed similar help?"

Nestle squirmed a bit. "He may have, I don't remember."

"For a lawyer, you have a very poor memory, Mr. Nestle."

Nestle's face turned red and he clenched his teeth and growled, "*You —*"

Pankow couldn't let his continue. "Objection! She's insulting her own witness!"

"I'm sorry," Tracy said insincerely. "But isn't that why you sent Mr. Brandice to see me, to learn some things about me?"

Pankow stood up again and started to speak. But nothing came out. He sat back down.

Nestle's anger returned — or was it panic this time. "Now you listen to me, I've made it clear —"

"Why did you call from your land line the morning of the murder?" she interrupted.

"I explained that —"

"Was it to establish your alibi?"

"My *what*?!"

"If you were at your office at 10:15 you couldn't have been at my client's shop at 10:25 to make the call to the victim."

"You're not making *any* sense!"

Tracy moved so that she was standing directly in front of Nestle. "Look outside that box of names on the board over there Mr. Nestle. I see you arriving in the morning, calling Max shortly after you returned to your office, and then going *back* to my client's store mere hours later the very same day. And you never even made it to the bank that afternoon."

"So *what*?!"

"So didn't you take Mr. Paganini's phone with you when you left in the morning, make the call to Randy Pepper from your office, and then return Mr. Paganini's phone to him in the afternoon?"

Nestle gulped. He looked to the jury. Then he looked back at her. "Why would I do something like that?"

"To frame Max Paganini for murder. You and Pepper were involved in illegal flipping. Walters, Brandice, and Pepper were involved in much more. I suspect you may even have helped out Walters and/or Brandice along the way as off-the-record legal counsel. So when Brandice found out Pepper was working with the FBI, he contacted you, knowing that Pepper was a threat to you too. And you came up with the idea to frame Mr. Paganini, the one person whose animus toward Randall Pepper was well known. So didn't you take Mr. Paganini's phone with you when you left that morning?"

Nestle stared at her for a brief moment. And then he smiled. "If what you say is true, then Max couldn't have answered his phone when I called him at 10:15, now could he, because I was by then back at my office. He couldn't have answered my call if *I* had his phone."

"You're right. But how do we know Max — I mean — Mr. Paganini *did* answer his own phone that morning?"

Nestle hesitated and then asked "What kind of question is that? The phone records prove he got my call on his *own* phone!"

"They prove someone made and received calls to and from Mr. Paganini's phone that morning. They don't prove *who* made and received them."

Nestle's body tensed up. He couldn't believe it. Had she figured it out? Impossible; his plan had been ingenious. Okay, she was smart. But how in the hell could she have worked it out?

Tracy moved away from Nestle and toward her associate. She nodded at Neal who handed her a small bag which she then placed on the defense table.

"You certainly wanted it to *appear* that my client received your call and then called the victim. But there is another possible explanation." She was

A Tracy Brubaker Mystery

rummaging around in the bag with her back to Nestle. When she finally turned she was holding two small items, one in each hand. Nestle nearly collapsed.

"All you needed were these, two disposable, also known as prepaid, cell phones, one of which looked similar enough to Mr. Paganini's phone so that this man with poor eyesight would hardly have been able to tell the difference." She was now moving toward the jury. "With the first phone, you downloaded Mr. Paganini's ringtone and programmed the phone number of the *second* disposable phone with your name. You switched the first phone with Mr. Paganini's phone when you were there in the morning, leaving the decoy on the table by the charger. You then returned to your office."

She turned from the jury to face Nestle. "While you were at your office, you called Mr. Paganini's actual cell phone — the one you took — from your land line, thereby establishing your alibi. At the very same time, you called the first disposable phone, now on Mr. Paganini's desk, with the second disposable phone, the one whose number you programmed into the first phone, so that your name would display on the screen when you called, as a precaution. Mr. Paganini would not likely have noticed anything was wrong."

Tracy was suddenly aware of the silence around her. It seemed that people had stopped breathing. Nestle looked at her in what she swore could only be described as terror. She jettisoned her friendly tone as she continued. "When Mr. Paganini answered the dummy phone, you opened up his actual phone, the one you had with you right there at your office, to answer the land line call and basically had a brief conversation over *two* phones. When you were done, you ended both calls simultaneously, effectively creating the illusion that Mr. Paganini had been talking on his own phone at his office when in reality he was using a different phone. Then, at 10:25 a.m., you used his actual phone to call the victim, did the best Massimo Paganini imitation you could muster, and summoned Randall Pepper to the meeting where you then killed him later that evening. You had returned Mr. Paganini's phone to him that afternoon after lunch, when you showed up again, ostensibly to pick up the signed papers and check, thereby establishing that the 'fatal' call had been made at a time and place where you couldn't possibly be suspected. And you lucked out that most people are at the shop on Wednesdays, which would provide a lengthy list of alternate suspects in case Mr. Paganini, for whatever reason, suddenly stepped out of his office in the 10 minutes after you called him at 10:15 a.m. and came up with his own alibi." She folded her arms. Now she would make it a little personal. "You've been Max's attorney and friend long enough to know all there is to know about how the shop runs; that Max would be working late that Wednesday. You could easily have had key copies made. You're single and looking for a girlfriend, so I doubt you'll have an alibi for the night of the murder."

The quiet continued. All eyes were on Nestle awaiting some kind of response. He straightened up his chair, and leaned forward. There seemed to a return of confidence to his expression. Then he grinned at her. "That's quite the imagination you have there, counselor. But even if you're right about everything, there's no way you can prove such a fabrication." Nestle then leaned back in his chair.

Tracy straightened herself up again. She faced the jury briefly, and then turned back to Nestle. And she returned his grin for a spell. Finally she said, "I wouldn't have said all that I said unless I thought I could prove it." And the grin left Nestle's face. He jumped a bit when she suddenly shouted, "Props!" at which point Neal Bennett stood up, and removed what looked like a rolled up banner from the defense table. Tracy and Neal unfolded the 'prop' and showed it to the judge and Pankow. "I'd like this entered as defense exhibit three," she called out, and then she and Neal moved toward the dry erase board. The two of them unfurled the banner and clipped it to the structure. After Neal returned to the desk, Tracy positioned herself next to what was a map of Baltimore City and Baltimore County.

"I'd like to draw your attention to this map, Mr. Nestle," she began. "You will notice the symbols of three small triangles, each colored differently." She paused and withdrew a laser pointer from her suit jacket pocket. She pointed the bright beam at the top yellow-covered triangle. "This triangle here is your office, Mr. Nestle, the one from where you called Mr. Paganini the morning of the murder. The office is located in Baltimore County." She then moved the beam down so that it highlighted a green triangle near the center of the map. "This second triangle is Mr. Paganini's office from where he *allegedly* called the victim." The beam then made its way to the blue triangle near the bottom of the map. "And this, Mr. Nestle, is Randall Pepper's office, where he received the much-debated call." She paused, turned to face her witness, and then asked, "Does this look right to you, Mr. Nestle?"

"I guess," he murmured.

A Tracy Brubaker Mystery

She again faced the map, and then started moving the beam over the entire canvas. "Now I'd like to point out these various black 'x' marks that represent the cell phone towers utilized by Mr. Paganini's service provider. You can see for example, there are no less than 10 towers that belong to or are leased by the provider within a five mile radius of Mr. Paganini's office. And if we broaden our radius you can see there are approximately 30 towers that fall within a 15 mile radius. Do you see what I mean, Mr. Nestle?"

"Yes."

"Before I continue, I'd like to introduce you to someone, Mr. Nestle. Will Ms. Dana Rosen please stand?" A young woman dressed in a blue business suit rose from the gallery. "This is Ms. Dana Rosen," Tracy said pointing. "She works for Mr. Paganini's cell phone provider. I will be calling her to testify as an expert after I'm finished with you to further corroborate what I'm about to discuss, lest the State think my evidence is less than compelling or inadmissible. You can sit back down Ms. Rosen." So Dana Rosen sat.

Tracy moved away from the map and faced the jury. "Do you know about what's called 'pinging a cell phone', Mr. Nestle?"

"I've heard of it," he tersely answered her.

"Pinging is how cell phone companies or other parties can determine the location of someone's mobile phone relative to the cell phone tower being used to either make or receive a call. Cell phone companies can provide information on the tower used when a call is initiated, and when a call is terminated. Were you aware of that?"

Nestle was aware of it. He also was aware that using such information as evidence was semi-controversial given that the tower used wasn't always the one closest to where the call was actually placed, as various factors could cause a signal to bypass the nearest tower and look for the next closest one available. But he wasn't quite sure where she was going with her questions. And he didn't want to say anymore than he had to. So all he answered was, "Yes."

Tracy then returned to the map. She aimed her pointer at a circled 'x' close to Nestle's office. "Now, Mr. Nestle, I would like to draw your attention to this map for one final time. Do you see this tower with the dark circle around it near your office?"

Nestle felt the blood drain from his face. *Now* he knew *exactly* where she was headed. He shifted uncomfortably in his chair as he, again, simply said, "Yes."

"According to Mr. Paganini's service provider, this circled tower, the one that is less than two miles from your office, is the tower where the cell phone signal 'pinged' when Mr. Paganini ended his 10:15 a.m. call with you. And it is the tower where the cell phone signal 'pinged' when the 10:25 a.m. call was placed from my client's phone to the victim. In other words, it appears that the call my client took from you and the call he allegedly made were both received and made very close to your office." Tracy was staring at Nestle now. She paused long enough so that he would squirm some more. Then she slowly turned to make her way back to the defense table; she turned to face the jury. "Now it's true that sometimes signals can skip over the nearest tower for sundry reasons and pick a tower further away. But your office is more than 15 miles away from Mr. Paganini's, and there are almost 30 towers to skip over in order to reach the one by your office. In other words, on the morning of the murder, based on the provider information, which will be substantiated when I call Ms. Rosen, the signal from Mr. Paganini's cell phone signal had to skip over those 30 or so towers not *once*, but *twice*. What are the odds of that I wonder?" Before Pankow could object or Nestle could opine she continued. "Do you still maintain you did not make the call to the victim, despite what the map shows?" She again did not pause long enough for Nestle to answer. "Before you answer, Mr. Nestle, I want to make you aware of something else."

Tracy turned back to her desk and reached for a spiral bound set of papers. "Defense exhibit four," she began. "This is a study that my office conducted over the weekend. I, my associate, and my administrative assistant were very busy on Friday and Saturday. We requested permission from Mr. Paganini to be set up with his provider to have the right to ping his phone, which we were granted thanks to a patient customer service person. This report represents the results of our study after we received permission to ping Mr. Paganini's phone." Tracy paused a bit, realizing how, um, improper that sounded. "The report was signed this morning before court as to its validity by me, my associate, my administrative assistant, and Ms. Rosen in the presence of a notary public — although I am sure the State will want to conduct its own study."

Tracy started to move toward the center of the courtroom and faced the jury. "Between the three of us we made and/or received calls to and from the three key locations on the map, my client's office, the victim's office, and your office, each of us at one of those locations. I had Mr. Paganini's phone and was in the very same office he was in the morning of

A Tracy Brubaker Mystery

the murder. My associate was outside of your office, Mr. Nestle, and my administrative assistant was kindly granted use of Randall Pepper's office by his staff. I placed calls from Mr. Paganini's phone to the phone my AA had. And my associate called me on Mr. Paganini's phone from your office building location. In all Mr. Nestle, utilizing my client's phone, I made 40 calls to Randall Pepper's office and received 40 calls from my associate. After each and every call we phoned the very patient and understanding service provider and recorded the cell phone tower that was pinged." She paused again, turned to face Nestle, and raised the report in the air. "This report documents the results of that study; documents that show which cell tower received the signal for each and every one of those 80 calls; documents that will be corroborated by Ms. Rosen."

Tracy turned and threw the report back on the defense table, twisting her wrist a bit so that the report landed with a dramatic flourish. She put her hands behind her back and slowly began making her way back to Nestle. "Mr. Nestle, would you like to know how many of those 80 calls resulted in signals bouncing off the tower by your office, the tower where *both* signals pinged the morning of the murder?" She stopped to glare at him. She then stepped back and turned to the jury. "Not a single…solitary…one. In not *one* of those 80 calls did the signal hit a tower *anywhere* near your office. In fact the signals never traveled more than *five miles* from my client's office. Isn't technology grand?" She faced her witness. "As I mentioned, Defense will be calling to the stand Ms. Rosen who will verify the results, as well as corroborate that the tower outside your office the morning of the murder received the two signals. So I ask you again, Mr. Nestle, do you still maintain you were not in possession of my client's cell phone the morning of the murder, and that you did not make the call to the victim using my client's phone despite what the map shows and the study basically confirms?"

There was silence. Nestle looked down at his hands, which were folded on his lap. He then lifted his head and looked at Tracy who was now standing directly in front of him. "At this point," he began, "I don't think I'm going to answer any more of your questions, Fifth Amendment and all." They stared at each other a bit more, and then Tracy started backing away. She stopped and once again folded her arms.

"Then I guess I have no more questions." She took another quick look at the jury, and then seated herself next to Max, who reached for her hand. She turned to look at him. She saw a look on his face that she had faked during the set up of Carlton Brandice, betrayal. Max's tears were genuine however, so she released his hand and put her arm around him.

"Marty?" he mouthed, without actually saying his betrayer's name.

"I'm sorry, Max," she whispered. And he rested his head on her shoulder.

Judge Reynolds noted this exchange, and then he looked over at the jury and saw they too were noting the same thing. Some of the jury members had tears in their eyes. Others were shaking their heads. Still others were glaring at the still-seated Martin Nestle. Then Reynolds looked over at Martin Nestle. Next he looked at Pankow. Reynolds cleared his throat and moved forward in his seat.

"Ms. Rosen," the judge said. She once again stood. "You work for Mr. Paganini's cell phone provider as Defense indicated."

"Yes Your Honor."

"Are you going to confirm the accuracy of the information that Defense just presented with respect to the tower outside Mr. Nestle's office?"

"Yes, sir, Your Honor," she answered.

"I see. You may sit back down, Ms. Rosen." The judge pondered a moment longer and took another look at the jury. "Mr. Pankow," he began, at which point the State's Attorney stood up, "I don't see how, after what just occurred and what will be confirmed by Ms. Rosen's expert testimony, that a jury could render any verdict *other* than not guilty in this case. Therefore, I am directing that a verdict of not guilty be entered and the defendant be released immediately." Reynolds turned to the jury. "I want to thank the jury for their service in this matter. Please don't think my actions in any way diminish your importance to these proceedings." Reynolds looked back to Pankow. "I'll leave you to decide how to proceed with Mr. Nestle."

"Yes, Your Honor," Pankow said.

Reynolds looked at Massimo Paganini. "Mr. Paganini, you are free to go; Godspeed to you, sir. This court is adjourned." And then Reynolds brought the gavel down. And then Max embraced Tracy, oblivious to everything else happening around him.

"Is that really it?" Max asked her.

Tracy answered, "That's really it, Max. It's all over. Now let your family take you home." Max looked up to see his wife and sons beaming, tears in their eyes, standing behind him. Tracy helped Max navigate his way to

A Tracy Brubaker Mystery

his loved ones, and let them guide him from the room. Pankow then came over to her as she was returning items to her briefcase. "Great job, Tracy; I mean that."

"Thanks Art, and *I* mean *that*."

"I should have checked that signal stuff myself. But Max never denied the phone was in his possession, and when the phone records confirmed the calls I didn't even think to go to the next step."

"Well, using tower signals as evidence *against* a defendant versus using it to raise doubt *about* a defendant's guilt is legally speaking a lot trickier. But feel free to use my study if you think it will help you prosecute Nestle." She smiled as Arthur Pankow patted her shoulder and exited the courtroom. She noticed Agent Roper approach Pankow at the doorway, and then she turned her attention to Neal. "You solved it Neal. You did it. I can't thank you enough."

Neal shook his head. "No, Tracy. I may have thought outside the box and mentioned switched phones, but I never would have thought of two disposable phones in a million years. That was all you. So we both solved it. I still don't know how you figured it out."

She zipped up her case. "You were the one who reminded me of the possibility of a decoy phone. And then when I realized that Nestle could have done something like that I kinda just backed into it. I mean, there've been disposable phones popping up in this case practically the whole time. So I thought why not take a look at tower signals the day of the calls. After that, the only theory I could come up with was the two phones."

Neal nodded. "Well, I still can't believe it."

Tracy put her arm around Neal and gave him a light jostling. "Neal, buddy, you gotta have faith; sometimes that's all you can have."

Chapter 18

Tracy was in the courthouse hall when the Paganini clan caught up with her. "Tracy!" Max called out. "I want you to come home with us. Gloria's preparing a feast. You should celebrate with us."

"Oh, Max," Tracy began. "You've been spending so much time with me lately. You should celebrate with your family."

Max's expression turned serious for a moment, and then the smile returned. "Tracy, you *are* family; you have been since the first day you stepped into my shop." He paused, and then said, "Tracy, I don't know how much time I got left. So don't argue with an old man who doesn't know how to thank you properly for all you've done for him. You come and eat with us."

Tracy felt herself tearing up. "Okay Max. It would be an honor to dine with you and your family."

"Terrific!" Max shouted. "You can be Jerry's date." Tracy let out a laugh.

His youngest son heard what his father said. "Pop, I'm seeing Laura now."

"You need to find a smart girl like Tracy."

"Laura's smart," the son said, his tone defensive.

"Well, there's smart, and then there's *smart,*" Max said. Then he added, "and Laura's neither of them," at which point he slapped Jerry in the stomach and started guffawing. Everyone else joined in, except Jerry, who just shook his head.

"Pop, you need to be nice to Laura. I think she's the *one.*"

"Ah, you know I'm always nice to her."

The Paganini clan continued moving forward toward the courthouse doors. There was more merrymaking and good-natured ribbing. Their laughter echoed through the sterile halls. Tracy watched them, moved by their displays of affection. Here was a family that was most likely to value each and every moment they would have together from now on. They had been through a horrible experience, but they would prevail. She found herself thinking of her mother. How she wanted to see her right at this moment. She would spend a few hours with Max's family and then she would visit the most important person in the world to her right now.

As the family exited the building, Tony Paganini suddenly turned. "Oh Tracy, I just wanted to thank you, and I don't just mean about Pop's trial."

Tracy cocked her head slightly. "What do you mean, Tony?"

"Jeff came to me Friday. He told me about Craig and Sonny. It's true isn't it?"

Tracy nodded. "Yes; they're not the most upstanding people."

"Well, Friday was their last day with us. I kept Jeff of course. Now we're down to one sales person and one tailor, just like Lester wanted."

Tracy laughed. "Hey, that's right. Lester must be pleased."

"He is. I don't know what the future holds, but I think I should sit down and listen to Lester's ideas. I've decided I really do want to run the store."

Tracy smiled. "I'm really happy to hear that, Tony. It's really kind of amazing how things worked out in the end. I hope things continue to work out for your family, Tony. What are you going to do about Paul Iris?"

"Keep him on the payroll for now."

"Good. He's trying to care of his daughter. I like Paul."

Tony smiled and nodded. "Again Tracy, I'll never be able to adequately thank you for everything you've done for us. If you ever need anything, and I mean, *anything*, you call me." Then Tony Paganini embraced his father's lawyer tightly and warmly. "Oh, I want you and your mother to be our guests for Easter dinner. And I won't take no for an answer."

"We'll be there Tony. I look forward to it."

"Great—oh and thank your staff for me too. I bet they helped out. I'll see you later at the house."

"You have no idea," she thought as Tony moved quickly to rejoin his jubilant family.

"Ms. Brubaker!" a voice called out as Tracy opened her car door in the courthouse parking lot. She turned and saw Agent Roper approach her. "Glad I caught you."

She gave him a skeptical look. "What can I do for you?" she asked without really meaning it.

"I just want to thank you; that's all."

Now he had her full attention. "Whatever for?" she asked him.

"Look, you don't have to play coy with me. I'm not like Lennon. But I think you already know that."

"Yes; and I know you helped me when you probably shouldn't have."

"And I know you took a risk allowing your own mother to be used as bait to nab Brandice."

"*If* I did something like that it was only because I trusted Detective Tanner and the department."

Roper nodded. "Still, that couldn't have been easy."

"No, *hypothetically* speaking of course."

Roper grinned. "We've taken Martin Nestle into federal custody. His former employer Mark Mustabaugh was listed in Brandice's journal and so was someone named Mr. C. Bar. Every time Brandice wrote Bar's name down he wrote a smiley face next to it, like it was a private joke."

Tracy thought a bit, and then she started laughing. "You think C. Bar stands for Crunch Bar. Martin *Nestle*, a lawyer—passing the bar. Double rim shot."

Roper nodded, laughing himself. "That's pretty much what we're thinking yeah; or maybe Candy Bar."

"Well that explains why El didn't recognize any names when he scanned the journal. I always felt the killer had hidden his motive pretty well. And there I was telling Marty almost everything, thinking there's no way he can be involved in this since he couldn't have made that call; I'm an idiot."

"Well, nobody thought Nestle killed Pepper."

"But you knew he worked with Pepper on securing the appraisals," Tracy said giving Roper a slight scowl.

"Yes, but Pepper never implicated him. Nestle got hooked into the Walters crew via his old boss and must have continued helping them out on the sly. You worked out the rest. Once we start looking into his financials I'm sure we'll find something."

"Good luck with that. I hope you *fry* his ass."

Roper gave a hearty laugh. "Anyway, I just wanted to assure you that, given everything that's happened, and how you did help us get Walters, we won't be bothering Tanner, Pankow, or you about anything, unless we need help connecting some of the dots."

Tracy extended her hand. "I'm really glad to hear that Agent Roper."

"Sure," he told her while shaking her hand. "I told Lennon he should be the one telling you this but he mumbled something about eggs and decided to pass. I don't know what that means."

Tracy started laughing again. "Well, don't worry about it. Have a safe trip back to D.C."

"Thank you. It's been a pleasure." Roper released her hand, turned and made his way back to a nondescript car that was waiting for him, engine running. Tracy saw Lennon sitting in the front. She bent over a bit and

A Tracy Brubaker Mystery

waved vigorously at him, big smile on her face. He looked at her and then turned to face his windshield, returning neither her wave nor her smile.

"Oh, well," she thought. "I'm not getting the wave from that prick. I guess he'll never be a member of the Tracy Brubaker fan club." Tracy proceeded to enter her car and make her way to the Paganini family feast.

Tracy's mother was back in her Aberdeen apartment. Even though it wasn't the weekend Tracy was feeling the need to see her, not really to boast about her latest victory, but instead just to sit and talk—or even be totally quiet—with her. She managed to escape the Paganini household just after 7:00 in the evening, but not before Gloria Paganini had supplied Tracy with a care package for Violetta Brubaker. Now it was nearly 8:00. Mrs. Raccio greeted Tracy after a few rings of the bell.

"Your mother's in her room resting now. We were watching TV up until a little while ago."

"I have a lot of food here courtesy of Mrs. Paganini. It's all for you and Mom."

Mrs. Raccio's eyes widened. "Oh that dear woman; thinking of other people at a time like this."

"Don't you know, Mrs. Raccio? Max is a free man as of late this morning. It's over."

Maria Raccio gave a big smile. "Oh, how wonderful! There's been some stuff on the news but we were, oh how do you say that? We were channel waving."

Tracy chuckled. "Channel *surfing*."

"THAT'S it."

"Who are you talking to out there Maria?" Violetta Brubaker called out from her bedroom.

"It's Tracy. She's come to see you."

Tracy put the bag of deliciousness on the counter near the refrigerator, and then made her way to her mother's room. "Hi Mom!" she cheerfully greeted. "How are you feeling today?"

Violetta opened up her arms and mother and daughter embraced, one that lasted longer than usual. When Tracy was freed she looked at her mother closely. Violetta put her hands on Tracy's cheeks. "What a joy to see you, dear child." She then kissed her daughter on each cheek. "I didn't know you were coming. Otherwise I would have waited for you."

"I didn't know I was coming either, Mom. I just wanted to see you."

Violetta's face suddenly showed panic. "Tracy, what's wrong?"

Tracy couldn't help but laugh. "Nothing Mom; nothing at all. Honest."

Violetta's expression was slightly skeptical. "Well, if you say so."

"I was thinking about you. When Max was with his family, well, I just wanted to be with my family."

"Tracy, what are you talking about?"

Tracy sat in the chair beside her mother's bed and took her hand. "I won the case Mom. Max is a free man. And we've been invited to Easter dinner by the Paganinis. The federal people have the real killer in custody and I think they'll have enough to send him up the river."

"The river?"

"Prison, Mom."

Violetta smiled broadly. "Tracy, that is wonderful."

"That's what Mrs. Raccio said."

Violetta looked at her daughter—the former happy little girl who was, at present, a happy big girl. "I wish I could go back to the hospital and tell those know-it-alls a thing or two."

Tracy was still smiling. "What do you mean, Mom?"

"I'd hear them, reading their papers, or watching their TVs, saying how Max was guilty, there was no hope for him, and all of that. But I'd say, 'My daughter says he's innocent. She'll prove it.' They'd just nod, like I didn't know what I was talking about. And now I'm not there to accept their apologies."

Tracy laughed. "Oh Mom, don't worry about it."

Violetta looked at her daughter. "I've always loved your laugh. It reminds me of your father. You remind me so much of your father."

Tracy promised herself she wouldn't cry tonight. But she wished her father was there with them, knowing how proud he'd be. She gulped and then kissed her mother's hand.

"Tracy," Violetta said. "I need to talk to you."

"Sure Mom. I'm all yours—at least for an hour. I want to be home by 10:00."

"Tracy, I'm being serious."

Tracy paused. "What is it Mom?"

Violetta pushed herself up in the bed. "Tracy, I know what you did for me."

"What do you mean?"

"I know you wanted to be like your father; to be a police detective."

     A Tracy Brubaker Mystery

Tracy gulped again. "Mom, we don't have to get into that."

"But I want to. I know you gave up your lifelong dream because you were scared for me."

"Mom…"

"And yet within a year you've been involved with and solved two murders."

Tracy put her head down. "I know Mom. But they were special circumstances, where I knew the people were innocent. I promise it won't become a habit."

"Maybe it should."

Tracy lifted her head. Did she hear that right? "Mom, I…"

"Look, Tracy. Parents are supposed to make sacrifices for their children, not the other way around. And if the Good Lord gave you a gift, then it is wrong not to use it. It's a *sin* not to use it."

Tracy broke her promise to herself. The tears started to make their way down her cheeks. "Mom…"

But Violetta interrupted her again. "Tracy, I was able to let your father go out the door every morning because I knew he was doing right. He was using his gifts to help people the way he best knew how to. The bible says that laying your life down for someone is the ultimate gift. And I take great comfort in the fact that I *know* your father is in heaven. You should think about that too."

Tracy was sobbing now, so she just nodded her head. "I do," she managed to say.

"So since you're so much like your father, then you should use your gifts the way you do best. If someone comes to you and says they need your help, even if it involves a killing, and you think you can help them, then you should help them. I know you told me you would stay away from all that, for my sake, but I don't think it's the right thing to do. Who would have helped that boy if you hadn't have been there? Who would have stood by Mr. Paganini if you didn't? Are you hearing me dear child?"

More sobbing, more nodding, and then through tears, her answer, "Yes."

"What are you crying for?" Violetta reached for her daughter's face. "Tracy, I love you. You are the most precious thing in the world to me. And I'm proud of you. And your father's proud of you. So what is there to be sad about?"

Tracy shook her head. "I'm not sad."

"Then give me another hug. Then maybe we play a game, huh?" So Tracy hugged her mother with as much gentle strength as she could.

"I love you too Mom," she was finally able to say. She didn't want to let her mother go. After almost 32 years on this earth Tracy had gained an understanding of her mother she never had before. Their relationship would be forever changed now—for the better. The stroke had been minor, but it no doubt would have a major impact on both mother and daughter.

But then, just because Violetta Brubaker was Violetta Brubaker, she said, "Of course, I wouldn't mind some other precious things to love; little ones."

Tracy chuckled gently. "Me neither."

Violetta pulled away to look at her daughter. "Well nothing's ever going to happen if you spend all your time at work or your apartment."

"Condominium," Tracy corrected.

"Don't be disrespectful."

"I've got some things in the works Mom, a Plan A and a Plan B; or rather a Plan BS, and a Plan PI."

Violetta didn't understand the addendum—probably another one of her daughter's attempts at self-amusement—but she smiled broadly. "It's about time."

Tracy just shook her head and laughed. She wasn't going to fight with her mother; not tonight.

Tracy left her mother a little after 9:00. There had been no games as Violetta had felt tired. So Tracy had spent most of her time there watching her mother sleep; and being thankful for every minute of it.

The oven clock said 10:13 p.m. when Tracy finally arrived home. She was completely exhausted, physically, mentally, and emotionally. But she couldn't remember the last time she felt so *good*. She couldn't help wonder though how Neal and Rebecca would feel when they learned they would most likely be handling more murder cases now that Violetta Brubaker had spoken. Rebecca would be fine with it. Neal would grumble but he would come around. He had to. She certainly didn't want to lose him.

She let her mind wander from the business realm. The case was over. Now it was time to make good on the deal she had made with herself. Plan Brian Shane would be tested first. And if that didn't seem likely, Plan Paul Iris would be enacted. The latter would be calling her soon probably. It was only fair to him that she give him some definitive answer.

     A Tracy Brubaker Mystery

But thinking about all of that could wait. She wouldn't be able to stay awake much longer, so why not just sit on the couch and allow herself to feel happy? Enjoy the moment…the day was almost over and thus wouldn't be getting any better.

Tracy's phone started ringing. She had drifted off so it took her a moment to realize she was being summoned. "Probably Mom seeing if I got home okay," she thought. She reached around her and grabbed the receiver and sleepily said, "Hello."

"Hi Tracy. It's Brian."

She paused a moment and rubbed her eyes; realization then set in. "Brian…Hi!"

"Hi! I've been trying to reach you all evening."

"Oh. Yeah, well I just got home a few minutes ago. And I turned off my cell at some point in the afternoon and forgot to turn it back on. I'm so bad about that."

Brian Shane chuckled. "I always liked how you never let mobile phones interrupt your fun, Tracy."

She laughed. "Yeah; it's been a good day; it's been a *very* good day."

"I know; that's why I called. I wanted to congratulate you. You're something of a celebrity. I thought you may be somewhere giving interviews."

Tracy laughed again. "Well, there was some press outside the Paganini house during his victory party. But Max told them to go away because he wanted to spend today with his family. And then he basically said that the press was nowhere near being considered his family and that they should all go the hell home." And then there was laughter on the other side of the line too.

"He sounds like a real character," Brian finally said.

"Max is family."

"Speaking of family, how is your mother doing? Rebecca at your office brought me up to speed."

"She's back home. She's wonderful; and she's feeling much better too." She paused a bit and then asked, "How are *you*, Brian?"

Brian stopped laughing. "I'm great, Tracy. I'm really great. I haven't had a drink for almost a year; well 10 months, anyway. I go to my meetings. In fact I've lost more than 10 pounds."

Tracy smiled. "Did you really?"

"Yup. And I moved out of the house. I've got my own apartment now."

"Brian—why did you do *that*?"

"I wanted to start taking care of myself. I cook, I clean, I shop; and I'm taking night courses in computer technology or whatever they call it. I work during the day at the company, in the IT department. I enjoy it, and Crystal's been super supportive. I mean, we're the only family each other have now."

Tracy was practically speechless. Brian had done it—at least, he was doing it, getting his life in order, setting goals, living sober—the whole shebang. She finally said, "Brian that's great. I mean, that's all *really* great."

"Thanks Tracy," he responded. "Tracy…Tracy I'd like to see you again, even if that means making an appointment to see you during office hours."

Tracy laughed, but she also felt a flutter in her stomach, something she hadn't felt for over 10 years. And that's when she realized Paul Iris hadn't made her feel that flutter. "You don't have to do that, Brian," she finally told him.

"Okay then; can I take you to dinner? I KNOW you eat dinner."

She laughed. "At least seven times a week."

"How about this Friday?"

"Let me check my calendar. Friday sounds perfect."

Another laugh from Brian. "That's great. I can pick you up at your home. Do you prefer 7:00 or 7:30?"

More flutters. "Oh you don't have to pick me up. I can meet you somewhere."

There was a brief pause. "But I want to pick you up, Tracy. I want to hold the car door open for you like I used to."

Tracy's mouth went a little dry. Suddenly she was feeling 17 again, just like she felt at the July 4th party where they first met. Maybe it was because she was so tired; maybe it was because this *was* a beginning. "Okay Brian. Let's make it 7:30 then."

"Great Tracy; really great. I'll make the reservations for 8:30. Well, I can tell you're tired. So, congratulations again and I'm glad your mom's okay. I'll be at your place Friday at 7:30."

"Okay Brian."

"I can't wait to see you again. I... Goodbye, Tracy."

"Goodbye, Brian." And then she heard the click on the other end.

Tired? She had been; in fact she was asleep when he called. But now… now every part of her was awake. All the ugliness, all the awfulness of the past several months was gone, given the heave-ho, on the train to Splitsville; outta here. She went to look out her balcony window, but it wasn't

A Tracy Brubaker Mystery

the lights of the Inner Harbor she was seeing. She was gazing into her future, the glass rectangular door acting as a crystal ball. Suddenly the life she had always wanted was a possibility again. Her mother was doing well. Tracy could pursue the cases she wanted with her mother's blessing. She could perhaps really help someone again, like the way she helped Max Paganini today, the way she helped reunite him with his family. Family, she still wanted her own family. Once upon time she thought she'd have one with Brian Shane. Then the personal tragedies and drinking destroyed that dream. But the dream *hadn't* been destroyed after all, had it? No, it lived again! She felt it again. Maybe she always knew it was never truly dead. Maybe that's why she had stayed single for all this time—didn't immediately accept the dinner invitation from Paul Iris—because deep inside she knew this day would come. She had had faith. She thought, "You gotta have faith; sometimes that's all you have."

A Tracy Brubaker Mystery